THE STATION

A Novel

Rebecca J. Kelly

For Tim, Jack, and Lillian.
I love you to low-Earth orbit and back.

Preface

They say the fall only takes a few minutes, just a few minutes; then it's all over.

I hope that's the case. As I sit here waiting, hoping, thinking, doubting, mentally double-checking, and internally freaking out, I realize I'm not afraid. Well, I shouldn't say that. There's always fear. But in this case, fear isn't what's driving my mind forward. It's the anticipation of the event that's gnawing at me. I'm mostly curious about what it will feel like.

My heart hammers against my ribs. The fall is coming and my heart knows it.

I wrap my fingers around my thumbs and squeeze them… hard. Over and over. I count backward in my mind from 1,000 to keep my heart from splitting in two.

999… 998… 997… 996…

This exercise works. My breathing slows, my heart slows, yet my mind continues to spin. I turn my head to look through the small window on my left. It's not much, but I'll still be able to see it when it happens. I'll see the fall in all its fiery glory as only a few humans in history have ever seen it. For a moment, I feel lucky.

Right now, though, as I look through the tiny, round window, there's no fall, only the surface. The ocean is spread out below me in shades of blue as far as I can see. This is probably the last time I'll see those colors presented in such a beautiful way. I crane my neck to get a better look.

I watch the clouds swirl around in brilliant patterns and wait for the fall.

Part I

Chapter 1

It's Monday morning. Today's itinerary includes running system checks, logging errors, whittling down my list of maintenance items, and performing a full visual inspection of the station.

I woke up late today so I'm already behind, but I pause after breakfast and take several minutes to put together the perfect Monday morning music playlist. The Delta Space Station computers have the largest informational and entertainment archive ever put into a space vehicle. Because this station was meant to serve as a base camp for long-term space missions, NASA scientists designed the archive to hold everything a group of astronauts might need to lead productive lives in the outer limits of the solar system.

The scientists also knew there would be times when the station wouldn't be easily accessible to radio signals from Earth. So, the archive was a way to give astronauts everything they would need to figure out issues with station mechanics, keep their minds occupied during long hauls, and further their education in the process. I can access millions of music files, movies, books, magazines, comic books, and news articles dating back hundreds of years.

I've found, after years of doing the same routine, that varying the music selection on Monday is the way to go. It keeps me from making a jump out of the nearest porthole. Today's playlist is a mix, mainly older stuff, but some new millennium stuff to keep me on my toes. I hit the play button and get to work, hoping the upbeat music I've chosen will stave off boredom for a few hours.

There's something to be said for boredom. Two weeks ago, the thermal lining, which protects the interior of reactor core number three, fried to bits. The incident was the biggest issue I've faced in a long time and it was unnerving, to say the least. I sent Nix out to fix it. He removed the busted lining and then I reprogrammed the other two reactors to bypass number three. It was a relatively easy fix for something that could have been much worse. Eventually though, I'll need to do a spacewalk to repair it because I won't be able to live on the other two cores forever.

Suffice it to say, the thermal lining incident isn't a good sign. It's held together well considering how old it is, but still, it's showing signs of age, and I'm not going to lie... it worries me.

Anyway, it's fixed now and things could always be worse. It's Monday, which means if there is something else awry on board this rickety old station, I'll probably find it today. Although, I don't think there will be any major issues today. That's because today is special and I feel lucky.

***

Today is my eighteenth birthday. In Earth years, that is. I'd rather measure time in revolutions, meaning how long it takes the station to revolve around the surface. It's quicker and more fluid that way. Revolutions slip by in such rapid succession. Considering time moves slower up here (Einstein be damned), anything that gives time a little nudge is okay with me. But despite my aversion to it, I have to keep up with Earth days and years, since that's how the station computers measure time. My station makes a little over fifteen revolutions in one Earth day. Every ninety-five minutes, the Sun rises and sets again and Earth swings from deep blues, greens, and browns, to total darkness, pockmarked by the occasional bundle of lights.

The lights weren't always there. They appeared about five years ago. At first, there were tiny spots, like the skin of the Earth had been pricked by a pin, allowing me a glimpse into the fires below. Then those spots got bigger, turning into little pools that faded around the edges. Then the pools of light multiplied and continued to get bigger still, and soon, they looked more like sprawling spider webs, creeping over the surface, connecting one pool to the next.

They're still not everywhere though. There are vast expanses of the surface with no lights at all, but it's nice to see the humans below me are lighting their way again after so many years of darkness.

Because of the station's orbit, nighttime is short and succinct. Of course, daytime is just as short, but that's good—I prefer darkness. My mother always thought this idea was ridiculous. She loved few things as much as the vast, bright surface of the Earth, painted in all its exotic colors by sunlight. I, on the other hand, find daytime much too vibrant. I prefer the darker, cooler times when the station is out of the sun's violent glare. It's during the night when you can see the stars, after all.

For eighteen years I've spun around in this never-ending orbit. That's 99,930 revolutions. The computer reminds me every Earth year on this day that it is, in fact, my birthday. It doesn't make much difference to me though. If I were a normal eighteen-year-old girl, I'd be celebrating with friends. Maybe I'd have a party with pulsing dance music and a tall, tiered birthday cake full of candles. I'd celebrate that I could now vote and drive, and I'd consider myself a full-blown adult. But I'm not a normal girl, and in reality, it's just another day here on the station.

"Happy Birthday, Eta," says a voice from over my shoulder.

I startle but quickly relax as my brain recognizes the voice and I turn to face him. "You scared me, Nix," I say. The slender robot holds onto the handhold on the wall behind me. "I see the computer alerted you to the day."

"Oh, I would never forget your birthday. It's unbecoming," he says.

Nix is a station robot. Nautical Intelligence Experiment (NIX) is his full designation. The NIX system was originally designed to work in an underwater laboratory, hence the "Nautical" part. Back in the day, space agencies used enormous swimming pools to train astronauts underwater. Water is apparently the only way to simulate zero gravity on the surface, which seems strange to me. I've never been submerged in water myself. Water is, of course, in short supply up here on the station. There is an excellent water reclamation system on board that filters and reuses all liquids, so I'm not in danger of running out of water, but I've never felt more than a few drops of it on my skin at a time. I've seen people in swimming pools in movies. Like in *Cocoon*, when the old folks swim in the pool with those big, hairy alien egg pods and soak up the alien juice, or whatever it is, and start acting like teenagers again. It's one of my favorites. So, I know what swimming in water *looks* like, but I can't imagine how it would feel like microgravity.

NIX units were used to aid in underwater astronaut training. The NASA engineers quickly realized that the robots might come in handy in space as well. They did some modifications, added some specialized equipment to help them stand up to the vacuum, and the station robot was born. I like to think of him as "nautical by nature."

He's not exactly intelligent, as his name might lead one to believe, but he is an impressive design. I don't think he would pass the Turing test, but he's programmed to provide occasional entertainment and a source of companionship, which is a blessing in this bleak and lonely corner of space. Well, technically, all of space is bleak and lonely.

Nix is about as tall as I am, a little over one and a half meters when fully extended. He's meant to function only in microgravity, so his thin gray legs sit folded at his chest where they rest when he doesn't need them. He mainly uses them for gripping the outer scaffolding on the station hull. His torso is shaped like a human's, with a chest, arms, hands, neck, and head. I guess the designers figured the more humanlike the robot, the better the actual humans would feel about sharing space with him. I'm sure it has something to do with the psychology of confined spaces.

On his back, he sports a battery pack that makes him look like he's on his way to the first day of school at Robot Elementary. Well, I've never been to an actual school before, so I wouldn't know for sure.

The best part about Nix, though, is his head. He looks like Iron Man. A gray version of the old Iron Man comic character. I used to read the comic books when I was younger, and, of course, I've seen all the Iron Man movies. The strange mask serves a purpose, of course. The front of the mask has a fused silica glass plate that houses multiple cameras. Giving him that silly mask defeats the purpose of shaping his body like a human's, in my opinion.

"I am finished with the weekly maintenance run along the outer hull. No additional patches this time. Good news, if you ask me. Is there anything else I can help with?" he asks.

"No. I'm happy your maintenance run went well. You really are Iron Man," I reply with a wink.

Nix is not all that useful inside. For the most part, he stays in his little docking bay and charges his batteries. He has his very own airlock, which allows him to come in and out of the station without compromising the atmosphere or using the huge, primary airlock in the Docking Module. Without Nix, my job would be much tougher, especially now that I'm alone.

"I am pleased with today's music choice," Nix says. He swings his arms in front of his body and bumps his Iron Man head from side to side, mimicking the electronic beat thumping out from the speakers. He looks hilarious and I laugh, as he expected I would. After a few seconds, the song fades out and blends into something new. "Would you like to do anything special today?" He moves out of my way as I float past him to check one of the holo-screens in the Service Module. "It is your birthday, after all."

"No. I'll be okay, Nix. But thank you for asking. I appreciate that." I tap the screen lightly and log the information as it comes in from various systems on board the station. The new song has picked up and I, too, am now ticking along to the beat.

"Righty-O!" he says and reaches up to grab the handholds above his head. He swings his arms from rung to rung and heads back to his adapter port to plug in. Some of my favorite videos in the archives are those showing animals in their natural habitat. Nix looks almost like a monkey swinging from limb to limb as he makes his way through the module. I can hear a faint click as he settles in and the slight whoosh of his fans as he powers down. I've never been on monkey bars, but it's always something I've wanted to do. Not because they look particularly fun, but because I'd like to know what it feels like to hang on a bar under the full weight of the Earth's gravity. What would it be like to feel the ground beneath me pulling my hands, elbows, and shoulders down, down, down? I pause for a moment to think about it before continuing on with my work. No sense in dwelling over the things that have never been... or may never be.

I turn toward the Viewpoint Module, also known as the VP, which is adjacent to the Service Module. The VP is where the windows are. They form the shape of an octagon sticking out into space, with eight windows making up the sides and one larger central window. I try to keep the external shutters drawn as much as possible to protect the windows from debris collisions, but today, I have all of them open. It is my birthday, after all.

I take in the view below. The sunlight glitters off the ocean in a way that looks almost like sparks flying off of a piece of blue green flint. I've never seen sparks, of course, but this is how I imagine they would look if I were to actually hold a flintstone in my hand.

Currently, the time is 0900 GMT. The station runs on Greenwich Mean Time (GMT) and I have day and night built into my schedule. I am human, after all. I must eat and sleep and work on a schedule, as does any other human. Because my schedule was set before I was born, I don't usually deviate from it, but today, my schedule is off. I woke up late, I spent too much time picking out today's playlist, and I'm playing it much louder than I normally do over the station speakers. Since I'm already behind for the day, I decide to spend a little extra time in the VP. I am working on something.

I start with Africa.

The continent is in full view through the thick windowpanes in front of me. The glittering edges of the shoreline pass beneath me. I press my hand to the glass, knowing I can't actually touch the shoreline below, but still wondering if maybe some miracle would bring it up to me. I've never felt sand before, but I have felt wet soil in the garden, and I think sand might be similar. Closing my eyes, I imagine the cool, wet, grittiness of it beneath my fingers. The miracle doesn't come, of course. The only thing I actually feel beneath my palm is the smoothness of the glass, the same as it feels every day.

The glass isn't cold as one might expect a space station window to be. The windows are made up of four panes of borosilicate glass with a layer of radon gas sandwiched between each to help with insulation. The innermost pane is there as a scratch panel to protect the outer three layers from floating experimentation equipment and the occasional bump of an astronaut's arm. The outermost pane is covered with tiny nicks, long scratches, and various rough patches, the battle scars of run-ins with space debris over the years. In the past, they would have replaced the outer panes periodically to make for smoother viewing surfaces, but there are no replacements here now.

I take my hand off the glass and return my attention to the holo-screen in my other hand. Pulling up the program I'm looking for, I type in the coordinates and start the scan. The playlist has now moved even further back in time, leaving the turn-of-the-century pop songs behind in favor of a more brooding and melodic rock-and-roll tune. I hum along.

My mother designed the program I'm running. It uses electromagnetic light waves to scan a hundred square kilometers of surface area. After it scans the plotted coordinates six times, it sends back data about surface movement. This repeat scanning gives six complete maps of the coordinate area. My mother knew it was important for us to find a way to track movement on the surface, so she created this program that uses multiple scans to compare changes from one scan to the next. The station does have a state-of-the-art (well, state-of-the-art about two decades ago) laser mapping system. She tweaked the coding on the mapping system so it scans multiple times.

The laser scanner is accurate down to a single square meter. But the closer in you run the scan, the longer it takes. So, I run each scan at an accuracy of ten square meters to speed it up a little. That means, if anything moves within a ten square meter area, the scan will pick it up.

We started a few years ago, around the same time the pinpricks of lights appeared on the nighttime surface of the Earth. That's when my mother was still here with me. She noticed it first during a routine communication scan. She picked up a radio signal from them, not directed at us, of course. Just a lonely radio signal indicating they were broadcasting again.

Since that time, I've been using the mapping scanner continuously. It's a time-consuming, mind-numbing process when you consider how incredibly huge the planet is. Earth has 510,000,000 square kilometers of surface area, about 82 percent of which is below sea level. When taken in 10,000 square kilometer blocks, that's 9,180 checks to search the entire surface. It takes the program about sixty minutes to check one full coordinate block and a little over a year to check all the habitable surface area on the planet. It seems silly to check certain areas, like the top of the Himalayas or Antarctica, but I do it anyway, just in case.

Of course, the Earth moves too. Rockslides, mudslides, avalanches, floods—all that stuff happens, but it's gotten easier for me to recognize and skim over these natural movements. As the years pass, human movements have increased. At first, it was a few major streams of highway travel, what looked like big trucks hauling building materials back and forth on the roads. They looked like ants marching single file along the ant bed, to and from the major cities. Then the cities themselves started humming. I could actually see them building new structures out of the burned-out rubble that once pockmarked the land. In some areas, cities cropped up where there had never been cities before. Perhaps the destruction was too great and they had to start fresh somewhere new.

The encouraging part was, it was happening pretty much all over the world. The humans were moving out from whatever underworld they had been hiding in to escape the devastation of the war. It was a true "world war" based on how long it took them to start recovering from it.

My job now is to find out how to communicate with them. It's not that I can't send a radio signal. There's nothing wrong with my antennae. I can send radio signals as much as I like, but if nobody's *listening* on the other end, they'll never hear them. That's why the surface scans are so important. If I can continue to document their growth, I'll know the best areas to direct my radio signal, and I'll know when they begin using satellite communications again.

The station has broadcast an SOS signal on a continuous loop for the last nineteen years. So far, nobody's picked it up. At least, not that I know of, because they've never sent anything back, and it could be their dish arrays were destroyed during the war, like the satellites.

Even if they did pick up my signal, I'm not sure what they could do about it. I doubt there is a functioning space program after all those years of fighting the war. But I hold out hope, and I continue to run my scans and keep detailed documentation about the building and growth I see on the surface. I hope they'll get their radio and satellite communications back up and running. I hope they'll start exploring the sky again, and when they do, I hope they'll find me here waiting for them.

The screen in front of me beeps. The first scan is complete with no substantial hits. I type in new coordinates and turn back to the windows in the VP. The surface slips away slowly below. Never-ending.

The 1100 GMT alarm squeaks on the bottom right of my holo-screen. It's reminding me to move on with my day. I've spent an hour longer here watching the program work than I usually would. You can't just "take a day off" around here, even if it is your eighteenth birthday. So, after I set up the next coordinate search, I head down to the G.

Chapter 2

The Gagarin Module or the G, as I call it, is the most important part of the station. When they first built space stations, they used supply vessels to bring food to the astronauts aboard. When the Mars mission started to become a reality, they knew delivering food would not work in the long run. Enter, the G.

It took them six missions to transport the pieces into low-Earth orbit and another twelve missions to assemble it. The G is, by far, the largest module on the station. Everything I do on a daily basis revolves around keeping it alive and functioning. It's about ten years past its proposed life span and I consider the fact that it's still operating one of my greatest achievements.

Not only does the G house my garden, but it's got something else going for it—*gravity*—or more accurately, it has acceleration. Good, old-fashioned centrifugal force provides me with Gs. The same way David Bowman was able to take a jog on the Discovery One in *2001: A Space Odyssey*.

The module itself is a big circular tube that revolves around a spherical chamber called the Node. The Node is about three meters in diameter and feels like a giant hamster ball. It's made of two aluminum hulls, outer and inner. The inner hull is stationary and connects directly to the access tunnel on one side, which connects to the Service Module. On the opposite side of the Node, there's another docking port that sits empty. The G spins around the Node.

This module is actually part of a larger spacecraft, one that was never built. The ship would have docked to the G through the docking port in the Node and taken the whole contraption with it on its journey, leaving the bones of the remaining station as a base camp for future deep space missions. At least, that's how I understand it. This plan never came to be, of course.

Along the middle of the Node, perpendicular to the access tunnel, the inner hull splits, with a half meter gap running along the entire diameter. The outer hull spins around this inner hull with the gap serving as the access point to the G tunnels. There are two tunnels, each with ladders leading down into the spinning tube that makes up the rest of the module.

It's all about forces around here. There is a nine-meter distance from the center of the Node to the floor of the G at the end of each tunnel. The entire module spins on its axis one full rotation every fifteen seconds and produces approximately 1.6 m/s squared, or about a sixth the force of Earth's gravity. It's comparable to the gravity on the Moon. The tunnels are also reinforced with an outer and inner aluminum hull to make sure the spinning apparatus doesn't threaten the integrity of the atmosphere.

Sometimes, for fun, I hang out in the Node and listen to the mechanics of it all. There are thousands of golf-ball-sized ball bearings between the outer and inner hull. If you stop and listen closely, it sounds like humming, kind of like a beehive. It sounds alive.

I stop to listen to it now, closing my eyes and absorbing the hum. The sound is constant and warm and makes me feel like I'm wrapped up in a fluffy, humming blanket.

The Node has no windows and no gravity. Whenever loneliness creeps in on me, and I can't count it away or shake it off, I come here to sleep. The noise and the microgravity are comforting in comparison to my sleeping compartment in the G. There is ambient noise all over the station, of course, but it is loudest here.

The G's hull has been intact and spinning for over eighteen years. At one point, we had to bring it down to a slow crawl to rework some of the internal wirings after a malfunction with the breakers. Another time, it stopped altogether for a few minutes while we did an EVA to repair some outer hull damage. Otherwise, it keeps spinning, like Earth itself.

As I enter Tunnel B, there is no gravity at first and I must float around to grasp the handles of the ladder. The farther down I move, the more the gravity takes hold. When I reach the bottom, I step onto a thick, rubber pad that lines the floor all around the module. I am able to stand now, and I feel my body weight pushing down on my feet. The tiny bones in them groan under the pressure.

It's a strange sensation, going from no gravity to gravity. I'm likely the only person left alive who's ever felt what it's like. All of a sudden, my organs feel heavy inside my belly. My heart pumps harder and I can hear it inside my ears, pump, pump, pumping to keep up with the new forces. The blood swooshes down from my head and chest into my legs in one great wave that I can feel rushing just below the skin. It's like an ocean wave, maybe. The new flood of blood makes my legs and feet feel warm to the touch and firm, like the difference between a ripe grape and an old soggy one.

I go through this process of passing between microgravity and gravity at least two or three times every day. Most of the time, I don't even think about it, but today, I take a moment to feel the change. It sends my mind wandering down to the surface. What does gravity feel like on the surface? Would it cause me to bend… or break? And how would it feel when gravity is omnipresent, like air? Not something you can choose to leave behind you, but rather, something you must fight against every day. The thought makes me shudder, not from fear, but from excitement. Maybe one day I'll get to feel it myself.

Now that I'm in the G, the music resumes through speakers built into the walls. You can't hear the music in the Node. There are no speakers in there, and it's too noisy to hear anything anyway. There are over ten thousand songs housed in the station archives, and just as many movies, television programs, articles, books, and comics. Since this place was originally meant to be the base camp for long-term space missions, they needed to keep a bunch of astronauts entertained for years at a time. So, they dedicated an entire database to entertainment and information material. The stuff is all outdated, of course, since the computer hasn't had contact with the ground for almost two decades. But it's something at least.

Directly off of the B tunnel ladder is the kitchen. The A tunnel, on the exact opposite side of the G, leads to the toilet and shower. The outer ring of the module is oval-shaped along the entire corridor, like an elongated tube, spanning about four meters wide. In the middle, the floor-to-ceiling height is about two and a half meters, narrowing at the rounded edges.

Along one side of the cylindrical hull are the kitchen cabinets and countertop workspace. There's also a sink and a small oven. No flame, of course. The oven uses microwaves. On the opposite side of the module, there's an upright pantry where I store dried corn, oats, and rice. Next to the pantry is a large, enclosed box which runs the entire length of the kitchen wall. It's called the cellar and it uses coolant circulated in from outside the station to keep foods almost frozen. It has three sets of doors for easy access. There's a smaller regular refrigerator sitting on top of the cellar.

Keeping up with the garden takes about eighty percent of my time, but it reaps a substantial amount of food. It also produces all the oxygen for the station. If there were more people here, we would have to rely on oxygen generation from other sources, but since it's only me, the garden does fine. In fact, I produce enough carbon dioxide to keep the garden alive all by myself. The station's atmosphere regulators keep the levels in balance so the plants thrive and I stay alive.

I make my way into the kitchen and get out my cooking utensils from their designated spaces in the cabinets. Then I turn to the opposite side of the module and pull out a large bag of dried rice from the pantry, a bundle of fresh cilantro, two cloves of garlic from the refrigerator, and a bag of roasted peanuts from the cellar. I measure the water and place the rice in the oven to steam. Later, before it's completely done, I'll add the chopped garlic and cilantro to season the rice as it finishes cooking. I use a small, electric burner to heat up a pan and sauté the peanuts in some oil to freshen them up. The fragrance they release enchants me for a moment, and I lean in and close my eyes to get a better whiff. For dessert, grapes from the grapevine.

After cooking, I sit at the round kitchen table and chew my rice. Again, like it does so many times during the day, the surface draws my attention. I wonder if rice tastes the same when it grows someplace other than on a space station. I wonder if the fresh air changes the way food smells. And I wonder what it would feel like to chew a steak.

Chapter 3

After lunch, I exercise. If I stopped exercising, my body would turn into space gel, so, I dutifully take part in this activity like any good astronaut. But it's fine by me. Exercise is one of my favorite parts of the day.

There is a stationary bike in the G and a weight lifting machine that uses piston-driven vacuum cylinders to approximate a higher level of gravity. Neither of these options appeals to me today. Instead, I choose the track.

The black rubber running track wraps around the entire floor of the G. I run in the direction of the module's spin because this increases the force of the artificial gravity on my legs. My bare feet squish into the soft rubber as I push off with each step.

After two laps, I stop briefly to punch some commands into the holo-screen built into the wall of the kitchen. These holo-screens are all over the station, so I can check the station status any time I want. They all feed into the main computer system housed in the Service Module. Anything I need to know about station operations, I can get on any one of the screens. Right now, I need to change the music to something more upbeat.

Long and narrow windows surround the entire perimeter of the module, each about twenty centimeters wide and about two meters long. The windows curve to follow the flow of the module wall, and they allow enough sunlight in for the garden to grow without overpowering the module with heat.

The garden is the closest thing I have to a pet. A pet is something you care for and love. Something that comforts you when you're lonely, or scared, or tired, or bored. This certainly applies to my garden, although technically it was here long before I came around. But, unlike a pet, the garden doesn't bark when I enter a room, and it doesn't love me in return. Maybe one day I'll have a dog, like Hooch, or Toto, or the beast in *The Sandlot*. I could handle that.

The original garden in the G was simple. It was only meant to take up half the module, with the rest of the area devoted to the crew's primary living quarters. Now that I'm the only one on board, there's no need for the extra living space, so the garden has taken over everything except the kitchen, toilet, shower, my sleeping compartment, and my mother's sleeping compartment. I can't bring myself to go in there. It's been closed off for almost three years.

I could downsize the garden if I wanted to. It produces more food than I need, but I don't because, well, because I like it. Tending the garden is calming and I'll take calm where I can get it. My life is at risk every single day. The station won't go on forever.

Systems fail. Computers malfunction. Metal fatigues. Mechanics wear out. It all exists in a vacuum, the most volatile environment known to man. Tending the garden to ensure my food source, my oxygen supply, and my sanity remain intact is the very least I can do.

The garden spirals around me as I run, and I say a silent prayer to the universe for the abundance of food my garden provides. I keep pace with the spin of the module and watch the Earth moving through the windows. It makes it look like I'm standing still, or rather, running in place while the Earth moves around me. I've run so many kilometers on this track, and this view of the module and the Earth are such a normal occurrence, I rarely notice it. Today, though, I'm grateful and reflective, so I pay attention.

Each variety of plant has its own place in the garden. The largest section includes rice, corn, and cabbage, as well as multiple varieties of lettuce, peas, and cucumbers. Then there are the root vegetables: onions, potatoes, peanuts, and garlic. I have a small herb garden filled with thyme, basil, rosemary, ginger, and cilantro. Nearest the kitchen, I grow three types of beans, and a long grapevine winds around the windows and into the kitchen area.

My very favorite part of the garden is the sunflower bed. I eat the seeds and use them to make oil with the oil press, so they're extra useful. But mainly, I like the big flowers. They look like faces. In a way, they're the most human things in the station, aside from me... and Iron Man. The sunflowers stand tall with their leaves outstretched like arms and their heads held high, always facing the windows on the port side where the sunlight shines through. They even lean slightly toward those windows, each one trying to get a centimeter up on the others, reaching for the light and warmth.

I follow a tight schedule of watering, harvesting, seeding, and planting. It's like a delicate dance sequence that keeps them all alive and keeps me alive in the process. When I don't stick to a strict schedule, things get out of whack, and that's one complication I don't have time to deal with.

Rice, for example, is hardy and doesn't need as much care. It doesn't need as much water as, say, cabbage. Lettuce does much better when kept out of direct sunlight, while beans, corn, and cucumbers prefer as much sunlight as possible. Some plants, like sunflowers, enjoy regular pruning. They want me to cater to their every need while they stare longingly out the window, waiting for something wonderful to happen.

It might seem like the strange day-night passage coming once every ninety minutes might distress plants, but that's not the case. Like me, these plants grew up right here, and like me, they have adapted to the quirks of station life, including the many sunsets and sunrises and the limited gravity produced by the centrifugal force.

I keep running and thinking. Cyndi Lauper's voice is pulsing through the speakers that line the module. The rhythm of my feet matches the rhythm of the song flowing out of her cheerful, bright voice.

When I've done fourteen kilometers, I do some cool-down stretches and head to the shower. The G is a humid place, kept so because of the garden, and my clothes and hair cling to my body with sweat.

The station has a water reclamation system that takes moisture out of the air and recycles it to produce drinking water. It's set to regulate air humidity in the G to 91 percent to help plant growth. Because of the increased size of the garden and the high humidity setting in the G, the reclamation system has a hard time keeping humidity down in the rest of the station. Only when you get to the VP, which is the farthest module from the garden, do you reach an area that's somewhat dry.

The problem with this increased humidity is the place gets a little moldy. Mold in space stations was an issue in the past and because of this, they implemented a strict cleaning regimen here. I, of course, do not want a mold outbreak either, so I stick to the cleaning regimen, even though I hate cleaning. I dream of a time when I can go longer than a day without having to spray down every surface and wipe it clean.

After my shower, I brush my teeth and comb my hair. Then I get dressed—gray shorts, gray shirt. That's all there is here, an endless stream of gray walls, gray floors, gray ceilings, and gray clothes. Even my skin and hair look gray under the dim, artificial lighting of the bathroom. I look at myself in the mirror and sigh. The ever-present dark semicircles under my eyes look even worse today.

Sleep doesn't come easy to me these days. The weight of the station sinks in on me with each passing rotation, which is a funny idea because, technically, the station weighs nothing up here in orbit. Things break down and wear out, and it all seems like it might crash down around me sooner rather than later. The longer I'm here, the more I worry about it and the more it seems like those semicircles might turn into permanent pits of gray skin under my brown eyes.

I sigh again and click off the lights. No sense in dwelling on my strange face. It's time to clean.

***

I take the battery-powered vacuum around the module and thoroughly vacuum up anything out of place. I will sift the vacuum contents later to preserve any bits of soil and plant matter to go into the fertilizer bin. After vacuuming, I get down on my hands and knees with an old T-shirt rag and a squirt bottle. It's full of water and a super-concentrated soap mixture. It's the same type of soap I use on my body, and since the station was designed for long-duration space missions, it was stocked to keep a crew of six humans and their station clean for years. That's why I still have soap left. Not everything has lasted so long.

I work my way through each planting setup. The floors, the planters, the walls, and even the ceiling get a good scrub. I do this every day in different areas of the station. It takes a week to clean the entire station, and the process starts again.

After I get today's section clean, it's time to work on the plants. I inspect every plant and clip any dead leaves before adding them to the fertilizer bin. Fruits and veggies ready to harvest are picked and sorted into baskets. I take soil acidity readings and check for moisture levels and record everything in the nearest holo-screen.

Cleaning and tending the garden takes about three hours. When I finish, I feel satisfied, accomplished, even. I put away my cleaning equipment in a small closet next to the kitchen and head back to the tunnel.

As I ascend through the tunnel leading out of the G, gravity lightens up with each ladder rung. It's disorienting. No matter how many times I do it, moving from gravity to microgravity causes me to get lightheaded and dizzy. If I stay at the entrance to the tunnel for a minute or two, close my eyes, and focus my energy, the disorientation passes faster. Today, I'm lucky and the nausea only lasts a few seconds. Once the dizziness passes, I continue on through the Service Module and into the VP. It is now 1600 GMT.

I pull up the tracking program on the holo-screen set up in the VP. It has continued to track while I was exercising and cleaning. I watch the program work, constantly spinning through numbers of code as it searches. After a few minutes, the lack of gravity and the faint light from the holo-screen make my eyelids heavy. My muscles relax as sleep takes over. Before I realize it, I doze off.

I don't normally remember my dreams, but I know I have them because I often wake from them so abruptly, it leaves my eyes wide and my soul in a panic. Usually, if I can remember the dream, it's because it was a bad one. Today's dream isn't good or bad, yet I still remember it vividly. It's strange because it's something I've never dreamed about before.

Fire.

I'm not sure why I'm dreaming about fire. Fire is really dangerous here, so I've never actually seen fire in person, only in movies. The fire in this dream seems strangely real. My dreaming mind is confident this fire exists somewhere other than in its own murky depths.

The fire starts as a distant pinpoint of light in the blackness behind my eyelids. I can barely see it at first. It dances around, many meters away from me, like a tiny, fuzzy dot, ebbing and flowing between red and orange. Squinting, I try to capture the details, and even though I can't make out the individual features of it, there's no question in my mind that it's fire. A *real* fire. The more I squint at it, the more I can tell it is, in fact, moving. It's coming closer to me, morphing from a tiny, wavy blotch into a larger, more solid mass.

I reach for it, but it is still much too far away from me. It continues to dance and vibrate off in the distance, slowly growing larger as it moves toward me. It must be so hot, my dreaming mind thinks. It's still so far away. Maybe it's a star.

I find myself wishing it would get closer, hoping I'll feel the heat of it soon. I can see it coming toward me, spreading through my frame of vision. It grows faster and faster and before I know it, it's close to me and enormous. It fills my entire field of vision, leaving only blips of darkness poking through around the edges.

As it grows and swells, the heat hits me in dense, fluid waves. Mild heat, at first. Then quickly becoming more intense. I wince away from it and put my hand up over my eyes. The heat and the light are almost too much to take. As hot as it is, I'm certain it won't burn me. Just like I'm certain it's a real fire, present in its pure form somewhere in the universe.

Peering between the fingers of my hand as it shields my face from the heat and light, I continue to watch it. The fire won't hurt me, yet as more time passes and the heat and light get more intense, I wonder if maybe I'm wrong about that. Could a fire in a dream really burn me?

Before I can think about it much more, the massive ball of fire passes right by me. Though I couldn't hear the fire until right when it passed me by, it now makes a whooshing sound so loud I touch my ears to make sure they aren't bleeding. It sounds like all the air is being sucked out from around me, following the fire as it goes. The sound only lasts a second. A millisecond, perhaps. As soon as it's gone, there is no longer any sound, and the fire retreats. My skin cools almost immediately after the fire passes. There's no smell and no more sound. Only the heat and the light, and it's moving away from me at the same, incredibly fast speed. Racing on to who knows where. Getting smaller and dimmer and more orange, then red, as it goes. Now, it's so tiny in the distance, I have to squint to see its dancing dot of light. A moment later, as I'm squinting, desperately trying to catch one last glimpse of the fire, an alarm sounds.

Yes, it's definitely an alarm. I know I've heard this alarm before, but I don't know where. It's a light, bright, pinging alarm. I can't put my finger on it. And then, in an instant, I wake up.

My eyelids flutter and I look around me, momentarily stunned by the realness of the dream. For a moment, I forget where I am. I'm sweating from the heat of the fire and breathing quickly, in and out, trying to calm my body.

I take a moment to remember. I am in the station. I am in the VP. It is my eighteenth birthday. Reality slowly settles in on me like my bedsheet might settle around my body in my sleeping compartment. There is music playing from the speakers. It's Neil Young singing to me about a heart of gold.

I heard something that woke me from my dream. It's the alarm. It's pinging from somewhere near me. Suddenly, I am gripped with panic. Alarms are never good. What was I doing before I fell asleep?

I look around me, quickly whipping my head back and forth to get my bearings. For a moment, I forget I'm in microgravity and move way too fast, sending my body in a spiral toward the outer wall. My head bangs against one of the cabinets on the wall behind me. That'll leave a bruise. I rub the back of my head and close my eyes to clear the momentary pain.

What was I doing in the VP before I fell asleep?

Scanning. I was scanning. It's the scan alarm!

I immediately look toward the holo-screen that's mounted on the far wall. The program is there as it was before I drifted off, but it's no longer searching. It found movement. Significant movement. In fact, this is the most movement it's *ever* detected.

Florida.

It was scanning a portion of Florida. I see it on the small map in the corner of the screen. I punch in a command, asking it to narrow the results.

Central Florida.

I continue to type and narrow down options. It found movement somewhere near the coast, the Atlantic coast, not the

Gulf. My heart is racing, but I keep my focus. I've learned after years of near misses and close calls that keeping my cool is important. In the microgravity, I can feel the blood generally pooled in my chest pounding up into my face, making my cheeks hot. Finally, after punching in a few more commands, the computer lands on the exact location of the movement and two words pop up on the screen. I am stunned.

Cape Canaveral.

That's the launch complex. They are launching again.

Chapter 4

"Whoa!" Alexandros Bakas jumped back as the thick steel and glass door to the office in front of him swung open in one sudden movement, surprising him and his cup of hot coffee. The coffee splashed over his right hand, burning his tanned skin and leaving it tender to the touch. He gritted his teeth at the initial shock of the burn. This did not help his morning.

"Alé!" Jade said as she came around the edge of the door, surprised to see him but not seeming to care that she almost knocked him over as she bolted through the doorway. Jade Stanton was Alé's boss. "What the hell are you doing standing behind my door?"

"Scalding myself, apparently," Alé said, a sly, crooked smile curling at the corner of his lips.

He preferred the nickname. Only his mom called him Alexandros. He felt the name Alé (pronounced how a matador

- 34 -

might taunt a bull: *Alé!)* made him sound foreign, even though he was born and raised in Baltimore.

Alé had dark curls that hung down over his forehead. They loosely crowned his head but skidded to an abrupt stop above his temples where the fade began. He was particular about the fade of his hair. He paid regular visits on the fourth Thursday of every month to Orlando, the only barber in town who could cut it the way he liked it. The fade started longer at almost a half centimeter and seemed to vanish halfway down his head, ending in a perfect shave at the neck. He pushed his uninjured hand through his rumpled curls, moving them off his forehead.

His olive skin and muscular build gave evidence to his Greek heritage and aided in his foreign appeal. Plus, he spoke English, Greek, and Russian fluently, so it made for a good parlor trick whenever he was out on the town. Pretend you could speak no English and the ladies would jump at the opportunity to help you translate. *How do you say, "Another gin and tonic?"*

Alé looked down at his sleeve and watched the coffee drip onto the floor. It had splattered all around the cuff of his white dress shirt. To hell with it, he thought, as he unbuttoned the cuff and rolled up the sleeve. Rolled sleeves were against NASA etiquette, especially in the main office hub of Goddard Space Flight Center in Greenbelt, Maryland. Down in the trenches, where most of the engineers and scientists worked, he could get away with it, but up here, the suits frowned on such a casual display. He didn't have time to worry about office etiquette at the moment. He was in the middle of the biggest project of his life, and as one of the lead engineers, its success or failure would make or break his career with NASA.

"I came to get the latest briefing on the launch. It's time to transfer this over to the coders to prep for commlink. How're the sats doing up there?" he asked Jade, shifting the stack of paperwork he carried to his right armpit and rolling up his left shirtsleeve to match the right.

Jade stared down at him over the top of her glasses, a pair of large, round, black-framed Guccis. She was a good six inches taller than Alé, making her six foot four in flats. A beautiful woman, she had dark skin that was smooth and clear. Jade liked to wear red lipstick and today was no different, with a bright red, almost orange color adorning her lips. It struck the perfect contrast to her crisp, navy pantsuit.

Her curly black hair was cropped short, right to her scalp, and her style, combined with her height and slender physique, made her look more like a runway model than a NASA executive. In high school, she was a promising track and field athlete and had hopes of going to the Olympics someday, but the war dashed those dreams.

Instead, she joined the Air Force and got her PhD in computer science and mechanical engineering. When the government fired up the space program again, a year after the war ended, Jade was at the head of the line for project engineers. She quickly worked her way through the ranks and was now the launch manager of the Tracking and Data Relay Satellites (TDRS) launch team. When it came to getting stuff done, Jade Stanton was all balls and no bull.

"So far, so good. Walk with me," she said, pointing out the direction and starting off at a breakneck pace. She liked Alé Bakas. He was one of the younger project engineers on the TDRS team, but he had a good head on his shoulders. She prided herself on her ability to spot top performers in an engineering bunch and Alé had some serious potential.

Of course, he needs to get his head out of the clouds, she thought, a sideways grin breaking from her red lips.

Alé, like most twenty-six-year-old men, was all about the sport and she could see it a mile away. After all, she had a full decade of life experience on him. Alé was in charge of the coding team for the first communications satellites to launch since before the war. During the fighting, they'd lost all communications satellites, forcing the world to revert to older styles of communication, using landlines and wires.

Over the past few years, many cell towers had been rebuilt, restoring cell service to almost prewar levels, but the world still lacked a broad, satellite-based communications network that worked independently of the cell phone companies. That was why this project was so important. It represented a lucrative cash cow, full of milk, and ready to make the government some big bucks through commercial communications contracts.

Jade pulled a folder from the outer sleeve of her briefcase, not missing a step as she continued down the office corridor. Alé easily kept up with her fast pace, which she liked. Jade was a firm believer in working nonstop, including walking time.

"The launch was successful. Separation went off with no issues," she said. "They're currently sitting in a low-Earth orbit awaiting the window for the boosters to fire. That's all I know so far. Your team has my blessing to begin the commlink actions. Take this to Nemo." She handed Alé the folder and motioned to it with a tick of her head while her eyes remained forward, scanning the hallway as she walked. Jonathan Nematokis, or "Nemo" as they knew him in the trenches, was in charge of the primary control group that ran the code to the TDRS. "He'll get the transmissions started. The boosters will begin firing within the next ninety minutes. Let's hope for six clean transfers."

The TDRS project was actually a grouping of six satellites, all launched on the same rocket, each bound for a different orbital position around the Earth. After the first stage of the launch put them into a low-Earth orbit, they had split apart using small, chemical thrusters. Now, each satellite waited to ride a separate booster out to its final orbital position. It was a tedious ballet, artfully designed to ensure the safety of all six satellites as they blasted off separately into the vacuum. The process required the orchestration of hundreds of engineers and coders working in tandem.

"Roger that," Alé replied. "I'll see what Nemo has to say. Oh yeah, I almost forgot." He leaned toward her as he turned to head down another hallway to the left. "I'll send you my dry-cleaning bill." He flashed a sideways smile followed by a wink.

Jade rolled her eyes and suppressed a smile of her own. She turned on her quarter-inch, Louboutin heel and started down the large, open stairway to catch the Metro into DC. NASA's administrator and his entourage wanted a briefing on the status of the TDRS launch. This was NASA's first launch in almost two decades and they were on the verge of firing up their crewed spaceflight program again, but first, they had to get communications in order, which was where Jade and her team came into the picture.

Each TDRS would come to rest in a geosynchronous orbit almost 36,000 kilometers away from Earth. Geosynchronous, meaning each satellite would orbit at exactly the same speed as the planet, 360 degrees in twenty-four hours, and would, therefore, remain stationary over a certain point on the globe. Anyone who knew where the satellite orbited could find it and use it for communications, as long as they had a hefty contract with NASA for commercial satellite use.

Boosters designed to carry the satellites to orbit and keep them in their orbits would fire at precisely the right window. Each satellite would leave its current orbit and venture into the void, still part of the Earth and its satellite complex, but much farther out than most orbiting vessels.

They would end up spaced out equidistantly around the planet to allow for constant communication between Mission Control and future crewed spaceflights. An orbiting space vehicle could bounce a signal off whichever satellite was directly in their line of site and switch to the next as the orbit continued. Constant communication was a necessity when working with humans in space, and it was up to this mission to make it happen.

Alé made his way down the straight hallway on the second floor of Building Thirty-Six, the New Flight Projects Building, located in the heart of the rambling Goddard campus. In its heyday, the building was known for its energy efficiency, suspended glass meeting rooms, and maximum use of light for a more natural working environment. Although it was now out of date as far as efficiency standards went, the architecture of the four-story office building went well with the rest of the buildings in the complex and was generally appreciated by its occupants. Alé wasn't sold on its looks. He thought it felt stark and overly sanitized with its white ceilings, slate-gray flooring, glass and steel stair railings, and light oak wall paneling.

After dropping off the memorandum and getting a brief rundown of the program status from Nemo, Alé returned to his desk and set down his holo-phone. The digital display read 1:32 p.m., another forty-two minutes before the boosters ignited, pushing the TDRS into the second phase of their orbital insertion.

It would take the satellites a further two weeks and five maneuvers to ensure they all made it safely to their orbits. After the communications satellites were in place, the real work would begin. There would be four weeks of diagnostic testing, coding, and bug fixes before they were fully functional and ready for regular use.

Alé sat at his desk and unlocked his holo-screen, pulling up his email with the flick of his index finger. The inbox held sixty-two new emails since he had left his desk thirty-five minutes prior. He shook his head and let out a sigh. Time to turn on the tunes. He reached for his holo-phone and found a playlist of what he referred to as "afternoon" songs, or those that kept him awake and had a good beat. He placed a pair of tiny buds into his ears and began to sort through the emails.

There would be no lunch break today.

Chapter 5

Breathe. Relax. Breathe. Relax.

I immediately work on calming myself. I've had my hopes up before, and so far, I have nothing to show for it. This might be another false alarm. I close my eyes and press my palms into my cheeks.

Breathe. Relax. Breathe. Relax. 10, 9, 8, 7, 6, 5, 4, 3, 2, 1...

I repeat the words and the numbers several times in my mind. My heartbeat calms. I catch my breath and the stress that built up in my muscles relaxes its vise grip. Counting backward is a little trick I've been doing since I was a kid. I mostly use it to help me sleep, but it works great for those times when the ship is falling apart, or when I find rockets launching from Florida.

When I open my eyes again, I'm calmer and ready to delve into this further. I run a basic diagnostic test to make sure the program is running correctly. Occam's razor says the simplest answer is usually the right one and this concept applies a lot up here in space. First step, make sure your computer hasn't created something out of nothing.

Everything checks out fine. Next, I take a few minutes to look over the readings carefully, thoroughly, to make sure this isn't some sort of user error. I've been the victim of user error before.

The coding program makes a map, but it's not like one of the old Google maps available on the station archives with lots of color and close-proximity detail. It's detailed, but it's not easy to read if you aren't a computer. You can't see what it found without taking your own pictures. The program helps you narrow down where you need to point the camera.

My camera just happens to be shaped like Iron Man.

"Nix!" I call up from the VP. I pause and listen for the sound of him detaching from his charging port mounted on the wall of the Docking Module. The Docking Module connects to the side of the Service Module. It houses dual airlocks and four docking ports and was originally meant for expansion, with new modules scheduled to be added to the docking ports and visiting ships docking there too. Of course, these modules were never built and there are no visitors now.

Nix has his own airlock inside the Docking Module. That airlock has a charging port in it and there's another charging port in the Service Module, but Nix prefers to charge in the Docking Module for some reason only he knows. That's how I know where to call for him. I hear the clicks as his batteries unhitch from the charging port. A few seconds later, he sticks his head through the hatch. "Yes? What can I help you with today?"

"I need you to go outside and take some pictures for me," I say, swiveling around so he can see my face. I don't know if seeing my face matters to him, but I like to think it does. "The tracking program found something interesting and I need to take a closer look."

"Oh yes, that sounds exciting," he says as he moves fully into the Service Module and looks at the screen. "What on Earth have you found?" he asks. Nix has a set of jokes programmed into his mind. Sometimes, I wonder if he's really trying to be funny or if he happens to get lucky. This time he got lucky and a quick laugh escapes me. He cocks his head to the side to show he's pleased with himself for making a funny comment.

"It found something in central Florida," I say.

"That's where they launch rockets," Nix says.

"You got it, buddy." I wink at him, then return my gaze to the holo-screen in front of me. "I could probably photograph it from inside, but the pictures will be much better from outside the hull. I want you to go outside with Hubble."

"Hubble" is a little pet name I have for the 1200 mm Nikon Space Camera mounted inside Nix's head. He has a direct wireless link-up with the station computers, so he can send the pictures back to my holo-screen moments after he takes them.

"I'll be out there in a jiff," he says.

"Thank you, Nix."

The station's almost in the dark now. He'll have to hurry. If not, it'll be a long forty-five minutes before the sun rises again, and with every rotation, the station gets farther away from Cape Canaveral. We must move fast.

I watch as Nix pulls himself into his airlock and closes the small hatch behind him. It's a tight fit. There's no way I could fit into the airlock, but it's the perfect size for him and the little tool kit he hauls along with him. The latches on the edge of the airlock click shut, and almost immediately, the air cycles out of it. All I hear from the inside is the faint hiss when the seals around the perimeter squeeze tight from the loss of atmosphere. Nix waves to me from the tiny window that looks into the lock. He opens the outer hatch and a fifty-meter tether unspools from a clip on his belt.

"Watch the tether," I say into the small holo-bud headset clamped to my ear. He already knows this, but there's no harm in being cautious. It's dangerous to have the tether too close to the antenna array. Not that the array does me any good since nobody's listening to my broadcast, but it's still nice to know it's there.

"Yes ma'am," he says, and I watch him from the holo-screen in the Service Module. He turns to the camera mounted outside his airlock on the hull of the station and raises his hand to his forehead to perform an army salute.

There are cameras at various places outside the station so I can see the outer elements of the spacecraft. I have several of the camera feeds pulled up on the holo-screen in front of me. I move the video tiles around the screen to get the configuration of shots that I want. In the top right-hand corner is a tile showing the Nikon feed from Nix's head. It's black right now, but when he starts taking shots, they'll appear here in rapid succession. He's working on getting his tether hooked up and I can see the blackness of space behind him as he works.

There's nothing quite as black as the void when you're looking at it from the station in the middle of the day. Only the very brightest stars and planets have enough power to pierce through the glare from the sun and the light bouncing off the planet below. Even those very bright few can't make it through sometimes. Right now, there's nothing. Just blackness. It's so black it makes me uncomfortable, and I minimize this tile and move it down to the bottom corner of the screen. It seems silly, yet I can't help but think that if I allow the blackness to take up too much of my screen, it might jump out into my station and consume me. This strange, unfounded fear rests in the pit of my stomach like a toad.

Nix gets his tether set up and makes his way to the starboard side of the station, moving in and out of several of the video feed tiles. The cameras are programmed to follow a target so they keep track of him as he circles around to the other side of the station. After ninety seconds or so, he's made it around and is facing the Earth below. Like a peacock spreading its wings in slow motion, the ocean passes below us in shades of blue ranging from the palest baby blue to the deepest dark, almost purple. Nix clips his feet into the handholds that surround the outer skin of the Service Module and retracts his legs to make himself more stable.

We are almost past the Pacific Ocean and the coast of California is creeping toward us in slow motion. The part of the surface I see during daylight changes with every new orbit. That's why we need to get these pictures taken now. After two more revolutions, Florida will be out of sight for another three Earth days.

The last remnants of the ocean slowly slide out of the camera's view. Now, the Grand Canyon lies sprawled out below, like an insect, a centipede with thousands of tiny legs twisting and turning in on itself through the red brown dirt of the desert. I've watched videos of centipedes squirming around and I can't imagine seeing one in real life. They look like science fiction space creatures. Well, I guess I'm more of a space creature than any bug on Earth.

I continue to watch the canyon slip by and notice it's flanked by forests of what looks like dark green moss. I close my eyes for a moment and try to imagine what it must look like from the surface, the canyon surrounded by vast forests of trees. I've seen pictures of it, of course, in the station archives, but it doesn't seem possible that a crack in the surface could expand almost thirty kilometers wide and 1,800 meters deep. I can't fathom the size of something like that. After a few seconds, I give up and open my eyes again. The expanse of green and brown continues below, occasionally cut into by rivers meandering toward the ocean. This orbit won't take me directly over the same spot in Florida, but it will take me close, through Texas, over the Gulf of Mexico, then out to the Atlantic Ocean.

"Nix," I say, "it's almost time to start. Are you ready?"

"Yes, ma'am," he replies. "You give the mark."

I wait a few more seconds, watching the orbital coordinates flash by on the holo-screen. Then I say, "Mark."

In an instant, he's snapping pictures. He can take them *fast*, about four per second during the five minutes the coordinates are in closest range. The pictures flow back to the station computers through his uplink. They're stored in a special file I set up to keep them separate from other pictures we've taken. I'll have around 1,200 pictures to go through by the end.

When he's done, it takes Nix about five minutes to make his way back to the airlock. I can hear his lock cycling, bringing fresh atmosphere in and pushing the scorched nothingness of the vacuum back out. I'm waiting for him there.

"Thanks, Nix," I say. "You did well. There are one thousand one hundred and ninety-seven photos in the database."

"Any time," he says. "Is there anything else you need me to do now? Maybe you would like me to dance some more for you on your birthday?" Now he's moving his legs slowly from side to side while pumping his arms in the air over his head.

I laugh out loud at this. "No, thanks. I appreciate it, but I've got my work cut out for me to analyze these pictures. I'll be in G."

He nods and heads out of the Service Module to find the warmth and peace of his docking port. I push myself along the handholds overhead. I've brought a small, handheld holo-screen with me so I can sift through the pictures while I take a stroll through the garden. I drop down through tunnel B, feeling the familiar pull of gravity making its way into my body, rooting me to the rubber mat on the floor. As I turn to head to the right and begin my walk, I glimpse something in the small mirror bolted to the wall over the sink.

I'm looking back at myself in the mirror, but it's a strange version of me. My dark brown hair is pulled back into a tight ponytail at the base of my neck. My clothes are rumpled but clean, as usual. Nothing looks like it's physically out of place, but there is something odd about my reflection that catches my eye. Something that I am not used to seeing. The plain brown eyes in the mirror take on a curious look and the nose wrinkles. It takes me a few seconds to realize what's different.

I am smiling.

I pause there only for a moment, shake my head, and start walking. This little development has taken the boring right out of Monday. Could this be some sort of cosmic birthday gift from the universe? I guess we'll see.

***

It wasn't a perfect pass over Florida, but the pictures turned out really well. It took me about two hours walking around the G to go through all of them, sorting them into files based on their clarity and position. Now I've stopped in the kitchen. I'm sitting at the little round table eating chunks of watermelon with the holo-screen propped up in front of me, going through the photos that are most interesting.

The movement detected by the program is definitely from a rocket launch. The photos include snaps of the launch complex at the Cape and there's the fuzzy outline of a cloud. It's a long, skinny cloud, like the tail of a fluffy, white cat spiraling up into the sky. It's a huge tail, and from the looks of it, it must have been a very large rocket.

Thoughts fill my mind. Ideas. Questions. Doubts. Fears. I file them away for now and focus on the facts presented in the pictures before me. Whatever they launched is not meant for low-Earth orbit. This rocket tail looks way too big for that. I did some research in the station archives to get a better idea of what the size of the tail might mean.

Communications satellites are often put into geosynchronous orbits, where they're synced with the Earth's orbit, directly over the equator. NASA used to have a massive network of these satellites for station communications before the war. Putting them into this farther orbit means that they're always in the same position over the planet. It makes it easy for Earth-based signals, or those in low-Earth orbit, to find the satellites, and it allows orbiting vehicles to stay in constant communication with the ground.

My station orbits anywhere between 350 kilometers and 450 kilometers above the surface, depending on the timing of the ion drive cycle. The geosynchronous orbit is 35,786 kilometers above the equator. It takes a big rocket to launch something out that far. I haven't picked up anything even remotely like that rocket blast on my monitoring program before. That doesn't mean they haven't been launching. It means that the few times I've scanned that portion of the globe, there was no launch going on. I got lucky with this one.

Whatever launched in that massive rocket is probably sitting in a parking orbit at the moment. Soon, they'll move it to a transfer orbit, which will then take it to its final orbital position. If it is heading toward a geosynchronous orbit, then I have a better idea of where it is, or at least, where to look for it.

It's not like I haven't been sending signals for help. The computer has been broadcasting a steady SOS signal since the start of the war. It's a simple SOS in Morse code. I added the dash dot dot for "D" or Delta, to indicate the call sign for the station. So far, nobody's been listening for communications from me because they don't know I'm up here. A communications satellite will be different though. It will be turned on to listen all the time. The chances of someone actually picking up the signal are much greater now, assuming I'm right about this hunch.

I pull up a tile on my holo-screen showing the station communications program. I set it to send any incoming signals directly to me, no matter the time of day or night. That should catch anything they may send back in return, and in a few weeks, if I haven't heard anything back, I'll direct my signal at 36,000 km to see if I can find my new friends in space. If I can, I may be able to direct a signal right at the new satellite. We'll see.

Chapter 6

Gina Lau sat back in her chair and raised her hands above her head. She tilted her head back, then bent her body from side to side, stretching her neck and back. It had been a long night. The digital time on her holo-phone said 2:03 a.m. She had four more hours of this graveyard shift before she could get some sleep.

What made matters worse was she hadn't slept much the day before either. Launch day was always hectic and every member of the TDRS team had been either at their holo-screens or on call. Gina was no different, coming in early and working through the evening, even though she only played a minor role in the team. Her official designation was communication coding engineer, specializing in satellite communications. Because she'd only been at NASA for about eight months, Gina drew the short straw when they scheduled shifts two months prior. The graveyard shift job duties amounted to keeping track of location readings while trying not to fall asleep. She was more like a well-paid babysitter than an engineer with a master's degree in computer science.

The satellite separation had gone off without a hitch earlier in the day, and the six satellites were now awaiting the next burn to boost them into transfer orbits. That burn was scheduled for 8:00 a.m. EST. If all went as planned, it would happen while she dreamed of chocolate fudge and Dante Sweeney (the guy who worked three cubicles over with the long nose and killer pecs) in her warm bed on the third floor of her apartment building.

NASA designed these TDRS satellites to be small and light so that they could all be launched on one large rocket instead of six smaller rockets. Each had an electromagnetic thruster instead of a traditional liquid fuel propulsion system. This allowed for much lighter packages. Once they reached their final orbits, each satellite would "unpack" itself, deploying a large, primary antenna along with solar cells for future power needs. For now, every satellite had a small transmitter antenna, just big enough to send signals to and receive signals from Mission Control.

The downfall of launching six satellites at once was that there was more room for error. Stuffing all of that instrumentation into one payload wasn't easy or cheap. Had something gone wrong with the rocket, they would have lost it all. But so far, the mission was on track with no snags.

Gina pulled up various tiles on her holo-screen, casually checking each system before moving on to the next. Each satellite used a different call sign, the last six letters of the Greek alphabet, tau through omega. Her current project was to send tracking signals to the satellites individually and have them mimic the signals back to her to make sure everything was running as it should. No issues. The satellites sent back their respective signals and promptly returned to standby mode, awaiting her next command.

Gina finished the last set of commands and sighed, rapping her knuckles on her desk. It was time for more coffee. Instead of going to the small break room at the end of the hallway, she decided to head down to the cafeteria. They had better coffee there and she needed to stretch her legs. Plus, the route would take her by Dante's cubicle. Not a big deal since he wasn't there right now, but still, maybe she could snag a peek of that picture of him surfing in California. Before she left, she gazed one final time at the tiles on her screen. Nothing going on. Nobody would miss her for a few minutes.

***

Exactly fifteen minutes later, fresh mug of coffee in hand, Gina returned to her desk. That's strange, she thought, tilting her head to one side. Her holo-screen was still on, pulsing under the soft fluorescent lighting of the workspace. Her screen was set to power down into sleep mode after a two-minute user absence. It should have gone off while she was in the cafeteria, unless someone had been there looking through it, or something had happened with the active tiles she'd left open on the screen.

She swiped her finger lightly over the display and brought up each of the six tiles monitoring the functions of the satellites. All six were still online, snoozing away as they'd been when she left a few minutes prior. Then she saw that satellite five or Psi, as it was known by the team, was transmitting something onto the tile. Again, she cocked her head to the side and pulled up the tile marked "Psi" so she could have a better look. It had picked up a signal and it was relaying it back to her computer. Her look became more puzzled. She hadn't sent it a signal to mimic back, and there wasn't anything else out there that could have sent it. Yet here it was, clearly broadcasting a signal that it picked up from somewhere.

"What'cha got goin' on here, Psi?" Gina said out loud, eyes narrowing even more as she peered at the screen.

She ran a series of commands with some basic diagnostic checks: position, orbital speed, proximity warnings. Nothing appeared out of line, but it had definitely picked something up. The signal was repeating itself at regular intervals, some sort of mass broadcast. But from where?

At that moment, another satellite, Omega, picked it up too. Now both sats were reporting the same signal and the same pattern of repeats. Gina checked proximities for all known satellites still in low-Earth orbit. Since the war, there wasn't really much out there to check. It could have possibly been some space debris, but she doubted that any prewar debris would still have power.

She reached into her desk drawer and pulled out a pencil and paper. This time, when the message began, she wrote it down. It didn't take her long to realize it was Morse code. She pulled up her reference guide on the holo-screen and scribbled down the letters as she decoded them. Her eyes grew wide and her mouth dropped.

"Oh my God," she said and immediately grabbed her holo-phone off the desk next to her.

***

Jonathan Nematokis lurched out of bed, bumping his head on the headboard shelving and immediately cursing. After a dazed, sleep-filled moment, he realized he wasn't dreaming. His phone was, indeed, ringing on the table next to his bed.

He picked up the phone. "This is Nemo."

"Nemo! It's Gina. I'm getting some," she paused for a moment, then said, "strange communications from the sats. I think you need to get down here. They're picking up a signal from low-Earth orbit."

"What?" Nemo asked. His brain was still foggy with sleep and he rubbed his eyes to wake himself. He'd heard what she said, but it made no sense to him.

"The sats picked up a signal from low-Earth orbit, Nemo," Gina repeated, slower this time, as if speaking to a child.

His thoughts crystallized and realization began to sink in. "Are you sure it's not an error?"

"Yes, I'm sure," she said. "I thought the same at first too because only Psi picked it up right away, but I ran diagnostics and everything's in working order. No errors. Then Omega picked up the same signal. I'm telling you, it's deliberate. It's being broadcast from somewhere near the satellites."

"What kind of signal is it?" he asked, his voice strengthening.

"A radio signal in Morse code."

"Well, what does it say?"

"It's an SOS. Followed by the call sign 'Delta.'"

"Delta? Are you sure about that?"

"Yes! I'm picking it up on both Omega and Psi and I've checked the transmission three times."

Nemo sighed. "I'll be down there in fifteen minutes. Keep a watch on it. I'll bring Stanton into the loop," he said, swinging his legs around to the side of the bed. He hung up the phone and rubbed his aching head before heading to his closet to get dressed.

Chapter 7

Troy poked his head into Jade's office. He cracked the door enough so she could see the bridge of his long nose and one eye peering over his long, delicate fingers. As her assistant, he knew she was busy and would *not* appreciate this interruption, but Nemo insisted.

"Ahem... Ms. Stanton?" He shifted his one visible eye nervously in her direction to see how she would react, like a child confessing to a crime.

"Yes," Jade replied, breaking her eye contact with the holo-screen in front of her to look at him with disdain. Troy was a nice enough guy, but she suspected she terrified him, which wasn't a bad thing, but it bordered on annoying. He was weak, always wanting to be liked, and never wanting to make waves. A great quality in a politician, but not in her assistant.

"Nemo is here to see you, ma'am. He says it's very important," Troy said in a soft voice.

Jade gestured for Troy to let Nemo in, then turned back to her holo-screen and continued to move tiles around the screen, typing here and there, lifting items into archives, and jotting notes down with her fingertips. Troy let out a nervous sigh as he moved away from the cracked door and Nemo walked through.

Jade paused and glanced at the time on her computer—8:00 a.m. on the button. No messing around, she thought with a crooked smile and a slight head nod. She had been there since 6:30 a.m., of course. As director of the TDRS program, the next few weeks would be tense and she wasn't one to shy away from an early morning work session.

"What's up, Nemo?" she asked, this time, not looking up from her screen.

Nemo slid through the doorway and walked into her office, standing in front of her shiny mahogany desk. He was thin and towering with brown, shaggy hair that hung over his eyes.

"Jade, I'm sorry to bother you, but we've picked up something that I think you need to know about," he paused and glanced off to his left at a vibrant painting of the night sky that hung on the far wall. "Something unusual," he added. His gaze broke from the painting and he slouched down into one of the thick, leather armchairs that stood in front of her desk.

Jade noticed that Nemo seemed disheveled, at least more than usual. He wasn't known for his ability to dress like an adult, but this morning was worse, like he had been there for hours already. Still, she didn't mention it. Lots of NASA employees looked like hell when huge projects loomed around them. It was practically part of the job description.

Crossing her arms at her chest, she repeated, "Unusual." It wasn't a question meant for him to explain; rather, it was her way of mulling the word over in her head before speaking. Nemo waited dutifully for his turn to speak. She didn't make much of the word though, because a short second later, she was back to typing. "What does that mean?" she asked at last.

"The satellites picked up a signal. Something broadcast from low-Earth orbit. It was first detected by Psi at about 2:30 a.m. Since that time, all of the sats have picked up the same signal at different times and at regular intervals. Whatever it is, it's orbiting up there with them. Not the same orbit though, but near them." He paused to scratch the beginnings of the beard scruff underneath his jutting chin. "From what we can tell, this thing is orbiting higher and faster than our sats. Of course, the sats are only in parking orbit for now, but based on how the signal is traveling, we know whatever it is, it's in a more stable orbit."

Her dark eyes darted up from behind the screen. Now, he had her attention. She snapped her fingers and the holo-screen disappeared as if it had never been there in the first place. The sound made Nemo jump. Not only had he been there for five hours, but he'd also had plenty of coffee.

"What are you talking about, Nemo? What could be broadcasting up there?"

"Well, at first, we thought maybe it was some space debris, but that doesn't make sense. Anything left over after the war should have run out of power long ago. Plus, it's a regular broadcast, you know, repeating the same thing over and over again. Space debris doesn't do that."

"The South Americans," she said. Again, this wasn't something she wanted Nemo to answer. She said this looking up at the ceiling as if trying to decide if it was a real possibility. Then she shook her head. "No way. They are under strict sanctions and the allies are watching their launch bases like a hawk with an evil eye. They couldn't have anything up there."

Nemo nodded his agreement. "You're right. The Trusted Allies would definitely know if the South Americans had something going on up there in orbit. We called up Martin Javi, the Trusted Allies' representative in DC, and there's nothing up there that they're aware of. We even considered that maybe it was one of the SA allies. Perhaps some rogue nation launching space probes from the desert or something." He swallowed hard. "But that makes no sense either, considering *what* the message says."

"For heaven's sake, Nemo, what does it say?" Jade hated playing games.

"It's an SOS, Jade. Followed by the call sign Delta."

"Delta? Are you sure? Who would use a Delta call sign?"

"Well, that's what we were wondering," he said, his eyebrows spiking toward the ceiling. "So, we did some research, looking back into the old NASA logs from before the war. Then we found this." He opened up a binder that sat in his lap. Jade hadn't even noticed it in his hands when he walked in. Inside the binder was a thick manilla folder. Nemo took the folder out and slid it toward Jade on the desk, right where the holo-screen had been moments earlier.

Her eyes fell on the cover. She looked back up at him and said, "You can't be serious."

But the look on his face said that he was dead serious. The label on the file read "Delta Space Station."

Chapter 8

"Have a seat, Alé," Jade said.

She sat on the opposite side of the desk in her big leather chair, legs crossed, elbows resting at her sides. She peered at him through her fingers, which were tented in front of her face. One finger moved forward slightly, and with a synchronized nod of her head, she indicated which chair he should sit in.

Alé always felt out of place in Jade's office. It was the office of someone with impeccable taste and style. He stared at the large painting that hung over the credenza on his left. It depicted the night sky in bold swaths of purple, blue, and black, dotted with stars of all colors and sizes. No doubt, it cost more than his truck and apartment combined. What struck him about the painting was that it wasn't a realistic view of the sky, but more like an artist's impression of what the sky might look like if it had color and texture, not simply light on dark. He had to admit it was beautiful.

Taste and style weren't his thing. Alé preferred more lighthearted office accessories, like the little plastic toilet he'd won at the department golf tournament last summer. He actually had the *highest* golf score, for which he won a prize: the little toilet to display on his desk, with pride, for a whole year. He had started taking golf lessons immediately after his coworkers bestowed that honor on him.

He walked around the chair to Jade's left and took a seat, leaning back and stretching his arms behind his head. "What's up?"

Jade slid a file across the desk to him without saying a word. It was a thick file with the words "Delta Space Station" printed in bold font across the front. "I want you to take a look at this. Nemo brought it to me this morning. He said the graveyard shift found a radio signal broadcasting in low-Earth orbit. The sats picked it up." She paused to take a sip of coffee, her eyebrows raised at what she was about to say. "It seems that whatever is broadcasting is orbiting up there with them."

Alé looked down at the file in front of him and flipped open the front cover, scanning the first page of contents with a furrowed brow and pursed lips. After a few moments, he said, "Is this a joke? You don't seriously think it's this space station. I mean, this thing had to have deorbited years ago when the war broke out."

Jade peered at him through her fingers again, one eyebrow raised and her head cocked to the side. The look said that she was certainly *not* joking. After a moment, her face softened into a look of understanding and she sighed, rubbing her hands at her temples.

"I know. I didn't believe it at first either," she said. "But yes, we think it could be this space station. Now, whatever it is, it's broadcasting a repeating SOS in Morse code, followed by the call sign Delta. I've got a call in to our guys over at the State Department to see if there's been any kind of launch by the South Americans, which was our first thought. If they were doing communication launches, the State guys would know about it. But frankly, I can't imagine why the SAs would launch a satellite and program it to broadcast an SOS using the call sign of a defunct space station. It doesn't make sense."

"When was the last time they had contact with the Delta?" Alé asked, raising his own eyebrows.

"They lost contact at the same time everyone lost contact... when the SAs took out the satellites, what, nineteen years ago? That's the last communication in the old NASA system logs. All hell broke loose after that. Well, you know how it was," she said.

Alé nodded. He *did* know how it was. He continued to leaf through the contents of the file, his face tight with concentration. At last, he put the file down on the desk. "So, what do you want me to do?"

Jade nodded and swiveled in her chair to face him. "Do some digging for me. Make sure it's not an error in the satellite program coding." He tried to interrupt her with an assurance that it couldn't be a coding error, but she wasn't having it. She put her hand up and shook her head. He stopped.

"I agree," she said, "I don't see any way that it could be an error, considering it's registering on multiple satellites, but I want to make sure this isn't something we've messed up on our end. I can't bring this to the administration on a hunch." Again, she paused to sip her coffee. "I also want you to do some more digging on the Delta. I want information on life support, power systems, size, structure, crew, you name it. Write up a report for me by tomorrow afternoon."

Now she relaxed a little in her chair and swiveled it enough so she could look out the big window behind her that peered over the rolling lawns of Goddard. "I agree, there's no way that thing is still flying around. Unless someone is up there running it."

***

Later, Alé stopped in front of Gina Lau's cubicle. He rested his forearms on the front panel and peered down at her.

"Gina Lau?" he asked.

"Yes..." she said hesitantly. She wondered what Alé Bakas was doing down in the coder trenches, which is what they called the vast room filled with cubicles where the lower-level engineers worked.

A sweet smile spread across his face. She blushed in return, looking down and taking a second to catch her breath under his gaze. He was handsome in a sharp kind of way, all angular and dark. It made her uncomfortable. Plus, Alé was at least two levels ahead of her in rank, and talking to superiors always made her stomach flip.

He continued to look at her, his eyes darkening slightly. Then he glanced away toward the north wall of the room. She could tell he wasn't actually looking *at* anything, almost like he was brooding over something, some task he wasn't thrilled about. After a moment, his thoughts must have skittered away and he looked back at her and cleared his throat. "I hope you got some rest today. I know you were on graveyard last night."

Gina nodded and yawned at the same time. She had gotten some rest, that was true, but not enough. It was now after 6:00 p.m. and she was preparing for another night on sat watch. The sats had been on the move that day, the first round of course corrections that would send them into their final orbits. They would require closer monitoring tonight. Because of this, two other engineers had joined her for the evening shift, but the room was so big that neither of them were near her desk.

"I have a little task for you to do tonight, if you don't mind," he said, flashing her another smile. His words weren't meant as a question of whether she minded but more like a courtesy. She wondered if he knew the power he had with that smile. Again, she blushed and looked at her desk, embarrassed that he had such an effect on her. "You picked up a signal last night. Something broadcast from low-Earth orbit. I need you to do some code checks for me. Stanton's got me looking into this, and I want to eliminate the possibility of a coding error. Would you mind?"

"No, I don't mind. But I assure you, there is no..."

"Thanks, Gina," he cut her off and turned to leave her desk. Pausing, he turned his head back to her slightly. "Oh, and we should probably keep this one just between us for now"—he glanced around the mostly empty room—"until we know what we're dealing with."

"S-s-sure," she said.

He nodded, flashed her one final grin—a thin, slight one this time—and dropped a pile of paperwork on her desk. There were dozens of form letters in the pile detailing what tests he wanted her to run. They were long, boring, and were to be tested in triplicate. Gina watched him as he walked down the aisle and out the main door, shaking her head. She didn't want to run the tests because she knew it was a useless search. There was no way a computer error had produced those radio signals. She mentally berated herself for not protesting more, but that smile had gotten to her. Instead of dwelling on it any further, she sighed, reached for the pile, and got to work.

Chapter 9

Alé was eight years old when the war started, but the memory was still sharp in his mind, like it was fixed there with a straight pin on his mental bulletin board. The unrest had been brewing for years, under the surface of the world's political systems. That summer, the summer of the bombings, would turn out to be one of the darkest times in human history.

It actually began years before with the Summer Olympics held in Sao Paulo, Brazil. South America had long been a host of the FIFA World Cup, but the Olympic games had only been held on the continent one time prior to that, the 2016 games in Rio de Janeiro. Those games had been plagued with rumors of cash deficits, poor construction quality, and blown deadlines. When Sao Paulo won the bid many years later, heavy controls were put into place to ensure that these same issues did not occur again. The government of Brazil had grown stronger in the years since Rio, and they intended to redeem themselves with this new bid.

The Brazilian government still lacked the funds necessary to make a successful bid without help. To fix this problem, they leaned on the shoulders of powerful drug cartels from all around the continent to provide money and labor. This meant that billions of dollars of drug money flowed in and out of the country in an effort to have the city ready in time for the opening ceremony. But just as they'd done so many years before in Rio, they quickly ran out of time and money, and desperation set in. The cartels capitalized on this desperation. Cartel leaders began to occupy high positions of power in the Brazilian government and a new family of drug lords came into the picture.

The Guerrero family had control over the historic drug cartel called O Comando. Juan Guerrero, who was actually a native of Columbia but had migrated to Brazil in his youth, was elected president of Brazil in a corrupt, violent election, only six years after those fateful Olympic games. It did not take long for Guerrero and O Comando to turn the government into a dictatorship. As the drug money flowed in, Brazil became one of the strongest and most repressive governments in the world.

This scenario was not unique. Violent dictatorships had risen up more often than not in the history of human civilization. Guerrero was a brilliant man, hardened by years in the cartel trenches. He knew that what Brazil needed to become a world superpower was weaponry, and he had his sights set on creating a nuclear arsenal. But if he wanted nuclear power, he needed help.

North Korea had been developing nuclear technology for decades, to the detriment of their international relations. They were hungry for a meaningful trade partner, and on the other side of the planet, nobody paid much attention as Juan Guerrero and O Comando rose to the pinnacle of power.

The meeting with Kim Yong Ho, the dictator of North Korea, and Guerrero, took place under the radar. Guerrero came in to Pyongyang under cover of a shipping vessel up the Taedong River. Once there, he had a quiet meeting with the aging dictator, and Guerrero got his first glimpse of the magnitude of North Korea's nuclear program. He realized he'd struck gold. North Korea had the technology, the engineering power, and the materials to create a powerful nuclear arsenal. The world knew that the Koreans were dabbling in nuclear arms, but only Guerrero knew the strength and depth of what they'd developed in Pyongyang. The two dictators reached a deal and Brazilian drug money started flowing into North Korea in exchange for nuclear technology.

In the years following the secret alliance with North Korea, Guerrero quietly took control of the countries around Brazil. He got his deputies elected to political positions in the other South American countries through bribes, corrupt elections, and strategic murders. By the time the world took notice of the little government down in South America, the entire continent was under the control of the Brazilians through political partnerships. They called themselves the South Americans or the SAs for short. Deep in the jungle, Guerrero created his own state-of-the-art nuclear weapons manufacturing facility. He'd now set his sights on bigger goals.

When observed from space, Amazonia is usually shrouded under a thick cloud of condensation. It's like looking at a river of clouds flowing through the sky. Locals knew about the high-tech facility located several kilometers northwest of Manaus, but the story went that the structure was built as a laboratory for habitat research. Much of it was underground, to avoid being seen by airplanes, and the river of clouds provided the perfect cover from the prying eyes of satellites. Construction workers and nuclear engineers alike were quarantined, unable to leave the facilities under penalty of death. It was from this facility that the first attacks originated. They came in the middle of a steamy night in late June.

Five stealth drone bombers launched from the secret facility, each carrying a twenty-megaton thermonuclear bomb. Four of the drones were remotely piloted to New York City, Los Angeles, London, and Paris. The fifth drone was headed to Washington DC but never made it. A radar malfunction caused it to fly off course and detonate over the Atlantic Ocean.

They hit Los Angeles first and approximately one hour later, New York City. By the time the London bomb fell six hours later, armed forces all over the world were on alert for the drones. An ICBM caught the Paris bomber before it made landfall, and it detonated over the northern Atlantic Ocean. The bomb was so powerful, that even though it hadn't hit its intended target, nuclear debris and radiation spread throughout the west coast of Europe, burning and poisoning millions of people.

The bombs caused four matching mushroom clouds that rose nearly thirty-five kilometers into the sky. The fireballs and resulting radiation clouds were so big, they were visible from space. By the end of the night, millions were dead, and the world had changed forever.

Unfortunately, the nuclear attack was only the beginning of the story. After the bombs dropped, the cyberattacks began. Guerrero was a competent military man and a ruthless leader. He knew he'd need more than a few flashy bombs to start and win a world war and employed hundreds of hackers at his jungle compound for that purpose. After all, the cyber battle was just as important as the military battle.

Not only did Guerrero have the Amazon hackers in his corner, but they sent word out to their rogue counterparts throughout the world. Every cyberterrorist on the globe was part of the arsenal. After only two days, they had taken out all satellite communications by implanting viruses into the computer code that controlled the satellite systems. Communications satellites became glorified hunks of metal.

Guerrero was then ready for the next phase in his plan. He had amassed an army of over two million soldiers, all well-versed in alternative forms of guerrilla warfare communications. The officers of his army went through extensive training deep inside the underground passages of the Amazon facility. Then, those officers spread throughout South America, training fleets of soldiers stationed in strategic places around the continent.

The satellite blackouts devastated the world on many levels. Computer servers depended heavily on precision timekeeping. GPS satellites were the primary means of keeping accurate time around the world. Within a day after the satellites went black, time itself faltered. A half a second here and half a second there, and soon, computer systems failed. The internet crashed. Power and other utility companies were unable to control transmission networks. The planet went dark. Travel ground to a halt as commercial airliners, which depended on satellites for communication and weather tracking, couldn't function.

Two days after the initial nuclear strike, huge armies of SA soldiers rained down on the countries of Central America, taking them down easily. It was only a week before they were knocking at the US border with Mexico.

Militaries had to revert to World War II-era communications systems like telegraphs and Morse code. Since most of the landline phone cable network had long since been abandoned throughout the world, there was no way for the average person to communicate. Everything had to start from scratch, and it all had to be done fast to prepare for the counterattack of the advancing SA armies.

The events of those first few weeks marked the beginning of the deadliest war in human history. It lasted almost a decade and millions of people died in the fight. But out of the ruin, there was a silver lining. World powers that had formerly been bitter enemies, united to fight against the SAs. The resistance called themselves the Trusted Allies. Huge underground bunkers were constructed to house civilians and keep them safe from the attacking SA armies. People rallied together to find new ways to live and work in these underground habitats. They figured out ways to grow food, desalinate seawater, and restore communications with limited materials and almost no infrastructure. Men and women joined up in droves to be a part of the fight on the surface.

Eventually, the Trusted Allies made offensive moves, first into the bordering areas of Central America, where the SA stronghold had been almost invincible in the early years of the war. Little by little, the allies made progress, pushing the SAs farther back.

Although many wanted an eye for an eye, the allies never fired back with nuclear devices of their own. The fact that the attacks came out of the Amazon was especially important from an environmental standpoint. World leaders knew enough about global weather patterns to realize that destroying the Amazon with nuclear warheads was simply not an option if there was any hope of preserving the planet. So, the allies fought on the ground.

Alé didn't know it until much later in life, but he had narrowly escaped death by the bomb that was meant for Washington DC on that fateful June night. His memories of the time were of panic and disorder. People evacuated all major metropolitan areas, including his hometown of Baltimore. His father, Nick, enlisted in the army the very next day. It was the last time he would see his father alive.

Six months before his eighteenth birthday, the last stand happened in Sao Paulo, Brazil. A fitting place, since that's where all the chaos had started many years before with the Sao Paulo Olympic Games. Over one million soldiers lost their lives in the battle, but the Trusted Allies won the day, and the SAs surrendered on June sixteenth, almost a decade after the start of the war. All of the South American countries and their allies were now under the control of the Trusted Allies after the signing of the Sao Paulo Peace Treaty.

Not long after that day, people emerged from the underground shelters. The rebuilding ensued and the world economy actually boomed under the new flags of trust and unity. Alé spent two years helping out during the rebuilding effort, and when universities began admitting students again, he was one of the first to enroll. He earned a double master's degree in Aerospace Engineering and Computer Science, which led him directly to NASA.

Political leaders wanted to revive the crewed space program to provide a boost to American morale. NASA, with the help of commercial companies looking to contract satellite time, turned their attention to rebuilding the satellite communications fleet. Few satellites had survived the decade-long hiatus and of those, many were outdated and in rough shape. A total redesign was necessary to get communications back up to their prewar speed.

By the time Alé took the position as the head of the communications department of the TDRS launch, the war was a fading memory, making way for a new era of space exploration.

Chapter 10

"So, tell me. What did you find out?" Jade asked.

It was late the next afternoon. Jade had pushed back their meeting time twice because of issues with the TDRS orientation maneuvers. Now it was pushing 5:00 p.m. as they sat in her office going over the report Alé put together.

Alé pinched the bridge of his nose and squeezed his eyes shut. He'd been up most of the night sifting through various databases to put this report together, and his head wasn't happy with him. The pounding started after lunch, right behind his eyes. He'd kept the headache under control by chewing on ibuprofen, but it was creeping back into his eyes again. He'd need some caffeine soon.

"I had one of the coders run through a comprehensive series of checks and there are no issues with the sats themselves, which is good news," he said. "Of course, that does mean there's something else out there transmitting."

"Okay," Jade said, turning her neck from side to side and rolling her shoulders, exhaustion taking its toll on her as well.

He lightly tapped several times on the holo-screen he held in his hand to bring up his report. "The Delta," he began, "was a modular space station built about six years prior to the start of the war, an international collaboration involving multiple space agencies. Remember the International Space Station?"

Jade nodded in reply and Alé continued. "The ISS call sign was Alpha and there were two temporary habitats built between the time of the ISS and the Delta. They used the call signs Beta and Gamma. So that's how Delta got its name. Its primary function was to serve as the long-range stopover point for deep space missions. They built the station in low-Earth orbit, although the plan was to move it out farther, to a cislunar orbit... you know, between the Earth and the Moon."

"I know what cislunar means," Jade said, irritated. "Continue."

Alé cleared his throat. "It started in low-Earth orbit because it was to be the building base for the Deep Space Research Vessel, or DSRV," he said. "The DSRV was the ship that would take astronauts to other parts of the solar system, starting with Mars." He turned to the large holo-screen sitting on the conference table at the back of Jade's office and tapped some commands into his handheld screen. The overhead lights dimmed and the screen on the table glowed to life. A 3D model of the Delta materialized on the table, pulsing and shimmering as if it were alive.

"The ISS had multiple modules and solar arrays all surrounding a support scaffolding, making it look like a giant Lego structure," Alé continued. "The Delta was built in a similar way but was more compact. It had a cylindrical primary module called the Service Module, here." He used the screen pointer to show which part of the station he was referring to. "Below the Service Module, here"—he pointed at a round module connected via a docking port—"this was the Docking Module where the airlocks and additional docking ports were located. On the starboard side of the Service Module, perpendicular to the Docking Module was a hexagonal module called the VP for Viewpoint Module. It had windows all around it for viewing... as you probably guessed by the name." Moving farther starboard from the VP, Alé pointed to a set of scaffolds that ended in a large, gray box. This box was labeled "NUCLEAR REACTOR/ION ENGINE."

"That must've been one hell of an engine. It's huge," Jade said. Ion engines were not new technology. Space programs had used them since the 1960s to power vehicles once they reached space, but she had never seen one on a space station before. They were great for providing slow, constant acceleration, but space stations had always used conventional, liquid-powered rockets to keep them in orbit.

"Yes, it was, and there is a reason for that... I'm getting to it," he replied and flipped the holo-screen sketch around to show her eight long rectangles sticking out from the scaffolding between the Service Module and the engine box.

"Solar panels?" she asked.

"Correct," he said. "The station used the ion engine to do course corrections instead of conventional fuel. Since the station was never meant to stay in low-Earth orbit, the ion engine was installed to move it out to its final orbit, closer to the moon. The nuclear reactors were located in the same power module as the engine. They supplied the fuel plus all electricity to run the Delta. The solar panels were there as a backup power source in case something went wrong with the nuclear reactor."

On the port side, opposite the engine, Alé pointed to a narrow tunnel that ended in a sphere with a cylindrical module that looked like a doughnut circling the sphere. "This spherical module was called the Node and it was surrounded by the G."

"G for gravity?" Jade asked. She was in high school when the Delta was built, so she had some fuzzy memories of it based on news reports. She remembered there was a centripetal spin element included in the design.

"No," Alé said. "G for Gagarin. As in Yuri. This was a collaborative effort after all. Roscosmos was part of it too. I suppose they figured the first man in space should have a module named after him." He shrugged and set down his screen.

"The Delta was a critical part of the deep space mission plan," Alé continued from memory. "It had a fully functioning, centripetal force vessel. They needed the microgravity for long-term crew health and crop growth. It was the first spacecraft of its kind. Really phenomenal engineering. They successfully created a garden big enough to sustain a crew of six using the limited amount of gravity created by the spinning module. But this..." He pointed at a small portal on the side of the Node. "This was the crucial part. The RV would dock right here at this international docking port, and this was where they planned to build it. They'd do it all in a low orbit to save on costs. When it was complete, the Delta would use the ion engine to push itself and the DSRV out into cislunar orbit. Once there, the DSRV would leave the Delta and take this with it." He gestured at the G.

"The G," he continued, "had the capability to operate on the Delta or on the DSRV. Or they could all operate as one unit. And even better"—he pointed to the engine on the other side of the screen now—"the DSRV could rotate around after grabbing the G and pick up the large ion engine on the other side. This way they didn't have to build all that stuff twice. While the mission was underway, the Delta would go into a kind of... snooze mode, I guess you could call it, using its solar panels to power the minor systems. No orbital boost was necessary because of its position far from Earth, and even if they needed a boost, they planned to send crews to and from the Delta during the interval time periods anyway as part of ongoing scientific research. They could use conventional rockets brought by the visiting crew to change the orbit if necessary."

"Sounds complicated," Jade said.

Alé nodded and continued, "While the Mars missions were still in the building and training phases were on Earth, astronaut crews, who tended the garden and performed scientific experiments, occupied the Delta one hundred percent of the time. Similar to how the ISS was set up, crews would take the Russian Soyuz spacecraft up to the Delta three at a time, replacing a crew that would then leave in their own Soyuz. At any given time, there were between three and six astronauts on the Delta."

Alé picked up his holo-screen again and tapped a few commands into it, pulling up his report again. "So, that's the basics on how it worked, which brings us to the war." He looked at Jade to make sure he had her attention. He did. With her chin tilted up at him, she watched him curiously, and he continued. "There were three astronauts aboard the Delta on the night the nuclear bombs dropped. Obviously, this wasn't a problem for the astronauts, but when the SAs took out the satellite network with the computer attacks, well... that meant they couldn't talk to the ground anymore. The communications satellite network was how the crew of the Delta communicated with Mission Control."

"You mean they had no other means of communication?" Jade asked.

"Not from what I can tell. It all relied on TDRS transfer communications. They just never considered a complete failure of all satellites a possibility. It's probable that they had some rudimentary ham radios on board. But remember, after the nukes fell, all major cities were evacuated, including Houston and Mission Control. From what I gathered from these records, the astronauts were informed of the nuclear strike and advised that an immediate plan for return was in the works. Then, the computer hack left them totally without surface communications."

"But there was a return plan?" Jade asked.

Alé nodded. "There was, but they didn't realize how devastating the cyberattack was because they were never able to make contact again. They didn't get to relay the plan to the astronauts on the Delta. Then they found the debris."

"Debris? From the Delta?" Jade asked.

"No." Alé shook his head. "Debris from a Soyuz. Over Siberia. The Russians found a trail of Soyuz spacecraft debris a few days after the nuclear attacks. It appeared that the spacecraft had broken up in the atmosphere, but they never completed a formal investigation."

"Wait, they didn't investigate? How is that possible?" she asked.

Alé shrugged. "They assumed the crew tried to escape the Delta on their own and burned up. They found human remains in the wreckage, but there was no further investigation other than to clean up the major pieces of debris. You have to remember, the world was officially at war. They didn't have the workforce to check into it beyond that. After they found the wreckage, they assumed that without a crew there to make orbital maneuvers, the Delta would burn up in the atmosphere as it deorbited. I guess keeping track of an abandoned space station was not high on anyone's list of priorities."

When he finished, he looked at Jade, waiting for a response. She said nothing for a few moments, staring blankly out her window to the lawn below. As if snapping out of a daze, she spoke at last. "Well, that doesn't mean that it's still up there. Find out for sure. I want telescope pics. Bring in whoever you need for this, but keep the reasoning to yourself. If it's not the Delta up there sending that signal, then we need to figure it out ASAP. And if it is the Delta... Lord help us."

***

"Xander? Yeah, it's Alé."

Xander Kent worked in the astrodynamics department at Johnson Space Center in Houston, Texas. He managed the orbital motions team that was in charge of spacecraft trajectories and orbital maneuvers. Despite his fancy job title, Xander was not your typical mathematics geek clad in polo shirts and pocket protectors. He preferred Hawaiian print shirts and sported a fantastic mop of long, curly hair.

"Alé! What can I do for you?" Xander asked over the phone.

"I've got a question for you. Do you have a minute?"

"Sure. What's up?"

"Well, the TDRS are in transfer orbits right now, but they picked up a strange radio signal. I need some help pinpointing the source."

"Hold on a sec," Xander said as he put the phone down to bark something at someone standing in his office. "Sorry about that. It's like a zoo around here. Anyway, what are you talking about? How can they be picking up a signal right now? Are you sure it's not something that we're sending?"

"No, Xander. It's not from us. Trust me, I've checked."

"You think it's the SAs?"

"Well, it could be," Alé said. "For now, though, we're trying to rule out what we can. I'll email you the data that we got from the sats. They found the signal two nights ago and all six of them have picked it up. I want you to figure out where this thing is orbiting. After that, I'll try to get a visual of it."

"Ah, Doppler," Xander said, nodding his head in agreement. The Doppler effect was the frequency shift that waves made as one object moved relative to another object. Similar to how a police siren sounded different on its approach than it did when it was moving away. In astronomy, the Doppler effect was used to figure out the speed and distance of stars and galaxies, but it could also be used to determine the exact location of a radio signal. "Send over what you've got. I'll use our receivers here to pick it up and I can calculate the orbit from there."

"Thanks a bunch," Alé said, "I'd like to have that ASAP. Like today, if at all possible. Oh, yeah…" Alé paused and lowered his voice. "Let's keep this one quiet for now. At least until we've got it figured out. I would hate to put the world on red alert for a piece of space trash."

"No problem. Once I have a signal, I can get you the orbital data in no time," Xander said.

"Thanks, buddy." Alé hung up the holo-phone with a wave of his finger.

Part II

Chapter 11

She walked the four and a half meters from her living compartment to the small washroom in the middle of the G. After using the toilet and brushing her teeth and hair, it was time for breakfast. In the kitchen, she prepared a meal of oatmeal, grapes, and coffee.

She sat for a while, eating her breakfast at the small round table, and listened to the whirr of the electrical systems that kept the module spinning. The engineering never ceased to amaze her and she still couldn't believe she got to be a part of it. She sat in quiet gratitude for as long as she could before it was time to get to her work for the day. The tiny alarm bell dinged 0600 GMT on her holo-watch. That's when her day officially began and not a minute later.

As she moved up the ladder into the Node, the gravity released its grip on her body. Slowly, like skin slipping away from a snake's body, she shed the centrifugal forces of the G. The farther up she moved, the lighter her grasp on the ladder, until she no longer needed to hold it at all, but simply pushed herself into the spherical room above her head. She waited there, with eyes closed, holding her breath until the nausea dissipated, then continued on to the Service Module to begin her day of work.

"Good morning, Millicent," said a voice from behind her. She was so shocked by it that she jerked her head up. The sudden movement in the microgravity caused her to crash into a series of experiment racks attached to the wall behind her.

"Andrei, you startled me!" she cried. "Don't sneak up on me like that."

Andrei Fedorov popped his head in from the hatch on her left. He pulled his long body up through the hatch opening so that he was hovering beside her.

"I thought everyone was still sleeping," she said. "And you know I hate being called Millicent." She rolled her eyes in his direction to put extra emphasis on the statement, because she did, in fact, hate it.

He threw his head back and laughed. Although he usually wore his light blond hair cropped short, it needed a trim, and now it waved in the microgravity, matching the motion of his laughs. "Nu, then," he said. "Good morning, *Nu*. I heard you making breakfast. So, I decided to come up here and scare the you-know-what out of you." He winked at her with one pale, blue, Russian eye and floated over to an experiment rack on the opposite wall from the one Nu had crashed into.

The rack and corresponding compartments were part of the human physiology experiments that Andrei was in charge of while on board. It was full of equipment for drawing blood samples, taking eye pressure measurements, and gauging muscle mass. The tissue samples were flash frozen and stored in freezers to be sent home with the next supply vessel. Andrei looked over the equipment and checked off a list of items on his handheld holo-screen.

"Have you read through the schedule from Mission Control yet?" he asked in his thick Russian accent, glancing away from the screen to give her a brief look up and down.

"No, I was just about to," Nu said, turning away from the sideways look he gave her.

Millicent Shepard earned her nickname, Nu, in graduate school. It was the thirteenth letter in the Greek alphabet and the scientific symbol for the neutrino, one of the elemental particles in particle physics. The smallest particle of its class, the neutrino was also known to interact only through weak forces, like gravity. Nu was a small person, a little over five feet tall, and she had managed to lose an epic arm-wrestling battle with one of her fellow classmates at a local pub. From that moment forward, everyone knew her as Nu, and despite the weak nature of the name, she liked it. It gave her something to prove to herself. By the time she was in her midthirties, she was so used to the name that her given name, Millicent, seemed dull and outdated, like something out of old English literature.

She looked back down at her screen and said, "I thought I would get a jump on some of these experiments before the next crew comes this afternoon."

"Ahh, yes. We will have visitors soon," Andrei said. The next Soyuz, carrying three astronauts, was scheduled to arrive later that day. Liftoff was to be at 1100 GMT, assuming there were no issues to cause a delay, and they would be ready to dock at the station six hours later if all went as planned.

"The sun is rising," she said as she made her way through the Service Module into the hexagonal, windowed encasement of the VP. "I'll never tire of seeing that," she said and sighed as she gazed out over the wide expanse of the Earth beneath her.

Suddenly, she felt him behind her. Her breath became short and her heart rate ticked up. He put his arm around her waist with his hand at her stomach and pulled her body close to his. His breath was hot on her neck and she felt the slight trace of his lips as they met her skin right under her jawbone.

"Andrei... we shouldn't..." she said, trying, and failing, to push him away. She was powerless against him and he knew it.

"What were you saying?" he whispered in Russian, his mouth hovering over her earlobe. She had no words to respond.

Softly, he kissed her ear, her neck, her jaw. In seconds, and with great force, he wheeled her around to face him. This sent them both into an interlocked spin that only ended when they brushed up gently against the bright wall of windows. His right hand remained at the small of her back while his left hand traced the curve of her jawbone.

She looked up at him. Despite the microgravity, which usually caused astronauts to have a puffy, childlike appearance, his face was hard and chiseled, with a slight growth of stubble covering the skin. To her, he was almost more beautiful than the world below the windows.

Even though she was the commander of the station, she always felt soft and weak compared to him. She was slighter and significantly shorter than he was when they stood side by side in gravity. Even in Earth's gravity, he could pick her up easily with both arms.

She wore her dark hair pulled back tight in a bun to ensure it didn't fly all over the place in the microgravity, but one strand stood on end, waving lightly next to her face as they floated. He reached up and slowly twisted it in his fingers, then tucked it behind her ear, dragging his fingers along her neck.

"What were you saying again, my dear?" he asked, now bringing his lips to the base of her neck, right above her collarbone.

"Um..." was all she could muster as she wrapped her arms around his neck. Her body shivered and her heart hammered in her chest.

After one, frozen moment, she was finally able to get a grip on herself long enough to speak something other than a mumble. "What about Vincent?" she asked. As she peered into his blue eyes, a smile parted his lips.

"All right then," he said in Russian, shrugging. He switched back to English. "I'll get started on my work. If that is what you wish, Commander." He reached his hand up and gave her an army salute, more as a joke than anything else. Then he gave her a quick peck on the top of the forehead and let go of her, floating back into the Service Module.

It took her a moment to compose herself. The blood that normally pooled in the upper half of her body had shifted and she could feel it pumping everywhere, even in her toes. She shook her head vigorously to try to get him out of it. That was the problem with Andrei: he knew how to catch her off guard and totally incapacitate her. When he did this, she had to physically shake herself in order to free her mind of him.

"Oh yes, one more thing," he said in Russian. "You are beautiful, my dear." With that, a sly smile crossed his lips. She rolled her eyes at him and blushed, turning around to compose herself. It had been early that morning, perhaps 0500 GMT when he left her sleeping compartment for his own.

***

"Something's not right." Nu said, chewing her lip and staring down at the screen that stood in front of her on the kitchen table. When she was nervous about something, she chewed on her bottom lip. It was something she'd done since she was a child.

"What do you mean?" Vincent asked from his seat directly across the table. Vincent Cho was a flight engineer and the third astronaut on board the Delta. Also an American, he grew up in California and reminded Nu of an aging surfer. He was incredibly smart and easy to get along with, but he wasn't one to take life too seriously.

They were doing routine preparations for the visiting Soyuz spacecraft set to launch later that morning. The three crew on board that ship would replace Nu, Andrei, and Vincent after three weeks of training. But it was now 0900 GMT, two hours prior to the scheduled launch, and Nu couldn't reach Mission Control. Not only was the radio not responding, but she couldn't load the internet either. She had rebooted the system and even had the robotic NIX unit go outside and check on the antenna array. Everything checked out fine, but still, no communications.

It has to be a problem at Mission Control, she thought, drumming her fingernails on the kitchen table as she watched her screen, waiting and hoping she was right. Maybe Mission Control lost power, she thought again, trying to rationalize the absence. But she shook her head, knowing that was almost impossible. They had contingency plans for power loss. It made no sense. She explained this to Vincent and looked up at him, hopeful for some advice.

"Have you tried the ham radio?" Vincent asked, although he knew as well as she did they would not reach Mission Control at their current orbital position. Because of the line of sight, they only had about nine minutes to contact Mission Control when they passed over North America. The view that rotated outside the G windows was of the Pacific, in all its bright, blue, uninhabited glory.

"Yes, during the last revolution," she nodded, her face twisted into a pinched look of concern, her lip buried under her teeth. "I got nothing. I've tried everything else. Any thoughts?"

Suddenly, as if on cue, the radio connection crackled to life. "Delta, this is Houston. We have some news. Do you copy?" the CAPCOM's voice came booming out of the holo-screen. He had a thick Southern accent, no doubt a local boy from Houston.

Nu felt her body deflate with relief. Just as quickly, anger rushed into her head, all red and hot. She could feel it spread across her face. But, as any veteran astronaut would do, she let the anger flow right through one end of her and out the other, and in a calm voice responded, "Roger CAPCOM, we're here. What have you got to tell us?"

"There has been a nuclear strike on US soil. I repeat, a nuclear strike on US soil. Los Angeles and New York have both been hit. Copy that?"

Time stood still for a few moments. The CAPCOM's words were sluggish, not only because of that Southern accent but because of the weight of the message they carried. Nu looked over at Vincent, who had heard the transmission too. His head cocked gently to one side, he looked right into her eyes with a look of contemplation on his face. Her own mouth hung open, frozen in place.

After a moment, she muttered, "What...?" the word losing power as it escaped her lips. It was all she could manage. She shook her head from side to side to snap herself out of her mental time lapse. She picked the holo-screen up from the table and punched in the commands for the closed-circuit radio loop that ran through the Delta and said, "Andrei, I need you to get up to the Service Module immediately." The corresponding voice boomed over the speakers throughout the station. Nu jogged over to the ladder leading out of the G. Vincent followed close behind.

"Houston, be aware," she said, her voice heavy with the swift movements. "We copy what you said. I've alerted the rest of the crew. We're gathering in the Service Module now."

***

Several minutes later, the three Delta crew members floated uneasily in front of the large holo-screen in the Service Module, listening to the news from the ground. Andrei had been working in the Docking Module, preparing for the arrival of the new Soyuz, when he heard Nu's page over the intercom.

"We have very little detail at this moment." The CAPCOM's voice broke and he paused before saying, "Guys, we're all really sorry that y'all weren't alerted sooner, but frankly, all hell has broken loose down here. After the first bomb hit, all major cities were evacuated, including Houston. We're radioing from Round Rock." In emergency evac situations, Mission Control would move to a temporary facility in Round Rock, Texas, north of Austin.

"To tell you the truth," he continued, "I'm scared out of my mind. It took us some time to get to the contingency site, which is why we've been out of contact with you for a few hours." He sounded like he was on the verge of tears. She'd never heard this type of emotion coming out of a CAPCOM before, and she'd be lying if she said it didn't scare her.

"What's the plan?" Nu asked. "This station runs through Mission Control. It will require orbital maneuvers soon and you absolutely cannot pull our comm again... is that understood?"

"Copy that, Delta," the CAPCOM said. "Listen, there's a skeleton crew around here. You'll need to keep up with your own systems for the moment. Orbital maneuvers should be good for a few more days. The plan is to bring y'all home ASAP. We need to clear it with Kazakhstan to monitor the drop point. They'll also have to get the military involved to make sure they don't send a damn nuclear missile your way when you come out of orbit."

"What about the station?" Nu asked, her voice cracked with worry and tension, a strange look of fright coming over her face. The station had been an ongoing part of her life for more than ten years. She was part of the original design team that planned and built the Delta. For over a thousand days, she'd called it home. They couldn't just let it go. It cost too many labor hours, too many dollars, too much of her life. The thought of seeing it disintegrate in the atmosphere was too much for her. Her bottom lip trembled and she bit down on it to keep from losing control.

The voice that came back through the screen sounded beat down. Not simply tired, but the kind of tired you feel after you've buried someone you love. "They're planning to burn the engines before departure and put the Delta into a higher orbit. Something that can buy us some time. But as of now, they want to get all personnel back on the surface ASAP."

"Okay, Houston, let us get our bearings with this for a minute. We'll radio back at 1100 GMT. Did you get that?" she asked.

"Roger. I can't tell you how scary this is, Nu. For now, get the station systems up on auto. When you evac, you'll need to have everything going, just in case Mission Control can't fly it," he said.

"Will do, over and out." She turned to face her crewmates, their faces ashen.

Andrei spoke first. "Nu, we must get out of here. I know we need to wait for Houston to officially send the word, but I think we should get prepped and ready for immediate evac." Vincent nodded in agreement.

"Yes. Yes, that's the best idea," she said, staring down at the floor and trying to mentally reassure herself. The question popped into her mind: Was it the best plan?

***

Twenty-five minutes later, at precisely 1105 GMT, Nu spoke into the main holo-screen in the Service Module. "Roger that, Houston. I am ready to relay the plan to the team. I'll be back in a few minutes for the final details."

She turned around to see the two men facing her, anticipation tight on their faces. If she hadn't been so worried herself, she would have laughed. Here these two men were floating, waiting anxiously for her direction. Her. The smallest of them all. A slight smile crossed her lips. She may have been the smallest, but she wasn't weak. Millicent Shepard understood her role as commander of this vessel.

"Okay, here's the deal," she said. "They're getting our reentry plan in place. We'll plan to take Soyuz capsule MV-54 at approximately 0700 GMT on Thursday. That's two days from now. We're going to squeeze a week's worth of prep into two days. It sounds like they are worried down there, but they've got the math guys calculating trajectories and will let us know when the exact time frame is for undocking. Let's get to work."

***

Nu couldn't hold it in any longer.

Tears now flowed down her face in thick, salty ribbons. Before she knew it, she was sobbing. Deep sobs from down inside her body. She detested crying, and it was not something she did often. She could name on one hand the few times she had actually sobbed in her life: when her father died, when her high school sweetheart broke her heart, when she was accepted into the astronaut program, and when she was told she would fly on her first mission to the Delta.

Folding her arms around herself, she curled her legs up to her stomach to make her body as small as possible and contain the flow of tears. Within a few minutes, the sobs stopped. She wasn't an overly emotional person, so when she did break down, it was quick and dirty. She grabbed the bottom of her shirt and dabbed at her eyes, the shirt soaking up what was left of the salty water. In one motion she stood, grabbed her holo-screen, and headed off to find Vincent.

***

"Houston, this is Delta. Are you there?" Nu asked for the tenth time. This is not good, she thought.

When a Soyuz capsule undocked from the station, there was a specific checklist of items that had to be completed, starting a week prior to undocking. Both Mission Control and the astronauts had a full list of procedures to prepare for during this time. The exact trajectory had to be calculated by the flight controllers on the surface and this information was uploaded to the Soyuz computers after the ship undocked.

Doing it this way enabled them to have the most up-to-date information to hit their reentry corridor. Without communication with Mission Control, they would not have the luxury of the brilliant mathematicians who served on the astrodynamics team in Houston. They would have to fly the Soyuz blind, using their own calculations for time, speed, and angle. It was a contingency they had practiced before, but not much, and not with a full breakdown of communication. It wasn't something they ever thought was possible.

Her hands were clamming up with sweat, so she wiped them on the legs of her pants to calm herself. Suddenly, she was cold. The hairs on her arms stood on end and she rubbed her hands over her arms swiftly in hopes of warming up.

More than anything in the world, she wished she could go back to the G and crawl into her sleeping compartment... with him. She longed for the comfort of the partial gravity and his arms around her body. But something inside her felt empty, and she knew she would never have that time with him again. It was a terrible, depressing, lonely feeling. Before it could spread through her body, she pulled up the intercom on her screen and spoke. "Delta crew, make your way to the kitchen, please. We need to talk."

Chapter 12

"We've lost contact with Mission Control again and I believe this time it might be for good," Nu said, shifting her eyes between the two men at the table.

It was now 2100 GMT and they all wore masks of exhaustion on their faces—sweaty, sunken-eyed, exhaustion.

"I've been trying to reach them for over an hour," she continued. "This happened earlier today too, but that was when they were moving Mission Control. Now, I'm not sure what the problem is. But I have a guess." She bit her bottom lip as she said this and glanced down, purposely avoiding their eyes.

"What is your theory?" Andrei asked. Of the two men sitting across from her at the kitchen table in the G, he seemed the most composed. This didn't surprise her. It was his strength, both mental and physical, that she loved most about him. Vincent wore a grubby Hawaiian printed shirt and a day's worth of stubble.

"I think there's an issue with the satellite network. I've tried all the radio frequencies and there's no internet connection either. Not just a weak signal, but nothing. Not a single blip. It's like the communications satellites aren't even there. Which sounds impossible." She shook her head at the notion.

"It's not impossible," Andrei said. "What could be a more effective attack than taking down the communications system of your enemy? No doubt the people responsible for these attacks have trained their men in some other, more primitive means of communication. This strategy gives the attackers the advantage."

"I think you're right," Vincent said, glancing at Nu and then at Andrei. He'd been quiet over the last few hours, working through his checklists and quietly whispering to himself, but now, his eyes darkened. "This 'doomsday' scenario has been hypothesized for decades. What would happen if a cyberterrorism attack took out the satellite systems? Frankly, it should have been taken more seriously."

"So, what do we do now?" Andrei asked. "What are the odds of these enemies, whoever they are, bombing us up here?"

Nu shook her head. "They have no reason to bomb us. Besides, with no satellites communicating, I doubt they could even locate our position and a bomb would have to be spot-on to actually hit us."

Andrei nodded. His feet were engaged in a nervous dance beneath him, bouncing and causing a slight vibration in the floor.

"I've got some ideas," Nu said, touching her holo-screen to pull up her notes. The two men straightened in their seats. "I suggest we wait twenty-four hours. Mission Control usually flies the Delta remotely, but we'll have to do it ourselves until they get back in contact with us. I'll work on reprogramming some of the systems to strengthen the station's ability to autopilot. Altitude is good, so we don't need to worry about course corrections for now. Vincent." She turned to him as she spoke. He had been staring at the far wall, seemingly in a daze, but his head snapped around to meet her gaze. "I want you up in the Service Module with me. We'll work through the reprogramming and keep trying to reach someone. We'll pull out the ham radio when we pass over Houston, Florida, Moscow, and Kazakhstan. Somebody somewhere has to be listening."

She turned toward Andrei. "I want you to take six hours of personal time, Andrei. We need to keep up our exercise regime and get some sleep. We'll go in shifts. The next twenty-four hours will be tough and we need our rest. At 0200 GMT you'll take over for Vincent so he can rest. I'll take the six hours after that."

The men nodded their approval of the plan. She knew there would be little rest, so she added, "If you need to, take sleeping pills guys. We *must* be at our best over the next few days. Sleep is essential. Does everybody understand?" Again, they nodded.

As they rose from their seats, she motioned for them to remain seated. "Before we do anything, let's have some supper," she said. "I don't know about you, but I haven't eaten in over ten hours and I'm starving." The tense energy in the room immediately dropped a few notches. Shoulders relaxed, faces turned up into partial smiles, and the stress of the day faded back down to bearable. Communal suppertime was always a part of their routine. It created a greater sense of camaraderie while adding some lightheartedness to the rigors of spaceflight. The three crew members of the Delta stood and moved about the kitchen, preparing their last supper together.

Chapter 13

At 0200 GMT, Andrei made his way from the Node through the tunnel to the Service Module. He had gone for a run, tended the garden, taken his blood work and medical measurements, and caught a few hours of rest after he showered.

Nu and Vincent stared intently at the holo-screens in front of them, punching in numbers, swiping here and there, pulling up various station computer systems.

"How's it looking?" Andrei asked in Russian. Vincent was on the far end of the module, not paying attention to his crewmates. Andrei cast a sideways glance at Nu, then smiled and winked. She blushed and a weary expression crossed her face.

"We've made some good progress," Nu said. "We have some additional programming work to do, but I don't think it will take too long."

"No communication though..." Andrei said, his voice trailing off. It was not a question and there was no response from the other two. They continued to work on their screens, typing and clicking and punching in commands.

"Andrei, we need to start seriously working on a plan to fly home without the help of Mission Control," Nu said, not looking up from her holo-screen. "We'll have to do all our own course trajectory calculations and ship preparations. You're the one who knows the most about the Soyuz. We'll need your help through every step of this process."

"Yes." He nodded. "It has never been done before. Or simulated. With no ground communication, once we land in Kazakhstan, there will be nobody there to find us. God only knows what we might find there."

"I know," she replied. "But it might be our only option. Do me a favor, Andrei. Start doing the math. See what you can come up with." Her eyes were tired and had turned dull with concentration.

Andrei flashed her a reassuring smile. "You look exhausted. Perhaps Vincent wouldn't mind switching shifts with you so you can rest now." He looked over at Vincent who stared deep into the screen in front of him. Vincent nodded without looking up and gave a simple wave with two fingers to indicate she should go. Andrei turned back to her. "Go. Get some rest." He gave her a gentle push in the direction of the G.

***

Nu's sleeping compartment was about as exciting as a broom closet. It was a bland cubby hole with gray carpet covering the floors and walls. The whole room was two and a half meters long by two meters wide. On the far wall, a sleep sack hung suspended over a small desk. Track lighting circled the perimeter of the little room in an effort to minimize harsh, overhead lighting. Opposite the desk, there was a small sink and mirror, and some shelving to store clothes, toiletries, and personal items.

Exhausted, she flopped into her sleep sack with a grateful sigh. The sleep sack was kind of like a hammock hanging from two aluminum struts at either end of the room. It was meant to hold one person, but it could hold two, as she well knew. Although it was thin, it was actually quite comfortable considering the limited gravity in the G. She didn't need thick mattresses and heavy blankets to sleep comfortably there.

The hammock swayed under her for a few seconds before coming to a rest. She pulled the cotton blanket up to her chin and curled into a ball. For some reason, she was cold, although her room was balmy with warmth and humidity from the garden. Rolling back onto her back, she reached up and felt her forehead. It felt warm, almost too warm. Her stomach was upset too.

You ate too much. Go to sleep, she thought.

She closed her eyes and enlisted the help of a mind trick that had served her well for many years. On the black background of her closed eyes, she imagined the number 1,000. Then the number 999. Then 998. Then 997. Then 996. And so on.

Counting backward was the most effective way she had ever found to force her body and mind to relax. It was a way for her to outrun her waking mind and force it to shut down. She made it to 236 before she finally outran wakefulness.

"I've got an idea and I want to run it by you," Nu said to her two crewmates a few hours later. It was 0800 GMT and they were gathered around the kitchen table. Each had breakfast in front of them. For Andrei, it was scrambled eggs, bacon, and a bagel. Vincent had yogurt and fruit. Nu had her usual: oatmeal with brown sugar and strawberries.

"Lay it on us," Vincent said, leaning back in his seat, balancing precariously on two chair legs with his hands over his head.

Nu sat opposite Vincent with Andrei to her left. Her abdomen ached and she could feel a headache coming on, but she pushed it out of her mind. She'd gotten four hours of dreamless sleep and her mind had taken on an odd fuzziness over the last few days. Like there was a thin veil between her and her thoughts. Thankfully, the sleep helped clear it some.

She clasped her hands in front of her. "I've been thinking about this for the last few hours and I can't shake the feeling there's a better plan," she started. "When we last spoke to NASA, they told us they wanted us to evacuate immediately for safety reasons. They were concerned that whoever sent the bombs might go after the station too. They planned to keep the station running remotely until this mess on the surface got sorted out. This is obviously not the case now. If we can't reestablish communication, they can't run the station or help us reenter the atmosphere."

Nu paused and shifted in her seat to gather her thoughts. She wanted this to come out the right way because she knew there would be backlash. "I believe it's dangerous to stay up here without knowing what's going on down below," she said. "But it's not quite as dangerous as it was before. Without the satellites, they can't tell where we are, which means they can't send missiles up here to us. That said, I don't want my crew hanging around up here. I also don't like the risk of flying the reentry blind. So, weighing all of these factors, I've come up with a new plan."

"And that plan is...?" Andrei asked. His words had a bite to them. She didn't like it.

She took a drink from her water bottle, trying to quell the urge to vomit. "I think the two of you should take MV-54," she said. "I'll stay behind and help you undock and guide you to the reentry corridor. We can do it remotely from the station."

The two men sat silent, staring at her, eyes wide.

"There are procedures to help a reentering ship from the station if there is a radio loss with the ground," she continued. "It's something we've trained for. The odds of the Soyuz making it through reentry with no help from the ground or the station are slim. I can't justify the risk of losing my crew and I think this is the safest way to get you two back to the surface and to protect the station."

Andrei rose so fast from his chair, it tipped backward and hit the floor with a muffled thud. "It is out of the question!"

She furrowed her brow and puckered her lips like she often did when something displeased her. Placing her hand on his arm, she guided him back down to his chair. "Communications will come back up. They *have* to. They will send another crew up here. There's no way the world's space administrations will abandon a two-and-a-half-trillion-dollar space station."

Andrei's face bloomed pink with anger. He brushed her hand away from his arm. "It is out of the question, Millicent! We will all leave together. As we discussed!"

Nu ignored this comment for the moment and turned to Vincent. "What do you think?"

"Well," Vincent said carefully, looking at Andrei from the corner of his eye. Andrei stood, fists balled up, his face pink and puffy like pastry dough. "Technically speaking, yes, this is an option to consider. We know if we leave the station unattended, it will certainly be lost, a situation nobody wants. Nu is right. The odds of a successful undock and deorbit are higher if we have help from someone inside the station, especially since Mission Control is not with us." He trailed off and turned toward Nu. "But are you sure this is something you're willing to do? Nobody has ever run something this large and complex by themselves with no help from the ground. And to be totally alone… it's not a good idea."

"Of course," she said without a moment's hesitation. "I've dedicated a decade of my life to this place. I'm not going to see it burn up, and I won't risk losing the Soyuz with a blind reentry. It's not an option."

"You are out of your minds! Both of you!" Andrei hissed. There was no trace of calm left in his voice and he was practically screaming now. "You want to stay up here to save the *station?*"

"Listen to me this second!" Nu roared in response. She stood and planted her hands firmly on the table. She'd kept her anger tucked neatly away, but now she could do nothing to keep it from pushing its way out of her mouth. She looked directly at Andrei. "You are not the commander here! If I make a call that I believe is correct, you must obey my command!"

"Let's all calm down, okay?" Vincent said. He stood and placed a hand on Andrei's arm, urging him to take his seat again. He nodded at Nu to do the same and they both obliged, grudgingly plopping down in their chairs. "There is obviously some tension here," Vincent continued. He looked first to Nu, then to Andrei, and back again to Nu. She could see it in Vincent's eyes—he knew about their secret. Her face flushed with anger and embarrassment.

"All I'm saying," Vincent continued, "is that we need to look at all the options here. We won't dismiss an idea because we have an emotional reaction to it." His small, dark eyes shot a look at Andrei, who quickly looked at the floor. He understood exactly what Vincent was referring to.

"I agree, this new plan gives us the best chance at making it back intact," Vincent continued. Andrei grumbled something in Russian under his breath and Vincent ignored it. "Assuming we can get the calculations correct and Nu can help us undock and fly into the reentry corridor remotely from the station, then yes, it is the best plan."

"Not an option," Andrei said. Clearly, he was not dropping this. "I will stay here with her."

Nu sighed. "No, Andrei. You and I are the only ones qualified to command the Soyuz. You must go with Vincent."

"I will not go," he said. "I refuse." Then he stood, grabbed the back of his chair, and slammed it into the table. Without another word, he left the kitchen.

Vincent turned to Nu. "You'd better talk to him. I understand your plan and think it makes sense, but he won't get on board with this if you can't convince him."

She nodded, stood, and walked out.

Chapter 14

Andrei was furious. How could Vincent, a *man*, vote in favor of leaving their commander, a *woman*, behind? It made no sense to him. Being in love with the woman in question didn't help his fury.

Andrei grew up on a small farm outside of Moscow. His father was a violent alcoholic, and to claim their family lived in poverty would be a dire understatement. As the eldest son, Andrei went to work at age fifteen, hauling hay and manure for other local farmers to help provide for his family. He also held down a part-time job as a bookkeeper for a grocery store in the local village. This was in addition to his schoolwork and tending their own farm.

A head-on collision took the life of his father and the other driver, a young woman from a neighboring village who was pregnant with twins at the time. His father was, of course, drunk when he died and because of this, the courts awarded the family of the victim all of his father's remaining farm assets. Andrei was only seventeen years old when he found himself homeless in Moscow and supporting a family of six.

He secured a job at a company that manufactured construction equipment and moved his family into a tiny apartment in Garage Valley, a notoriously dangerous, run-down Moscow neighborhood. Andrei's mother was ill by then with advanced breast cancer, and with limited income and four siblings to raise, there was no money to treat her. She eventually died in the local hospital's homeless ward. the day before her thirty-ninth birthday. Andrei was twenty at the time. Her death left him heartbroken and enraged.

A year later, he joined the army, leaving his younger siblings in the care of their aunt, his mother's sister. Through the army, he supported his family and continued his education. After a promising first few years of service, he enrolled in flight school and became an accomplished pilot, which eventually led him to Roscosmos, the Russian Space Agency.

Andrei was absolutely capable of making tough decisions. He had done it many times in his life. But something about this decision didn't seem right to him. He couldn't wrap his head around leaving a crew member behind... especially her.

He pumped his fist in anger at the wall over his cot, which did nothing but leave his hand and ego bruised. Behind him, he heard the slightest rustle and whipped his head around to find the source of the noise. There stood Nu, with her beautiful face twisted into a sad frown.

Andrei shook his head and cursed under his breath in Russian. This was not what he needed. He needed to calm down so he could think of a better option. He needed time to get himself under control before he spoke to her. Based on the look she now shot him, time to calm down was not in the cards.

"Listen, Millicent," he said through gritted teeth. "I really don't..."

She interrupted him in a firm voice. "I didn't come here to listen, I came here to speak." She usually wore her dark hair in a bun at the base of her neck, but she had liberated the hair from the bun and it now hung freely around her face. "I understand you have a problem with this plan, but frankly, you're not the commander of this ship. I don't want to see this behavior from you again. Blatantly disrespecting your commanding officer is out of the question."

She moved closer to him. He turned his back to her, his forehead settling against the wall. Closing his eyes, he concentrated on breathing deeply. She reached up and rested her hand on his shoulder. "I do not want to be left alone up here anymore than you want to leave me alone. But I am certain this is the best idea. I won't be alone for long. They'll get communications back up soon. I am confident of that."

He let out a bitter laugh and turned to face her. "You're so sure? You really think everything's going to be okay? This isn't a game, Millicent!" Again, he swore under his breath in Russian and turned away from her.

"Enough of this, Andrei!" her words came out harsher than she expected and she saw his body tense. "I genuinely feel this is the best idea. They will get the communications back up and you will land the Soyuz safely. They will know I'm still here. They will come up with a plan."

"And what if we don't land?" he asked.

Her hand fell harmlessly from his shoulder and she looked down at the floor. "You *will* land. That's why I'm doing this. To give you the best odds of making it home to safety."

Andrei turned to face her again. This time, his eyes weren't harsh or cold; they were begging her to change her mind. "What if we end up in the ocean or out in the wilderness? What if they never find us, Millicent?" He took hold of her shoulders and looked her straight in the eye. "How will anyone know you are still here?"

It pained her to see the look of desperation in his blue eyes. She physically winced away from it as if she was staring at the Sun. Gently, she took his hand in hers and squeezed it. "You'll land safely. I will do everything in my power to see that happen. You are an exceptional pilot. I have no doubts." She smiled and looked down at his hand. It was the rough hand of a man who worked hard for what he wanted. She truly believed his hands were the best hands in the solar system to guide the Soyuz down to the surface safely.

He let out a long sigh and gently took his hand out of hers. "Millicent, I do not agree with this. Simple as that. I do not believe in abandoning a crew member."

She sighed, rolled her head back on her neck, looked up at the ceiling, and planted her hands on her hips. "You won't be abandoning me," she said, still staring at the ceiling. "There's enough food, water, and life support here to keep me alive for many months... even years! I know every cubic centimeter of this place. If anyone is qualified to spend a few months up here alone, it's me."

He stepped back from her and crossed his arms in front of his chest. With knitted brows, he said, "Oh yeah? What if something breaks outside? You can't do a spacewalk by yourself. What then?"

She shrugged. "I have the NIX unit," she said, releasing her stoic stance and leaning on the wall to her left. "It can keep up with the routine stuff. Maybe I'll even give it a name."

"Hal?" Andrei suggested. It was a reference to the classic space movie *2001: A Space Odyssey*—one of their favorites. This comment brought smiles to both their faces.

"Not Hal." She shook her head. "It looks kind of like Iron Man. Maybe I'll name him Tony." The smile on Andrei's face did not last. He wanted an actual answer to the question. "Seriously though, larger repairs can wait until there is a supply ship or another crew. I'll handle it."

He reached up and cupped her left cheek in his right hand, drawing her face close to his and settling his forehead on hers. He closed his eyes and breathed in deeply, allowing her scent to permeate his lungs. "It's not only the thought of leaving a crewmate behind, you know. It's you. I can't bear it," he said, his voice not much more than a whisper.

She wrapped her arms around his neck and he pulled her close to him, holding her tight. There was nothing more to say. She had no desire to leave him either, but her loyalty to the station, her life's work, was too great, even for his love to overcome. He seemed to understand this and it made him squeeze tighter.

After a few moments, they heard Vincent walking along the corridor of the G outside Andrei's sleeping compartment. They immediately released each other in a reflex reaction. The sudden movement made her dizzy and she sat on his desk chair, dropping her head down to catch her breath.

He knelt down next to her and lightly touched her chin. "Are you okay, Millicent? You're so pale."

The dizziness passed after a moment and she looked up at him. "Yes, I am fine." She gave him a reassuring smile. Standing, she walked the few steps to the compartment door. As she pulled the door aside, she looked back at Andrei with a smile and said, "But I *hate* it when you call me Millicent."

Chapter 15

"Soyuz MV-54, this is Delta. Please confirm undocking," Nu said, floating in front of the large holo-screen in the Service Module.

She was watching the video feed from the cameras mounted on the exterior of the station. Various video tiles were stacked here and there on the screen in front of her. She also had several programs pulled up showing her the current status of the critical systems and orientation of the Soyuz.

"Undocking is complete, Delta," Andrei replied from inside the capsule.

It had been three hours since Nu closed the hatch and unlocked the clamps on the station end of the docking port. During that time, the two astronauts inside the Soyuz dressed in their space suits and ran through a complete undocking checklist. Everything was working as planned on the spacecraft.

A few minutes earlier, a set of spring-loaded pushers gently nudged the Soyuz away from the station and it was now moving slowly outward at about two meters per minute. At this point, in a normal undocking, Mission Control would upload the pertinent data for reentry based on the location of the station at the exact time of undocking. Since this wasn't possible, Nu uploaded the data before the capsule undocked based on where the station should be relative to the coordinates last obtained from Mission Control.

When the Soyuz was about twenty meters away from the Delta, Andrei initiated the preliminary fifteen-second burn of the Soyuz engine to bring it into a lower, and slightly faster, parking orbit. This would ensure the two spacecraft did not intersect at any point in their next few orbits. Nu and Andrei did some checks of the systems over the next two orbits. She made some adjustments to their trajectory based on updated location information. When they both felt the timing and position were perfect, Andrei ignited the engine again for the deorbit burn, which would last about four and a half minutes. The burn slowed the ship down enough to allow it to enter the reentry corridor.

"How do we look?" Andrei asked, radioing back to the station.

The Soyuz spacecraft had been in operation since the mid-1960s. The design was simple and efficient, which was why it had been in use for so many years. Other countries attempted to create their own similar space capsules to ferry astronauts to and from space stations, but nothing worked as well as the Soyuz.

It was composed of three parts. The Orbital Module was a round module perched at the top of the spacecraft and used to hold gear, equipment, and experiments during the ascent. The Descent Module was a bell-shaped module located in the middle of the craft.

This was the most important of the three Soyuz modules because it was the only part of the spacecraft meant to make it through reentry. The crew seats were in the Descent Module, along with the parachutes and heat shield. The final piece of the Soyuz, located at the bottom of the ship, was the Service Module. It held all of the primary support systems, including the spacecraft engine. Moments before the ship would begin reentry, the Orbital and Service Modules would break away from the Descent Module, leaving it and the crew to make the fall alone.

"It looks great," Nu replied. "All systems are go. You boys will have a smooth ride home."

A moment after she said this, a round of explosive bolts surrounding the Soyuz burst in succinct order. For the astronauts belted down inside the Descent Module, it sounded like there was a spaceman standing outside, beating the hull of the ship with a sledgehammer. This was a normal part of the separation process, but it still made Andrei jump with nerves. He watched out the small circular window to his left and caught a glimpse of the two discarded modules drifting off into the distance, destined to burn up in the atmosphere and become part of the Earth once again.

Nu watched the screen and chewed on her fingernails. She was nervous. The location coordinates they were working with were not the most current. Mission Control was in charge of plotting the exact location of the station within its orbit, and without their precise tracking, she didn't know where the Soyuz would land once it made it out of the atmosphere, or even if it was sent into the atmosphere at the right trajectory. They could only work off of what they'd learned two days ago at the time of their last contact with Mission Control. All their calculations were based on a "best-case" scenario with two-day-old data.

Even if the spaceship landed where it was supposed to, there would be nobody there to meet the returning astronauts. They would be in the middle of Kazakhstan, a flat, windblown grassland with very few people and even fewer cities. Andrei and Vincent prepared ahead of time by taking extra food and water rations from the station stores. They could radio the launch base once they landed, but they had no idea what they would find when they got down there. Odds were good that they'd have to make a long hike, perhaps many kilometers, to reach any sort of civilization.

Nu was proud of the work they had done getting the ship ready. Vincent was one of the most organized people she knew and he oversaw the rushed departure, with Andrei doing a thorough final walkthrough of the spacecraft.

A half hour before they were scheduled to close the hatches, Andrei found Nu in the Docking Module with Vincent going through a final check of the computer.

"Millicent," he said, clearing his throat. "Can I speak to you in the G?"

She turned to Vincent, who gave her a knowing nod and turned to follow Andrei. He led her down the G ladders and past the garden to his sleeping compartment. As soon as she pulled the door closed behind her, he was there with his arms around her. The top of her head barely came up to his chin and the height difference allowed her to bury her face into his chest. To her surprise, hot tears rolled down her cheeks. Before she knew it, she was sobbing into his T-shirt.

He held her and they stood there for what seemed like an hour, although it could only have been a few minutes. She eventually gathered her ragged emotions and looked into his dark eyes. "I'm sorry, Andrei. I don't know what came over me. I'm just very… emotional about all of this."

"It's not too late. We can all leave today," he said with a hopeful look in his eyes.

"No." She shook her head. "No, this is the best plan. I am certain of it." She smiled at him and backed away, smoothing his shirt down where she had rumpled it with her fingertips.

He chuckled and pulled his hands forward to hold her face between them. "You're no good at this brave face stuff," he said.

She laughed and brought her right hand up to cup his left hand. He pulled her face to his and kissed her, softly, as though trying to soak up every last drop of her.

The kiss evolved and became more aggressive for a moment before finally tapering off into a series of soft pecks. "You really shouldn't worry," she said. "We'll have plenty more of those soon enough. I will be back on the surface before you know it."

A somber look flashed over his face. "*Da.* You make sure of that."

She nodded in agreement and they left his sleeping compartment together for the last time.

As she watched the small craft fall toward the Earth below, she remembered the intensity of their last kiss. She touched her lips softly and closed her eyes, hoping to conjure up the smell and feel of his skin.

***

Andrei pulled on his seat strap nervously. Although not normally an anxious person, he figured it was natural to be a little jittery now. He watched the Delta smoothly moving away from them out the small window. He shook his head and squinted his eyes. He needed to get the Delta, and its human inhabitant, out of his mind. The real work was about to begin.

Inside the station, Nu watched the screen in silence. She could no longer see the Soyuz as it plunged into the atmosphere and she'd lost radio communications thirty-two seconds earlier. They were on their own now. But she was calm, knowing she'd done all she could to ensure they made it safely.

"Excuse me, Nu," said a voice behind her, making her jump with surprise.

"Oh!" she said when she realized it was the NIX unit. She clutched her hand to her heart and reaching out to grab a handhold on the wall to steady herself. "You scared me."

"Yes, I see that and I sincerely apologize. But I wanted to let you know I finished the maintenance you requested this morning on the hull of the ship. I ran the diagnostic checks on the antenna array and it appears everything is in working order." He turned his head to the side and pretended to cough, something he was programmed to do from time to time to make him seem more humanlike. "There is one minor issue I thought I would bring to your attention though."

"Oh? What's that?" she asked.

"I noticed that MV-54 undocked from the station earlier this morning, but you are still here, which confuses me." He tipped his head to the side as if perplexed.

With all the bustle of the morning, she totally forgot about the NIX unit being outside the hull while they undocked. "Yes, that's right. We decided it would be best if the two of them went to the surface and I stayed back to look after the station." She paused, and with a hesitant voice said, "Mission Control will get communications up and running soon and I'll have further instructions."

"Ah, yes," he said. "Well, I thought I should mention something to you. When I was out on the hull, I noticed the thermal blankets surrounding MV-54 came undone beneath the Descent Module."

It felt like a hand tightened over her throat as she struggled to comprehend the words. "You mean, they weren't secured to the hull of the Soyuz?" she asked, panic gripping her. They ran all the tests. They performed a detailed and complete visual inspection of the inside and outside of the ship. There had been absolutely no sign of the thermal blankets coming loose. She shook her head in disbelief. "We checked everything before the ship undocked. How is that possible?"

"I saw it after the capsule pushed away from the station," he said. "I would have missed it completely had I not been on my way back to my airlock. The blankets were most definitely loose."

"Why didn't you say something sooner?" Her voice was high and cracked.

"I apologize," he said. "I did not realize this was a time-sensitive issue."

The Soyuz had multiple layers of protective blankets that looked kind of like sheets of tinfoil attached to its hull. These blankets served as a method of thermal control, protecting the capsule during ascent and docking. The harsh environment of space called for shielding to protect the delicate features of the Soyuz while it sat docked at the station. Although the blankets were not necessary for the heat shield to work properly during reentry, the fact that they'd come loose was not a good sign. It meant something wasn't right with the exterior of Soyuz MV-54.

Nu brought her hands to her face and closed her eyes in disbelief. There was nothing she could do now. She no longer had radio connection with the departing ship and they were already deep in the atmosphere. She had sent them in a defective ship... possibly to their deaths! What had she done?

Suddenly, she spun around, grabbing a medical bag strapped to the wall next to the holo-screen, and vomited.

***

Unknown to the crew of Soyuz MV-54, a bolt holding down a thermal insulation blanket sheared during the vehicle's ascent, almost six months earlier. This was not a normal occurrence and would not have happened had the ship been built six months prior. The bolt in question was part of an upgrade to the Soyuz and this style of bolt was not part of the spacecraft until the MV models rolled off the line.

There were six of these bolts used to hold down the insulated blanket surrounding the spacecraft. Because the modules of the craft separated at reentry, the blankets around the exterior skin were arranged in pieces that would separate with their individual modules. The faulty bolt was part of the Descent Module, the only one meant to survive reentry.

A failure in one bolt would not have been much of an issue, but it happened early in the ascent phase when the spacecraft was still hurtling through the thick atmosphere. Without one of the bolts, additional force transferred to the other five bolts surrounding the module. They weakened under the pressure and they, too, failed in quick succession. An error in the logging system missed the failure of these bolts and therefore, it did not show up on system checks of the Soyuz.

After the craft came to orbit, the thermal blankets stayed in place only because of a thin layer of glue used to keep them tight during the manufacturing process. Because the bolts were still glued down, when they failed, the crew didn't notice. But the glue was never meant to withstand the rigors of space, and within a few days, it failed too, loosening the blankets.

Without the blankets there for protection, the ablative heat shield covering the bottom and sides of the spacecraft was exposed to enormous temperature swings, space debris, and radiation. A tiny crack, only a few millimeters in length, formed on the third week the Soyuz sat parked at the Docking Module of the Delta. Another chip formed a few weeks later when a piece of space dust nicked the side of the craft, under one of the windows. By the time Andrei and Vincent boarded MV-54, the crack had grown to three centimeters, long enough to weaken the heat shield and doom the crew.

***

The ship broke up in a dazzling display of fire and lights over the Siberian tundra. Almost nobody saw it because it happened in such a remote location. Some reports made to local officials noted the occurrence of strange lights over the remote area. Fearing more bombings, Russia dispatched army troops to check it out, but all they found was debris.

Since the debris field from MV-54 was over thirty kilometers long, it would have taken the Russian and American space agencies months to comb out all the ship's pieces. Roscosmos released a preliminary report stating a "majority" of the craft was found and it appeared to contain the remains of at least two individuals, although medical evidence was inconclusive because of the severity of the burns and disintegration of the bodies.

The Russians had much more to worry about than investigating the crashed Soyuz. Ground attacks began a day after they lost satellite communications. Governments around the world prepared to move huge populations of people underground. That meant pushing back the investigation of the lost Soyuz, and eventually, it was forgotten.

They held a memorial service for the dead astronauts in Star City, the base of operations for Roscosmos launches. All three astronauts were honored at the service. Soon after the brief ceremony, the memory of the three lost astronauts faded into the wind as everyone braced for the inevitable fight.

Chapter 16

Thump. Thump. Thump.

I am nervously drumming the end of a pen against the table in the kitchen. I pause a moment to look at the pen. It's blue and has the letters NASA written across it in bold, white font. It also has my name, Eta, scrawled in my own messy handwriting on a small piece of tape around its perimeter. I can't remember the last time I put my name on anything around here.

I've finished supper and I can't think of anything else to do but sit here and drum this pen on the table. It's because I'm nervous. Although, I don't know why I'm nervous. It's been two days since my birthday and so far, nothing has happened except the same old, boring stuff that always happens around here.

But I'm happy to say my suspicion that there was a communications satellite launch is correct. Except there were six satellites launched from a single rocket, instead of just one. Here's how I know.

The station is equipped with radar so the computers can detect potentially hazardous debris. There's a ton of stuff floating around up here: everything from paint chips to rocks to large, broken-up pieces of satellites. According to Nu, there was no radar system built into prior space stations. They had to rely entirely on ground control to find potentially dangerous, orbiting objects so they could get out of the way in time. The station gets hit by space debris all the time. You can hear it. Bits of dust make metallic pings when they come up against the outer hull. The little objects aren't the problem. It's the big stuff the computer watches out for.

Because the Delta was meant to occupy an orbit much farther away from Earth than any space station in the past, they gave it a radar system to detect space debris on its own. But a radar system like that requires a lot of power to run it. All previous space stations relied on solar energy for most of their power. Not that the Delta doesn't have solar power. There are actually four solar arrays on the starboard end of the station. If necessary, they could provide the power necessary to keep me alive in here. However, they wouldn't provide enough power to keep the G running, or keep up with the long-range radar search. That's why they gave the Delta its own nuclear power plant.

It's equipped with a nuclear reactor that can run the station for over a hundred years. I'm not sure exactly how long it will last... but long enough. I'll either be gone or dead by the time the reactors run out of juice.

The reactor uses two uranium 235 tubes, about the size of baseball bats, to produce the heat that's then converted to power. It's also what powers the ion engine.

The Delta has an ion engine, which is how I perform orbital maneuvers to keep the station in a safe orbit. Ion engines allow you to produce a tiny bit of acceleration over a long period of time.

The radar runs on power produced by the reactors and it does a constant scan of the area around the station. It's set to keep track of a fifty-kilometer sphere of space, and it searches for objects bigger than ten centimeters as those cause the most damage.

So, as an experiment, I increased the bubble to one hundred kilometers. And there they were! Six objects launched to relatively the same area. This makes me think they were all launched on one rocket and split up after they got to orbit.

Well, to clarify, there *were* six objects. They have all since left my little search sphere. From the looks of the paths they took, they are on their way to geosynchronous orbits, which makes perfect sense for my communications satellite theory.

So, what to do now? Sit and wait. It's all I can do. Disappointing, for sure.

I call it a day and go to bed. It's only 1930 GMT, which is pretty early for me, but I can't concentrate on anything right now. My sleeping compartment is on the other side of the G from the kitchen, next to the bathroom. It only takes about thirty seconds to walk from one side to the next. I look into the mirror after I'm done brushing my teeth and hair. There's the girl again, looking back at me from the other side of the glass. She isn't smiling now though. She looks worried. This doesn't surprise me. She's always worried about something.

The Sun is out, so I cover up my little porthole window with a blackout blind and close the compartment door before flopping down on my bed. I know if I spend too much time lying here, I'll never go to sleep. It's time to start counting. My mother taught me a little mind trick many years ago. Count backward from a thousand to put yourself to sleep. I roll through many numbers, but finally, sleep takes over.

***

Seven days. That's how long it's been since I first found the rocket tail from the satellite launch.

It's Monday again. Nix and I are working on maintenance and system checks. The same checks we do every Monday. He's outside right now, checking the outer hull for punctures. I'm working on an orbital maneuver.

My station orbits between 350 kilometers and 420 kilometers above the surface. Even though I'm out here with what seems like a perfect vacuum, that's not exactly true. The Earth's atmosphere is farther reaching than you might think and tiny atmospheric molecules hit my station daily, causing it to slow down.

The real problem with this slowdown is that it's not constant. There's no way to predict how much it will slow down over time. The size of the atmosphere depends on the activity of the Sun, which causes the outer atmosphere to expand and contract like a sponge. At certain times, the atmosphere where I am is thicker than at other times. To counteract this atmospheric drag,

I fire up the ion engine from time to time. I can't set the engine up on autopilot, turning on at a specific time and at specific intervals. As I said, the drag isn't constant. It's something I have to monitor to keep the station's altitude from getting too low.

Frankly, it's not my favorite thing to do... fire up the engine, that is. If something fails in the burn process, I'm toast, literally. Without the atmospheric boost, the station gets lower and lower in the atmosphere, and the lower it gets, the slower it gets. The station can technically orbit as low as 260 kilometers, but anything lower than that is risky business. The ion engines wouldn't be able to lift it out of an orbit lower than 160 kilometers and it would start to break up at 100 kilometers. It's an exponential dance with death.

Today's orbit is showing just short of 350 kilometers, which means it's time to give it a boost.

***

The ion engine on the Delta is the first engine of its type ever built and put to use on a crewed space vehicle. Heat from the reactor routes to the engine where it's used to heat liquid hydrogen and create ionized gas. The engine then shoots the gas out the back of the spacecraft in a steady stream.

There are four tanks of liquid hydrogen strapped to the station that the engine uses to create its thrust. They were fueled up about a year before the crew lost communication with the surface, approximately nineteen years ago. I'm down to about half capacity, so it's still got some juice in the tank for orbital boosts. If all else fails, I can use the water reclamation system to isolate hydrogen, but it isn't an ideal situation because water, too, is a pretty important resource.

The ion engine works differently from the old-fashioned chemical thrusters would. It takes a little more time to push the station into a higher orbit, which is another good reason to keep the altitude well above the minimum. The amount of time needed to boost the station depends on how low the station is. Problem is, if it doesn't have enough time to produce the necessary thrust, the station could dip too low to recover. It's a delicate and exhausting balance.

I'm in the Service Module working from the main screen. I pull up the proper program and initiate the commands to warm up the engine. Being that it'll take a while to get her up and running, I head down to the G for an exercise break. Today's exercise will be the stationary bike. I *hate* the stationary bike. I'd better pick out an old movie to watch so I don't die of boredom atop the bike.

***

I'm pedaling through the steepest part of the virtual course, when down in the corner of the holo-screen, an email icon pops up. The computer is programmed to email me when it requires any sort of action on my part. It's a generic alert email, so it doesn't give me any specific information. I power down the bike and head up to the Service Module.

Once there, I immediately see what the issue is—there was a failure with the engine startup command. That's strange. I look through the system for a while and discover the command was sent to the engine, but the engine failed to initiate. The nuclear reactor is online because the station power is running as normal, but the propulsion system didn't respond to the computer command.

Great.

I try the secondary and tertiary backup initialization systems. No luck. Technically the nuclear reactor and the propulsion system are separate machines. The reactor can power either the propulsion system or the electrical system. I manually cut the station power so it's not drawing on the reactor. It can run on batteries for a while with no issue. This is usually what the reactor does when it powers the engine, but it normally does it automatically when I initiate the burn sequence. Again, no luck.

There are fans in the reactor that help dissipate heat. I check each fan, thinking maybe there was a problem with heat buildup. The system shows the reactor fans are working fine. The propulsion system has separate fans. I check those and bingo—no response. The propulsion fans aren't getting any power.

Next, I run a full diagnostic check on the connections between the reactor and the engine. It's showing a total failure. How could I not have caught this when I last checked the reactor? I suppose, if the reactor is working properly, then the engine itself wouldn't show any issues being it wasn't activated. My routine maintenance checklist does not call for a check of the engines, only the reactor. Damn.

"Nix!" I call out from the Service Module.

After a brief moment of silence, I hear Nix moving about and the latches releasing from his charging port.

"Yes, dear?" he says as he pops his Iron Man head through the tunnel leading to the Service Module.

"I'm having an issue with the engine," I say. "There's no power making it from the reactor to the engine. It's showing a total failure, almost like the engine isn't there." I bite my lip. It's a weird, nervous habit I've had all my life.

"Oh my, that's not very good news," Nix says. "What can I do to help?"

"I want you to go out there and have a look. You'll need to actually enter the reactor from the outside and see what might be causing the backup between the reactor and the engine. I've got a checklist here that I pulled up from the system files for how to go about troubleshooting it."

"Yes," he says. "I have the checklist right here in my memory stores. I will go out and take a look."

***

Nix has been outside a long time. I imagine it takes a while to go through the checklist. There's a ton of complicated circuitry between those units. I asked him how he was doing a few minutes ago and he said he was almost done and had yet to find the issue.

His voice pops into my ear. "Well, all seems to be well with the reactor. I believe the issue lies with the fans meant to dissipate heat away from the engine. The engine must have overheated during the last orbital maneuver. It looks as though there was a short circuit in the wiring. This caused the fans to quit working, which then caused the engine to overheat."

"What about the backup system? Isn't there a backup form of heat dissipation?" I ask.

"Oh yes, there certainly is," he says. "But it appears even the backup system has failed. Nothing on page sixteen of the checklist is functioning due to the shorted wires."

"Okay. Come back in." I sigh, defeated.

"Yes ma'am."

***

I am in big trouble.

I should have seen this coming. I can't expect something like a complex ion engine to last forever, considering it was only supposed to last ten years when it was originally designed.

I did some math. It will take about six months to slow down enough to drop the orbit to 200 kilometers. After that, the orbital decay will speed up a great deal. It's exponential. Complete deorbit will take place in about nine months. But really, if I'm still on this thing after six months, anything is game because, the truth is, I have no idea how fast this thing is going to crash.

Much of the atmospheric drag has to do with the Sun, and I can't predict what the Sun will do. I've never been all that great at math anyway and it's possible my calculations are wrong. I remember Nu mentioning what happened to the ISS when they allowed it to deorbit. It happened much faster than they anticipated because it was so big. The atmospheric drag took over at a greater rate than they thought it would, and it nearly broke up over an urban area. It was a big deal and gave NASA a huge scare before it finally came down harmlessly over the Indian Ocean.

So, that's that. I've hit a deadline. I have six months to get off this station or get the engine working. I must continue to try to reach those communications satellites and pray someone on the other end is listening.

Chapter 17

It had been four days since the Soyuz left the Delta. Nu spent much of that time carrying on station maintenance. She wasn't a spiritual person, but she did spend the first few hours after Andrei and Vincent left trying to drum up some positive vibes for the spacecraft and its occupants. Only she had known about those thermal blankets coming loose and just because they were loose, didn't mean the ship wasn't in perfectly good shape. She figured a little thoughtful meditation focused on a safe landing wouldn't hurt.

The truth was, she didn't know if they'd made it to the surface alive and she wouldn't know until she had surface communication again. Having no control over it was beyond frustrating, so she concentrated on work as much as possible.

The Delta was never meant to function totally on its own. Mission Control was supposed to support it. Now, Nu had her work cut out for her to "fool" the computer systems into thinking that she was Mission Control. Many of the programs automatically deferred to ground control for reference when certain commands didn't execute properly. Things like orientation, orbital maneuvering, and solar shielding were usually calculated on the ground, with the commands sent to the computers through data uplinks.

So far, she'd done a good job of reprogramming the station computers and had everything in good working order. But, as each hour passed, she became more and more anxious about the safety of the men who had departed in the Soyuz. It wasn't a good sign that they had entered the atmosphere almost four days prior and she was still without communications. If they did make it back alive, they would have made contact with the space agencies by now and let them know she was still up there.

She had, of course, considered the possibility that they had landed somewhere unexpected. The math had put them at a landing spot in the heart of Kazakhstan, not far from the Cosmodrome in Baikonur. However, even a tiny miscalculation meant they could land hundreds of kilometers off course. If the calculation was far enough off, they could have landed in the ocean which would have been a disaster.

No, they landed in the steppe, she thought to herself, presenting the idea to her brain as if it were a fact. They landed in the Kazakh steppe, right where they were supposed to. Perhaps they camped for the night since the landing took place in the midafternoon. Then they made their way back to Baikonur, where no one expected them, but were given a grand welcome in the face of this sudden and horrific war. Now, they were working to get communications with the station back up and running. Yes, she thought, that's what happened.

It was Wednesday, 1911 GMT and Nu sat at the kitchen table in the G picking at her meal of Mexican-style rice and beans. She'd chosen a vegetarian meal because the thought of eating meat made her stomach flip. She was still trying to get over whatever was wrong with her stomach. A movie played on the holo-screen in front of her, but she wasn't watching it. She wasn't even sure what movie it was. For some reason, she had a hard time concentrating tonight. Instead, she stared across the module out the narrow window. The Earth spun around out there, keeping pace with the G.

After a few more moments, she gave up on the half-eaten meal and walked to the cellar for a banana. That made three bananas for her that day. She didn't even like bananas, but for an inexplicable reason, the idea of eating bananas appealed to her. As she chewed on the ripe fruit, she counted what remained of her supply: only six bananas left. The last supply ship had been up a week prior and had brought fresh fruit. These bananas had been a beautiful, yet bitter lime green when they came up. Now they were perfectly ripe.

She resumed her position at the kitchen table and watched the Earth through the windows again. She felt totally alone. She *was* totally alone, and that thought suddenly made her terribly sad. The tears started. Not hysterical, sobbing tears, but rather soft, rolling tears that flowed easily down her cheeks.

After she spent a minute or two mindlessly chewing her banana, the peel fell from her hand and hit the table with a thud.

She jumped up and ran for the garbage bag that hung on the hook next to the cooler and vomited. When the last of the rice and beans and banana lay at the bottom of the bag, her body fell limp to the floor and she lay there, squeezing her arms to her stomach, curled up in a ball, willing the nausea to pass.

She remained lying there for what seemed like hours before she finally peeled herself off the floor and walked, doubled over, to her sleeping compartment. It normally took her many minutes, sometimes hours, to fall asleep, counting the numbers down from a thousand. But on this day, she fell asleep almost immediately.

***

Nu woke up many hours later and felt as though she had been asleep for days. In a panic, she grabbed her digital watch off the hook where it hung on the wall and looked at it through sleep-filled eyes. It read 0532 GMT, which was exactly thirteen minutes before her alarm was set to go off and wake her for the day. Relief flooded out of her lungs in a single, long sigh.

As she moved to get up, her body groaned in protest. As much as her mind wanted to start the day, her body wasn't having it and she curled up tighter, letting the sleep sack support her weight. What was wrong with her? Sleeping in was not her style.

Millicent Shepard was a worker. When she was a teenager, growing up on her parent's dairy farm in rural Minnesota, she worked long hours milking cows in the barn before school, then working night shifts at the grocery store in the nearest town.

Actually, it could hardly be called a town as it had a population of fewer than one hundred people. Sometimes it was after midnight before she got home, but she never complained. Work kept her sane.

That's why she loved being an astronaut. The long hours, the years of mission preparation, the rigorous training... it was perfect for her.

But something was off now. She could feel it deep in her bones. The more time passed without communication from the ground, the worse the odds were that the crew of the Soyuz had survived. She wondered if they even made it through reentry. The thought made her insides squirm and she quickly pushed it out of her mind.

She decided to go back to sleep. Obviously, she was having some emotional issues from all these recent happenings. Perhaps it was her body telling her something. Yes, rest will help, she thought. With a brief sigh, she closed her eyes and slipped back to sleep easily, no counting necessary.

***

Another three days passed with no communication. Nu floated in the VP's microgravity and watched the Earth spin beneath her. In her hand was the last banana. She chewed on the fruit methodically. Bananas. What a strange thing to crave, she thought. The garden was not a tropical oasis and there were no banana trees growing in it. So, when this one was done, she would have to go without. She savored it.

The banana made her think of Andrei. He loved bananas. In fact, the reason the supply ship had carried so many bananas was because of him. He had requested them. Until now, she never understood why. She wondered if maybe her subconscious craved him. She knew her *conscious* mind did. He was all she could think about.

For the past three days, she had spent her time programming computer systems. It was a big project, but one that needed to be done. As the days ticked by, it became more and more clear that her stay on board the station would be longer than she expected.

Something else bothered her too. When the station swung around the Earth into the dark of the night, there weren't any lights on the surface anymore. Usually, she could see little bundles of lights spreading throughout areas of the globe. Many parts of the surface were always dark, like the oceans and the mountains, but now, there was nothing. Even over the most populated areas— London, Paris, New York, Rio de Janeiro—there were always lights. But now, there was nothing.

She wondered if it was possible that there was no electricity anywhere. The thought of it was so cold and terrifying that she tried not to let it occupy her mind for too long. There was a war going on, after all. She knew this. Maybe the people of the world were laying low. That's all it was. They were waiting it out.

In the meantime, she would remain prepared. She went through her supply of food and perishables. The water supply would be okay. There was enough water on board to support a crew of six for up to six months, and that included watering the garden. The water reclamation system was near perfect, with a 98 percent efficiency rate in recycling waste. Without the added burden of extra humans to support, it would last indefinitely as long as she kept it running.

Food was another matter. The supply ships usually came up once every two months, depending on how many crew members were on board. The garden was in the experimental stages, not meant to supply the crew with all its food yet. So, she needed to increase the garden capacity. She had already cleared out an additional twelve square meters of space to plant in the G. If she needed to, she could take over the remaining five sleep modules and use them as planting space too. The plants that were on board could sustain her for a long time, but she didn't want to take any chances. She would make this garden as big and lush as possible, given the limited space.

One problem was soil. There just wasn't much of it. She had a solution for this. Plants don't need a ton of soil to survive. Of course, that depends on the plant, but most plants will do fine with less soil. Limited space tends to make them smaller, but the space didn't concern her. She figured if she could cut the soil on the existing plants by a third across the board, she could easily fill up the extra garden space.

The garden already had the capability to recycle solid waste from the astronauts. The reclamation system took the waste and mixed it with a chemical cocktail that made it less smelly. Then deposit pipes moved the newly made fertilizer directly into the soil. In the past, it wasn't necessary to recycle everything. The system collected a quarter of the waste for use in the garden and the rest was freeze-dried and packaged into garbage containers. These containers were bundled into expendable supply ships that were deliberately burned up in the atmosphere. Now, she needed as much fertilizer as she could get. So, she reprogrammed the system to recycle everything. Nothing would be sent outside.

As she stared out the VP windows, thinking about her newly reworked garden, she took the last bite of her banana and tucked the peel into the pocket of her flight suit to take to the fertilizer processing unit. Enough thought. Time to get back to work.

***

In the G bathroom, there was a small bulkhead window that faced away from the rest of the ship. The designers decided that people might want to watch the world spin around while they did their business on the toilet. The Earth would flow in and out of the window as the module turned, and sunlight would do something similar, ebbing and flowing like water around the little room.

For a new astronaut not used to the spin of the centrifugal module, it could be a dizzying experience. But Nu was a seasoned veteran of the station, very much used to the sensation of the spinning light. So, it surprised her when she found herself laid out on the floor, puking into the toilet again. It wasn't the spinning. No, this had nothing to do with the ship and she knew it.

In the cabinet under the bathroom sink, there was a medical kit. NASA always included a pregnancy test in their medical kits as a "just in case" item. All the necessary precautions were taken to ensure that women were *not* pregnant when they made their way up to the station. But in case a quirk of nature caused something unexpected to happen, the test was there as an easy way to rule out pregnancy when a woman became sick on board.

After the nausea passed, Nu decided it was time to rule out pregnancy. She opened her eyes and pulled herself off the floor, reaching over to the small cabinet. Inside the medical kit, she found the usual: tweezers, bandages, gauze, tape, pain medication, antibacterial cream, tampons. The little kit wasn't there for fixing big medical problems. The station had a state-of-the-art med bay by the kitchen that was stocked with more advanced medical equipment and supplies.

There were always nicks and cuts happening on the station, as there would be in any workplace. Once, a cosmonaut broke her arm during a nasty run-in with the wall. They X-rayed it, set the bone, and it healed in a surprisingly short amount of time.

The absence of gravity is typically detrimental to bone health, but with the broken bone incident, they found that the cosmonaut's arm healed better than it would have on Earth. The G's low gravity offered enough resistance to allow the bone to heal, and because she could use the arm with less pain than she would have had in full gravity, it healed in record time.

Nu now held the small medical kit in her hands. She flipped open the metal clasps and opened the box. Enclosed in its own compartment under the lid lay the pregnancy test, noted so by its label.

With a resigned sigh, she slid it out of its holder and unwrapped it to find the instructions. She had never taken one before, so she wanted to get it right. Most women, by the time they had reached her age, thirty-six, would have had some experience with one of these, but she wasn't interested in starting a family. She was also very careful about this type of thing. Pregnancy was never optimal for female astronauts hoping to get flight assignments. She carefully read the instructions from beginning to end. She didn't want to taint the results because of user error.

Exactly eleven minutes later, she still sat on the floor, her knees drawn up to her chest. Her forearms rested on top of her knees and the pregnancy test dangled from her fingertips. As the G spun, the sunlight beamed into the small bathroom and quickly zoomed back out. It didn't want to be in there any more than she did.

The two pink lines on the center panel of the pregnancy test were undeniable.

Positive.

Of course, she knew the outcome before she even took the test. What she couldn't understand was how it happened. She was careful about taking her birth control pills at the same time every day. She knew for a fact she hadn't skipped a single pill. These modern birth control pills were almost 100 percent effective, yet here she was—pregnant. She wondered if it was because of the microgravity. Perhaps it affected the female reproductive system in some unknown way.

As far as she knew, nobody had ever had an affair while working on a spacecraft. So really, there was no way of knowing if birth control worked in this type of environment. The thought made her chuckle to herself. NASA was so meticulous about testing everything involved with space travel many times over, yet they had never looked into what might happen if two of their astronauts began a relationship.

With a sigh, she tossed the test into the bathroom garbage bag and pulled herself up off the floor. As she walked out of the bathroom, she glanced at herself in the mirror. She looked terrible. Her eyes were baggy, with dark circles hovering beneath them, and her face was thinner than it had been before her crew left. She may very well be pregnant, but she knew enough about space, and particularly the dangers of radiation, to acknowledge that this child of hers would probably not make it far without the safe protection of the Earth's atmosphere.

As soon as she thought about the radiation, sadness crept into her gut. She brought her hand down to her stomach and closed her eyes, letting her fingers rest where she imagined her baby to be.

"Be safe, little one," she said before opening her eyes and continuing with her day's work.

Chapter 18

"God, I sure could go for a banana right now," Nu said out loud as she rummaged through the cabinets in the kitchen, trying to find anything that looked as good as a banana.

She knew it was a silly craving, like ice cream and pickles, but she couldn't get the thought of bananas out of her head. With a sigh of defeat, she chose a bundle of grapes from the grapevine instead and settled into one of the kitchen chairs to eat her snack while she reviewed some of the computer logs for the day.

It had been one month since she found out she was pregnant. She kept a detailed log of her health and vitals on the station medical equipment. This was the right thing to do, she decided, since this unexpected pregnancy could offer a vital look into how a baby develops in space. She didn't kid herself, though, and knew the odds of carrying a healthy baby full term were minimal at best. Radiation would have a say in the matter, she feared.

Space radiation was always a hot topic when it came to prolonged human exposure to space travel. How much radiation could humans absorb before it led to fatal illnesses? The station had plenty of radiation shielding built into the protective material surrounding the hull, but this didn't protect her from all radiation. She was well aware that she, and her unborn child, were receiving much more radiation than they would receive if they were on Earth's surface, protected under a thick blanket of atmosphere and a dynamic magnetic field.

Nu also feared what was going on down on the surface. The regular patchwork of lights on the night side of Earth's surface was gone. What had replaced it scared her even more. Bright spots of light burst from the surface as if huge bombs were dropping like flies. During the day, she could see the huge clouds of smoke wafting up from the surface. Cities had been decimated from the looks of it. She'd never seen anything like it.

By this point, she was fairly certain the men had not made it safely to the surface in the Soyuz. If they had made it, someone would have contacted her. But everything was working as it should on the Delta. All systems were healthy and running smoothly without contact with the ground, and since she and her baby were healthy, she decided she could wait this out.

The baby continued to amaze her. He (she'd gotten into the habit of referring to her child as a boy) showed nothing but normal vital signs and measured exactly as he should at twelve weeks pregnant. Every day she took her blood, did an ultrasound, and monitored his heartbeat, recording all of it in the medical log, coded as "Shepard, Millicent, and child." This way she could keep her prepregnancy readings separate from the pregnancy readings. She was determined to turn this unplanned pregnancy into a positive learning experience for future generations.

To minimize the effects of microgravity on the baby, she spent as much time as she could in the G. Studies of mice and other mammals showed the baby could have issues with balance if it developed in a microgravity environment. So, she only left the G when absolutely necessary. The kitchen became her new workspace.

She cried a lot more now than she had at the beginning of her time alone. Maybe the pregnancy and ensuing wacky hormones caused it, or maybe loneliness was to blame. She tinkered with the idea of reprogramming the NIX unit to see if she couldn't drum up a companion.

Nu was a strong computer programmer and knew she could write a program to allow her to have a rudimentary conversation with him and probably even more than that. She had nothing but time, after all. The idea gave her comfort when the loneliness seemed to overtake her.

As she popped the last of the grapes into her mouth, she glanced over at the garden and noticed the little plants she had planted just a few weeks before had buds on them. Life was flourishing all around her. She touched her growing belly and smiled.

Chapter 19

Tucked away in his little office on the third floor, Alé sat gazing at the screen in front of him. He had several pictures pulled up in various places on the large holo-screen. There it was, the Delta Space Station. After Xander got back to him with the exact orbit of the signaling object, he did some math and, with his personal high-definition camera, took some pictures using a long-range lens.

Something orbiting that quickly in low-Earth orbit would be tough to catch on a telescope, but through a wide-angle camera lens or a pair of field binoculars, you could get a pretty good view of it. To get better quality pictures, he drove over a hundred miles north of Baltimore, into the northern Maryland countryside. He was fortunate that night because the sky was as clear as a bell.

First, he tried finding it with binoculars. He saw the object moving overhead, right where it was supposed to be based on the orbit Xander had given him. The naked eye can see almost all large satellites in the clear, night sky. But on this night, the Delta was particularly bright as it raced through the heavens.

Looking at the big, bright object, he experienced a moment of disbelief. How could nobody have noticed this huge object orbiting the Earth before now? He shook his head at the thought. It boiled down to the fact that nobody was really looking. Nobody would have guessed that the Delta Space Station could still be up there, continuing to chug along at orbital velocity some eighteen years after its crew abandoned it.

After looking at the object through his binoculars for several seconds, he was positive it had to be the Delta. It was definitely a space station with various modules giving the shiny object a geometric pattern, not a round blob of light like you might see if you looked at one of the TDRS through field binoculars. He could clearly see the round G Module sticking out at one end.

Alé took about fifty pictures of the object from various angles before it finally dropped below the horizon. These were the snapshots he now analyzed on the holo-screen in front of him.

As he looked over the pictures and compared them to his notes about the Delta, he became more convinced: there had to be someone up there running it. There was no other way it could have stayed in orbit for so long.

When Xander emailed Alé the orbital parameters, he mentioned that it was settled in an orbit that would definitely decay without regular boosting. Based on the size of the object that he now looked at, Alé knew this had to be true.

If a satellite was small enough and placed into a high enough orbit, say several thousand kilometers above the surface, it could, in theory, go many years, even as long as eighteen years, without an orbital boost. But the closer you got to Earth, the more atmospheric drag there was, and the larger the object, the more drag. Space stations historically orbited in lower orbits. Since they depended on regular supply ships, they stayed at a relatively low orbit so that these supply ships could reach them without needing bigger rockets. The object that Alé looked at in his pictures was orbiting low, perhaps 400 kilometers or less, he guessed. He leaned back in his desk chair, one leg crossed over the other at the ankle, hands pressed against the back of his head, and stared at the ceiling, thinking about the possibilities.

He considered the idea that someone was operating the station remotely. In theory, there didn't *need* to be a crew on board to keep the systems of the Delta running. Although they'd lost communications shortly after the war broke out, it didn't mean someone hadn't realized it in time and made contact with the station before it deorbited. But the odds of this were low for two reasons. First, there weren't any active space agencies running during the war. Nobody kept up with space exploration while they were fighting to save themselves. Second, somebody would have said something by now. The war had been over for years. He was confident that someone would have come forward and said, "Oh, by the way, remember that space station, the Delta? Yeah, we've been controlling it remotely since the beginning of the war. It's still up there. What should we do with it?" No, he didn't believe that was possible.

He considered that perhaps there was an artificial intelligence running it. From what he'd seen of the old NASA system logs, the Delta hadn't been equipped with a sophisticated AI. But those records were decades old and incomplete. They could be wrong.

One question tickled at the back of his mind: If the Delta was on autopilot with an AI keeping it up, why would it broadcast an SOS? It didn't make sense. He shifted forward in his chair, picked up his phone, and dialed down to the coding room.

"Hello, Gina?" Alé asked when she picked up her extension.

"Yes, this is Gina Lau."

"Hi Gina, this is Alé Bakas again. I've got kind of a weird request for you."

"Oh? Like running triplicate code checks on six satellites wasn't weird enough?" she asked. "What do you need?"

"How are the satellites doing?" Alé asked, ignoring her initial remark and avoiding the subject of his call for a second longer.

"Good so far," she said. "They are expected to be in their final orbits by Monday afternoon. Then we'll start running some basic checks and communications tests. They should be fully operational for commercial use within thirty days as planned."

"That's great. Good news," he said, hesitating. His next words would make him sound ridiculous, and he knew it but also knew it was the right thing to do. "I've got a special favor if you don't mind. Again, I'd like you to keep this one just between us. Think you can do that?"

"Depends on the favor," she said.

"I need you to broadcast a message," he said. "I want it to run through all six satellites and go on a continuous loop over the next twenty-four hours."

"I'm sorry... a message?" she asked. If he'd been able to see her face, he would have seen the look of a woman seriously doubting the sanity of the person on the other end of the line. He knew how bizarre it sounded. There was absolutely no reason for their shiny, new communications satellites to send out a broadcast, unless there was someone up there to receive it.

"Yes, a message," he continued. "I think there is something up there that can pick it up."

"Oh... wait, are you talking about that signal I picked up a few days ago?" she asked. "You don't think there's someone up there, do you?" But she stopped, because the sound of his voice indicated that's exactly what he thought.

"Well, yes and no," he said. "I'm not positive, but I think this is the best way to know for sure. Like I said, that's why I want this to be just between us for now. I know it sounds ludicrous and judging by the tone in your voice, you think I'm ridiculous for asking. But I need to know for sure. I certainly don't want to waste satellite time after they get into their orbits. That's when the majority of the troubleshooting will take place and a lot more people will be involved. So, we need to do this now, while they're still in travel mode. I'd like to do it tonight since you're working night shift and you're already somewhat involved."

She sighed. "Okay, I guess so. Wow, if there really is someone up there..." Her voice trailed off and she was silent for a moment, just long enough for both of them to shiver at their desks simultaneously. The fact was, if there was someone up there, that person had been alone for almost two decades and neither of them wanted to think about how scared and lonely and, perhaps, eccentric a person would have to be to survive by themselves on a space station for that long.

"What do you want your message to say? Luke, I am your father?" she asked. As soon as she said it, she regretted the remark. He would surely think of her as an enormous geek for cracking a ridiculous *Star Wars* joke at such a tense moment.

Alé snickered on the other side of the phone, happy that she'd broken the tension with a joke. He happened to be a big *Star Wars* fan himself. "Well, that's one way to go. But I'm thinking that we'll just send out a message asking... um... whoever it is to tune into a ham radio frequency. Then I won't have to use multibillion-dollar space communications satellites to do this little experiment. At least for now."

"Okay," she said. "That should be easy enough. Email me exactly what you want me to say and I'll send it out."

"Thanks, Gina, you're a pal," Alé said, which, of course, turned Gina's normally pale face, bright tomato red. She was happy he wasn't standing there. That would have been *truly* embarrassing.

Chapter 20

I am screwed.

I'm sitting in the kitchen staring out the window in defeat. I spent the last three days trying to figure out a way to fix the engine, running circles around the track (and inside my head) daring my mind to come up with something brilliant. But I'm right back where I started. Not brilliant and without ideas. Although, I did get in a hundred kilometers, something I haven't done in a while now. So, that's positive.

According to Nix's logs, the electrical components between the nuclear reactor and the engine are fried. This likely happened after the last time we ignited the engine, but since the engine was shut down after that, the computer received no error message. I keep trying to remember the last time I did an orbital maneuver with the engine. It was forty-five days ago. Maybe I didn't pay attention when the computer shut off after the engine burned. Or maybe the computer didn't even shut the engine down and it burned out on its own because of the electrical failure. I just can't remember anything out of the ordinary.

I've been through the last four months of log entries in the computer system related to the power supply and the engine. It reported nothing out of the ordinary. Nothing to show anything leading up to this failure. No alarms or error codes.

Nothing.

I continue to send my distress signal and positive thoughts out into the universe, hoping for a miracle. It's literally all I can do now.

I stand to leave the kitchen so I can check the broadcast on the holo-screen in the Service Module. As I do, a bowl of roasted sunflower seeds falls to the floor and scatters all over the place. I am defeated. I don't even stop to pick it up.

After I float through the main tunnel and into the Service Module, I notice for the first time today, I'm on the night side of the planet. I've been so wrapped up in my thoughts about fixing the engine, I haven't noticed a single rotation. I continue on to the VP for a little look around before I start working again. I must be over an ocean because as far as I can see there is black, nothingness. The loneliness rises up through me so fast it takes my breath away for a moment.

I force my lungs to inhale a deep breath and try to shake it out of my body by shaking my hands back and forth and exhaling loudly. Then I move back into the Service Module. A blue light glows from the holo-screen and the start program for the station systems appears as I hover in front of it. I pull up the communications programs and notice there's no change. No ping. No answer. No signals received.

Nothing.

I scrunch up my nose in frustration. Surely those satellites are picking up my signal! I've been blasting it right at them for three days!

The heat of anger radiates through my body. Maybe this whole idea of getting rescued is a hopeless dream. Something out of a science fiction novel. If they did send a signal in return, I would easily pick it up if...

Wait. Wait just a minute.

With renewed life, my fingers move lightly across the menus, opening files, then closing them again, pulling up documents and programs, then dragging them off to the side to look at later. What am I looking for?

There it is, the controls for the antenna array.

The station has two antennae dedicated to communications. There's a high-gain antenna meant to pick up and broadcast highly targeted radio signals. It was the primary communications antenna for the station when the crew was in contact with Mission Control. It's highly sensitive and can pick up radio signals as long as the signal is within its tight beam. In contrast, the low-gain antenna covers a lot of range but is much less accurate and can't pick up weaker signals. When you know where to point the high-gain antenna, the low-gain antenna is mainly there as a backup in case the high-gain malfunctions.

I've been trying to point the high-gain antenna at the area where I believe the satellites are: in geosynchronous orbit around the equator. I've been transmitting the SOS signal using both the high-gain and the low-gain for an all-around effect. But I realize now, I haven't been *listening* with the low-gain antenna, only broadcasting. If I'm only listening with the high-gain and it's off by just a little bit, then of course, I would miss a signal if it were being broadcast back to me.

I punch in a series of commands to bring up the low-gain antenna and the gyroscopes responsible for moving the antenna whir to life outside the station. I update the programming, telling the computer to listen with both antennae and to open up the range of the low-gain antenna as much as possible.

I wait. I listen to the hum of the station systems, working in tandem to keep me alive. After several minutes, the computer beeps.

It has picked up an incoming message.

"Nix!" I scream loudly enough that I jump at the sound escaping my mouth. "The computer's picked up an incoming radio signal!"

"What was that you said?" he asks as he pokes his head into the Service Module. I can tell he has been charging in sleep mode by his demeanor. I don't know if it's possible—he is just a computer—but I believe Nix actually experiences grogginess when he's been charging for a long time. He seems to be less "sharp" after he wakes from a long charge.

"I picked up a radio signal incoming from one of those satellites they launched last week," I repeat excitedly. "Hold on, let me pull it up."

The signal is a text file, not an audio file as I would have expected. But this makes sense, because whoever sent it would want the signal to be as small as possible, knowing I might be using a less powerful antenna to pick it up. The message is in a loop and after a few moments of uploading, words appear on the holo-screen.

Hello. I received your transmission. Turn on ham radio to frequency 145.2 MHz over DC

I turn and grab Nix by the shoulders and a scream of joy jumps out of my throat before I can stop it. Tears well up in my eyes. Tears don't "fall" in microgravity, rather, they pool up in your eyes, making it difficult to see. I wipe them clean with the sleeve of my shirt but I'm so happy I'm almost sobbing and the tears well up again almost immediately.

Nix stares at me with the same old Iron Man enthusiasm he always has. The smile on my face must be overwhelming because he says, "Oh, Eta, I am very happy to hear this!"

I catch myself and try to regroup my thoughts. "Nix, I've got to get to work here!" Releasing his shoulders, I open a fresh tile on the holo-screen and make some notes. The station is on the dark side of the Earth right now and, based on the location calculator in the computer, Washington DC is on the day side. So, I'll have to wait until we orbit around. The orbit will take about twenty-eight minutes. Once around to the day side of the planet, I should have nine or ten minutes of talk time before I lose signal. I can live with that!

Next, I rummage through cabinets in the Service Module to find the ham radio. I find it in a forgotten corner of the module where I store things I rarely use. It's been years since I dragged this old, handheld radio out. The Delta crew members used it to talk to people on the surface whenever they had a few minutes of free time. It was a way for them to connect with the regular people who were just hoping to catch a word or two with the astronauts. I plug the old radio into the station computers and begin the setup process.

Please God, let it work!

Chapter 21

"Hello? Anyone there? Do you copy?" Alé spoke into the Ericsson MP-X handheld amateur radio. He sat at his desk, twirling the thick cord of the device around his index finger.

The radio had seen better days. He had to dig through boxes in the basement to find it. From his research on the Delta, Alé knew the station had its own ham radio and could pick up the signal as long as they were both on the same frequency. This was, of course, assuming the antenna array on the Delta could still receive signals. Just because the transmitter worked, didn't mean the receiver was still functioning. And his theory also hinged on the assumption there was actually someone on board to receive the signal—a big assumption.

As he waited, his mind reeled. He played back all the evidence he had come across so far, which pointed to a human occupant driving the Delta through space for the last nineteen years.

Despite all the evidence, he was still skeptical of the idea that there could be anyone in that station. But he also knew there was no other explanation for some of the happenings over the last few days. He had to disprove this theory in order to clear his conscience, and this was the easiest way to reach the station and send them some parameters for broadcasting directly to the TDRS. Once they (whoever "they" might be) knew how to reach the TDRS, Alé could talk to them directly on an uninterrupted basis.

So far, only four people knew this was even a possibility and he didn't want to blow the lid off of something outrageous if, in fact, there was nothing outrageous to blow the lid off of.

As his mind wandered through this ridiculous idea, the radio crackled beside him, causing him to jump, and pulling his attention back to the task at hand. It was only a brief crackle before the radio sat silent again. He shook his head in disbelief that he was sitting here, at 7:22 p.m. on a Thursday night, waiting to hear from a derelict space station through a piece of equipment that was so old, he had to dig it out of the basement.

Alé took a sip of water from his mug and pulled up his inbox. No new messages. He rubbed his eyes and forehead. The TDRS had all made it to their primary geosynchronous orbits. He would have a hell of a next few weeks getting them up and running, and it all started the next morning. The last thing he needed was another long night before the real work began.

He had been listening to the static passing in and out of the radio for several hours and he was quickly tiring of it. Based on Xander's calculations of the station orbit, it had passed over DC three times since he started, and was about to make another pass over the area. Either nobody was home at the Delta or they hadn't picked up his signal yet. He wasn't sure how long he'd need to wait to find out.

Shhhh... Crack, Crack... Shhhh... Crack, Crack...

The radio static continued for several more minutes, just long enough for Alé to lean back in his chair and begin the initial stages of dozing.

Suddenly, there was a break. The static cleared for just a moment, bringing Alé out of his doze before returning to a regular stream of hissing and popping. He eyed the radio suspiciously, and after a few more seconds, as if it were waking up from a deep sleep, the little radio came to life. The static cleared again and...

"Hello?" said a voice from the other side of the radio.

Alé nearly fell out of his desk chair as he straightened up to give the radio his full attention. The voice was clear, surprisingly clear considering the age of the equipment it was being transmitted over. It was a woman; he was sure of that. A young woman probably, based on the high pitch of her voice.

"Um... Yes, hello," he said, clearing his voice and trying to shake the nerves. "This is Alexandros Bakas. I work at Goddard Space Flight Center near Washington DC. Who is this? Over."

The reply was short and sweet.

"I am Eta."

Chapter 22

The contractions were getting closer and closer together.

Nu sat on a chair in the kitchen with the stopwatch in one hand and a small holo-screen sitting on the table in front of her. She was keeping track of the time and it had been three minutes and forty-three seconds since the last contraction.

Labor began nearly four hours prior and Nu was managing it with the stoic composure of a seasoned astronaut handling any new predicament. She had done everything she could to prepare for this day, even preparing herself mentally for the idea that the baby would have health issues because of radiation exposure and limited gravity.

One of her priorities during her pregnancy was to work on reprogramming the station robot so it could handle more tasks. She started by giving him a name that he would recognize and answer to: Nix. When the baby was born, she knew she wouldn't be able to do any spacewalks or stick to her long and strict daily work schedule. She needed to give him more capabilities to handle the little things, leaving her more time to care for her child.

She did this by reworking his code and also by adding computing power to his systems, which she pillaged from some of the more advanced computers on the station. Nix was now functioning at a sufficient level to do all of the maintenance on the outer hull of the spacecraft. He was a work in progress, but she was happy with the headway she'd made.

Another contraction pushed at her insides and she started her timer. They were getting more painful and she put her head down on the tabletop, curling over her large belly, breathing deeply to help combat the pain.

She had done many ultrasounds on herself over the last nine months, yet she hadn't allowed herself to see the gender of the baby, hoping to keep it a surprise. As the baby grew, it continued to amaze her. She had learned through her research, how to properly measure certain areas of the baby's little body. Bone length, organ size, heart function—all of it was normal.

Of course, Nu had helped aid in the baby's development by taking every precaution. Since the loss of ground communications, she had successfully tripled the size of the garden and was living on a high-fiber vegetarian diet. There were no prenatal vitamins on board, so she concentrated on eating foods that were high in things like folic acid and vitamin D. Frankly, she was getting a little tired of eating beans and spinach, but she was willing to do it for her baby.

Exercise was still part of her daily routine, and she kept a nutrition journal to detail how many calories she and her baby were getting and what nutrients she needed more of. She spent almost all of her pregnancy in the G, only going into microgravity when absolutely necessary. Nix had been invaluable during the process, like a little gopher, fetching whatever she needed from the other parts of the station.

She had spent the last hour walking steadily around the module while the intensity of the contractions increased. After about three hours, when the contractions were eight minutes apart, her water broke.

She could feel the baby's head resting on her pelvis. At first, she was worried she'd need to do something to "augment" the gravity to get the baby to move down in her body. But as of now, she wasn't all that concerned with it. Nature seemed to be working its magic like it would with any birth on the surface. The pain had been bearable so far, and she couldn't help but wonder if it wasn't the lower gravity that caused her to be more comfortable. She continued to monitor her progress, ticking off the time and measuring each contraction, waiting patiently to finally meet her new companion.

***

The baby, a girl, came into the world at 0232 GMT, bright pink and screaming like any healthy newborn. The labor and delivery had been textbook. Before the birth, Nu worried about things like placenta detachment or a wrapped umbilical cord, but it hadn't been a problem.

After the baby made her miraculous entrance, Nu lay on the bed in the medical bay and held the child, crying right along with her.

"Eta," she said, between sobs. "That's what I'll call you."

***

Eta let out a long wail as she searched for her mother in the darkness. Not more than a moment passed before Nu was there to comfort her two-day-old daughter. Taking her baby in her arms, she sat on a thick cotton blanket next to the little homemade bassinet and fed her hungry daughter.

Almost immediately after Eta was born, Nu worked on getting her baby on a regular schedule. She strung up blankets covering the walls of the sleeping compartment that would be Eta's room to make sure that no light entered while Eta was supposed to be sleeping. Routine and structure were so important to survival on the Delta and Nu wanted to firmly establish this importance in her daughter's mind.

And the name... Eta. Nu figured, why not name her after a Greek letter, like her very own nickname? In physics, Eta represented a particle called a meson made of quarks and antiquarks that was known to work through both strong and weak interactions. She liked the idea of her daughter being associated with strange quarks and being weak yet strong at the same time.

Nu had been given a gift—a reprieve from the loneliness— and she cherished every second of her time on board the Delta with her daughter. Because she knew better than anyone how quickly that time could end.

Chapter 23

Nu sat at the kitchen table in the G, squinting as she worked with a program on a holo-screen, her face tight with concentration. She was working on something new that she'd been mulling over in her mind for a few months.

The new program was a tracking system to monitor activity on the surface. It was a way for her to take a more proactive role in communicating with the people on the ground—if there were any left. She had been broadcasting an SOS signal for years, but they still hadn't reached anyone on the ground and she needed some other way to track what was going on. She hoped this Doppler-based system would provide the answer to where the people were.

Something caught her eye and she swiveled her head around to look. Eta shot past her, running through the center of the module, her tiny feet making dull thuds on the rubber running track. Nu smiled at this, but only for a second. As soon as the smile touched her lips, she turned it around and a stern look came over her face.

"Eta, have you finished your schoolwork?" she asked, not pleased to see that her daughter was away from her desk so early in the afternoon. Nu had set her down only fifteen minutes before to read three chapters of her book *Journey to the Center of the Earth* by Jules Verne.

Although there was no children's fiction in the station archives, there was plenty of literary fiction. Nu put together a "summer reading list" for her daughter to work on over the next few months. Eta was only five, but she was already reading Jules Verne and Charles Dickens. Her very favorite book was *Little House on the Prairie* by Laura Ingalls Wilder. She'd read it three times already, once with Nu reading it to her, and twice more on her own.

"Yes, Nu," she said as she flew past the kitchen table again, on her way around the circular module at breakneck speed.

"Eta, please slow down so I can speak to you," Nu said, putting her hand out to catch the little girl as she came around the bend again. "How can you have finished already? It's only been fifteen minutes?"

"No, it's been thirty minutes and I finished five minutes ago. I even read ahead a little! And now I want to run!" she said with a satisfied smirk.

"Has it already been thirty minutes?" Nu asked, her eyes perked up as she questioned her own timekeeping abilities. Nu was all about keeping the schedule, so the fact that an extra fifteen minutes had gone by without her realizing it, surprised her. She checked her screen time and yes, Eta was right, it had been thirty minutes. Nu laughed to herself. She'd been so wrapped up in the programming project that she completely lost track of time. "All right then, if you're sure you read and understand the material, then you may run for a while before supper."

"Okay!" Eta said, and in the blink of an eye, she was off, bound to run dizzying circles around the G for the next hour until she collapsed in exhaustion. Running was her favorite thing to do besides quizzing Nix for little tidbits of random trivia.

Shaking her head, Nu caught Eta's arm before she could get going, smiled and added, "Don't forget, we are running through the orbital maneuver procedures tonight. I want you to pay attention to it this time. The last time you were like a silly goose lost in space." She made a silly face that caused a fit of laughter to escape from Eta's lips.

"I just don't see why I have to watch you do that. It's not like you won't do it again," Eta said, her face turned up into a sour look.

"Yes, dear," Nu said. "You're right, but what if something should happen to me? You must be able to run it yourself and since there's nobody else here to teach you... I guess I'm it!" Eta shrugged and Nu got up from her seat with her fingers outstretched in a threat of tickles, and she chased the little girl around the G. By the third time around, they were both laughing uncontrollably and exhausted.

"Okay, little girl," Nu said. "I'll keep working on this program and then we'll tend to the garden before supper. How does that sound?"

"Sounds great!" Eta said, and once again, turning her attention to the rubber track, was off in a flash of bare feet and long, brown hair.

Nu placed the value of education above all else. At the tender age of five, Eta was more advanced than most children twice her age. She spoke, wrote, and read English and Russian fluently. All astronauts had to understand Russian in order to operate the Soyuz, but Nu actually learned the Slavic language many years before she became an astronaut. Her mother was born and raised in Moscow, the daughter of a factory worker and a physicist.

A brilliant woman, Eta's grandmother earned her PhD in physics before the age of twenty-six. She married Eta's grandfather, an American chemist, when she was thirty and left her career in physics behind to raise her daughter. Millicent was an only child and her mother was her best friend for twenty-five years until she died of breast cancer at the age of fifty-five. The loss devastated Nu. She became deeply depressed and almost quit pursuing her goal of becoming an astronaut. A near-death experience in a motorcycle accident pulled her out of her funk. After the accident, she swore that life would be hers to live to its fullest, in memory of her beloved mother.

Eta's school schedule rivaled that of most high-end private schools. Nu put the vast amount of information available on the station archives to work for her. Every day, she and Eta sat down to work on reading, writing, advanced math, physics, and economics. To top it off, they had the best bird's-eye view of the planet to study environmental sciences and geography.

Nu told Eta what she knew about the war and about how they had come to be stranded on the Delta. Eta, of course, had no basis for comparison as to what life might be like on the surface. She'd seen movies, pictures, and read many books depicting a normal human life on the surface of the Earth, but the concept was not easy for her to grasp. She was born on the station and it was all she knew. For Eta, Earth held the same place in her mind as Venus or Mars. They existed, but they were very far away and had no real effect on her life.

Every evening, Nu gave Eta a lesson about the station and how to run the various life-support systems. She wanted Eta to have a working knowledge of the station systems by the time she was ten.

This served several purposes. First, it was a way to keep Eta occupied by giving her actual, real-time lessons about her home and how to keep it functioning properly. Second, if anything ever happened to Nu, Eta would be able to stay alive on the station until someone rescued her. Nu continued to hold out hope that the war would end and NASA would rescue them.

And then there was Nix. Nu had given him a name, a voice, a database full of practical information, and the ability to hold a conversation. Having Nix around had been incredibly helpful. He did all the work outside the station and was good at his job, doing thorough inspections and handling minor repairs with ease. He always checked with Nu before completing a task if he was not specifically programmed to complete it. But in almost every case, he was correct in his analysis of the situation and she simply told him to go ahead with it.

Eta had grown fond of the strange-looking robot and genuinely considered him a friend. Once, when Eta was about four years old, Nu found her sleeping next to Nix on his charging port. Since there was no gravity in that section of the station, Eta floated easily next to him, her favorite sleeping bag (which she dragged around like a blankie) connected to the port by carabiners. Nix had his arm around her and a lullaby played from the tiny speakers in his torso. It comforted her to know that if something did happen to her, Eta wouldn't be totally alone.

Nu continued to work on her program as Eta rounded the module over and over again. She hoped to have it up and running before the end of a week so she could begin scanning the surface and analyzing data. She was willing to do anything to get her daughter down to the surface safely.

Chapter 24

"Lord, help us," Jade said, her mouth hanging open. In her hand, she held the transcript from Alé's conversation with the girl on the Delta, which had taken place a mere thirty minutes prior.

"Yeah, no kidding," Alé said. He paced slowly, one foot at a time, replaying the conversation in his head, watching the floor as if it might drop away from underneath him at any moment. He'd had only about eight minutes to talk to Eta before the Delta's orbit took it out of contact, but it qualified as one of the most bizarre things he'd ever done. What she had told him in those few minutes made him shudder, even now, as he replayed it in his mind.

The transcript Jade held in her hands read as follows:

Alé: "Where are you, Eta?"

Eta: I am on the station.

Alé: "Do you mean, the Delta Space Station?"

Eta: Yes, that's the one.

Alé: Umm... Excuse me for being unprepared, but how is that possible?

Eta: Well, I guess I don't understand. I mean, I'm here. So, it's definitely possible.

Alé: How did you get there?

Eta: I have always been here. I was born here.

Alé: How old are you?

Eta: I just had my eighteenth birthday. My mother was Millicent Shepard. But I called her Nu.

Alé: Is your mother with you now?

Eta: (Pause) No, she isn't.

Alé: Oh, okay... um, what happened to her?

Eta: I would prefer not to talk about my mother right now.

Alé: Okay, I guess that's a question for another time. Do you operate the Delta?

Eta: Yes.

Alé: So, you are the one doing the orbital maneuvers to keep it in orbit?

Eta: Yes. But there's a problem. A few days ago, I discovered that the engine is no longer functioning.

Alé: Wait, what do you mean? You still have power up there, right?

Eta: Yes, there's power. The nuclear reactor is still working, but there was a problem with the last orbital maneuver I did about a month ago. It caused a short in the engine wiring and fried most of the cabling between the reactor and the engine. As far as I can tell, it's useless. I sent Nix out there to see if he could fix it—

Alé: Wait, who is Nix?

Eta: Nix is the station robot. He performs the maintenance outside of the station. He went out there to try to fix it, but this problem is too big for him.

Alé: Geez... that's not good.

Eta: No, it's not. From my calculations, I have six months tops before the orbit becomes unstable.

Alé: Eta, I assure you, we are doing everything in our power to help you. Okay? Do you understand?

Eta: I... I... I don't even know what to say. I'm stunned to be speaking to you, Alexandros. It's been so long since I spoke to anyone.

Alé: Please, call me Alé. That's what my friends call me.

Eta: Okay, Alé.

As he paced the floor in Jade's office, Alé was deep in thought, replaying the sound of Eta's voice over the crackling radio. It was strange because her voice didn't sound excited or happy or hysterical, like he imagined he might be after speaking to someone for the first time in years. No, her voice was calm, but more than that, it was plump with relief—the kind of relief you feel when you've narrowly avoided a car accident.

Alé couldn't pinpoint it, but something drew him closer to the microphone during their brief conversation. Almost like an invisible string reaching from his office chair to Eta's space station had suddenly become connected. The longer they spoke to each other, the tighter the string pulled, drawing him closer to the microphone. It was a bit unnerving to him. He'd felt nothing like it before.

Something else about her voice fascinated him during their conversation—her voice was *beautiful*. Even over the static of the radio, its bell tones pinged inside his mind, delicate and delicious. He realized, after only a few minutes on the radio with her, he would do anything, *anything* to save Eta.

As their signal faded, Alé had told Eta to come back to the radio during the next revolution, when he would give her more instructions for how to train her radio antenna to the location of the new satellites. Then they could have uninterrupted radio contact. When Eta heard this, her beautiful voice rose with excitement and longing. Alé had been so overwhelmed by the conversation, it almost brought him to tears, before the radio signal spit and sputtered and finally relinquished its grip, dropping the radio back into the dull thud of static.

Jade watched Alé closely as he paced the room in front of her. She could tell he was rattled by this development and the idea of it surprised her. Alé always seemed so confident and relaxed, flashing that big, handsome smile around. Even men found comfort in his presence. He was one of those people who knew how to interact with others and put them at ease, no matter the circumstance. But the man who paced in front of her was worried and frazzled, nothing like the confident guy who could give you a wink and a nod and assure you he had you covered.

"Okay," Jade said, waving her finger at the chair in front of her. Alé snapped back to the present and obeyed her command to sit. He linked his fingers together in his lap and waited for her to continue. "Let's take a rational look at this situation. When does the station orbit back around?"

"It'll be back in radio contact in about eighty-six minutes," he said.

"Good. I want to talk to her this time," she said, pulling up the holo-screen and jotting down some notes. "Then I'm going to have to bring this up to administration."

"Who?" he asked.

"Who do you think? Patrick." She gave him a look that implied he should have known better.

John Patrick was the current NASA administrator, as his father had been before the war broke out. Patrick was a fierce guy, intimidating to almost everyone... except Jade. She could finesse her way around his monster ego with the delicate footing of a ballet dancer.

"We need to get a better communication system up with her. The ground network is shot. We'll need to rely on the new satellites. Let's get one of the programmers working on it. Preferably someone who already knows. Maybe that Lina person?" Jade said.

"Gina," he corrected her. "Gina Lau. She's the one who found the signal."

"Yeah, whatever." Jade nodded. "Let's talk to her. I still want to keep this one to ourselves, and if she already knows about it, then keep her on a limited-knowledge basis. Let's see what our new satellites can do and get them up and running. I want twenty-four-hour ground contact with this Eta person by morning. I mean it, Alé, keep this one close. This Lina person needs to know as few details as possible. Make her understand."

"It's Gina," he said again.

"She could be Joan of Arc for all I care. Just make sure she knows," Jade said. "I mean, how is it possible a government as big

- 183 -

as ours could lose an entire space station? We need to figure out the answers to that question before the public finds out about this."

"Got it." Alé bobbed his head. "I'd also like permission to start working on the rescue. I might have to pull some more people in. I'm sure physiology will want a crack at this too—someone who's been in space her *entire* life. They'll salivate at the opportunity to learn from her." He paused a moment before adding, "Jade, her orbit is decaying. We don't even have a functioning space vehicle. Hell, there hasn't been a human in space, well, one we've known of, for eighteen years. I need to get started *now*."

Jade stood from her desk and slung her black Chanel bag over her shoulder. "Yes, get to work on it. I'll be down at your desk in eighty-four minutes to talk to her. Have it ready."

"Yes, ma'am," he said.

***

Gina Lau looked at the information on the holo-screen in front of her. Stunned didn't really capture her expression—it was more like the disbelief of a deer right before making contact with the headlights. She looked up at Alé and said, "You can't be serious."

"Trust me, Gina, it's not a joke. This project has now been upgraded to the highest priority level. Jade wants those satellites pointing at the Delta immediately." He moved his fingers over Gina's screen several times and pulled up a long list of coordinates. "These are the orbital coordinates I've plotted so far. It shouldn't be too difficult to program them to track this and relay back a full-strength radio signal."

"Wait. Just wait," she said. "You mean to tell me the *Delta* is still up there in orbit... after eighteen years? And the person running it is a girl who was born there? And after all these years, her ion engine malfunctioned and the station will deorbit within a few months? And we're just finding out about this now?"

"That's what I'm telling you," he said.

"Geez..." She fell back in her chair and let a long breath of air escape from her lips. Then, as any good engineer on a mission would do, she sat up, turned her attention to her holo-screen, and began pulling up the satellite interfaces. "Well, I'd better get started then."

Alé smiled. "Good. And you'll keep this to yourself." It was a statement, not a question.

"Got it," she said without looking away from her screen. She would spend the next six hours at her console working on the project of restoring full-time communication to the Delta.

Chapter 25

I've lived a fairly uneventful life. So, to say that today is the best of all the days I've had isn't really saying much. I spoke to another human being today for the first time in three years. I should be excited.

It's strange because I'm not *acting* excited. I mean, in the conventional sense. When I watch movies where people get excited about something or another, they express their excitement in relatively common ways. They jump for joy, or get all red in the face, or slap themselves as if they can't believe their own good luck. Someone who's excited might laugh or scream or let loose a whole slew of "oohs" and "ahhs" and "OMGs."

I didn't do any of that. Excitement just isn't something I'm used to.

When Alé's voice came through the old radio, my mind instantly calmed. One moment I was trying to get the radio set up, frantic and anxious and hanging on for dear life. The next moment, his voice boomed out of the little box and all was well. I felt stable and safe, and I was able to catch my breath again. It literally happened that fast.

And his voice! It was like nothing I'd ever heard. Even through the crackling radio, there was something special about it. It was beautiful. Not beautiful like bells chiming or violins playing. His voice wasn't smooth or fine or delicate. It was beautiful in a rough sort of way. In a *male* sort of way. Maybe it was just the radio, but his voice sounded to me like the lyrical equivalent of eating a delicious steak. I've never eaten steak, but it seems to be the sort of food men like a lot. That's what his voice reminded me of, a steak, all charred and buttery and full of flavor.

I picture him in my mind, standing on a porch in front of a big grill like I've seen in movies. He's smiling and flipping steaks. I have no idea what he looks like, of course, but in my steak fantasy, I imagine he's tall with dark hair, dark eyes, and dark skin. I picture myself standing on the porch with him, drawing in the scent of rosemary and crackling coals. My mind conjures up what the coolness of the breeze might feel like, coming off the huge trees surrounding the porch. And all around us is lush greenery.

I realize, for the first time in my life, I am actively imagining myself standing on the surface. I've never thought of myself as part of that world before. It's a place that exists, but not for me. Not until now. Until I heard his voice.

Our conversation was short because of the station's orbit, but Alé promised me he would be there, waiting for me with further instructions when the station revolves around again. I cannot *wait* to hear his voice again.

Now, finally, I am not the only person in the whole universe who knows my engine is blown. I'm also not the only one responsible to fix it. I can even allow myself to think about getting rescued. It's exciting. And terrifying.

Alé mentioned that since the war, there has been no crewed spaceflight, which means they will have to build something to come up and get me. That's okay. If the experts at NASA can troubleshoot my engine, then there's hope to get it fixed and continue to orbit until they come up to rescue me.

**

The radio crackles. I wait. As the seconds tick away, I get more nervous. Did I dream the conversation? Is Alé a figment of my stressed-out, overworked mind?

"Eta. Are you there?" His voice breaks through the static of the radio and my body and mind melt with relief.

"Yes, I'm here, Alé," I say into the receiver. I am in the Service Module and have steadied myself against one wall with the footholds.

"Ah, you remember my name!" he says.

"Of course, I remember your name," I say, a little too eagerly, and my face flushes with heat.

"Well, that's good because we'll be talking a lot," he says.

I nod and purse my lips to show him I'm grateful for this. Blushing, I roll my eyes at myself—it's not like he can see me.

"Listen," he continues, "I want to go over a few programming commands with you so your computers can locate the communications satellites. That way we won't have to rely on these ancient radios to communicate. But first, I've got someone else here who wants to talk to you."

Panic rises in my throat. Someone else? I can't talk to someone else yet. I'm having a difficult enough time dealing with just the one person. I mutter into the radio, "Um, no, no, I don't know if I want to talk to anyone else yet." There is silence on the other end. Realizing my comment might have sounded a little weird, I clarify it. "It's just that... well, I've never talked to anyone else before. I'm nervous."

There's a pause. I hope I've explained well enough to keep me from sounding like a total weirdo.

"It's okay, Eta," he says. "It must be difficult being alone up there. I promise I will try to be your primary contact, but from time to time, you will have to talk to other people. Trust me, I don't care much for talking to other people either." He laughs. "We're bringing in all the experts we can to get you out of there, and as much as I like to think it, I'm not an expert on everything. So, you'll have to listen to some other people from time to time. Is that okay?"

"Okay. Yes, I understand." I like how he asked my permission to continue, and oddly, I'm more at ease now that he's explained it in such a casual way.

"Good." He sounds satisfied. "Now, I will put you on with Jade. She is one of the directors here at NASA. She and I work on the same team and we will handle your rescue mission. Hold on one second and I'll have Jade come on and speak with you."

There's a pause, followed by the radio crackle as he's probably let the handset go for a second. My heart rate picks up in an instant. Why am I so nervous? I can't believe I'm actually speaking with people. Maybe I *have* dreamed all this up in my head. Have I finally lost my mind? The radio crackles to life again.

"Hello, Eta. My name is Jade. It's a pleasure to get to speak with you. You've caused quite the buzz around here since Alé came to us with this news," she says. "I promise you one thing, Eta. I won't sugarcoat anything for you. Figuring out how to fix your station and how to get you home will be difficult, but we'll do it. Do you hear me loud and clear? We will do it."

How interesting. She used the word "home" to describe the surface, like I've been there before and am taking a long vacation here in space. But I do like her style. Her voice is strong and dark, like Alé's, and I like how confident she sounds.

"Alé will be the leader of this project," she says. "Does that sound good to you?"

"Of course," I say.

"Good. Now, I know we're short on time, so I'll get Alé back on here to give you instructions about setting up the satellite communications. But before I go, I just want to say one more thing. You're a very brave girl. I appreciate bravery. And I'll make damn sure we get you back home. Got it?"

"Yes, ma'am. I understand," I say.

The radio breaks up for a moment until Alé comes on again. "All right," he says. "Now that we've commenced with the pleasantries, let's get down to business."

For the next few minutes, he gives me a list of instructions on how to find the satellites with my computer tracking program and then set up the broadcast channel. They are relatively simple steps, but he feeds them to me as if I've never seen a computer in my life. I'll have to make sure he knows I've been on this station for a while now and I'm capable of the basics. But I suppose he's being safe.

The communications satellites were supposed to go through a period of testing and troubleshooting, but Alé says they've pushed their engineers into high gear for my sake and got them up and running at full power three weeks early. Once I update my system, I won't have a single minute of lost communication going forward.

Just like that, I'm not alone anymore.

Chapter 26

John Patrick stared out the window of his ninth-floor corner office at Two Independence Square. The long-time NASA headquarters was in the heart of Washington DC's downtown business district, a few blocks away from the National Mall. The building held the gold-trimmed, leather-lined, mahogany-rich offices of anyone who was anyone at the world's most prestigious space agency.

Patrick had been the administrator for only three months when Congress had finally given the go-ahead to push forward with a new campaign to put humans back in space. That was six years ago and since that time, they had made great strides, a fact Patrick never left out in a press conference. He took great pride in the accomplishments of the organization under his command. That pride came with a pinch of smugness and a dash of bullying swagger. Bully or not, John Patrick had created a space agency that, unlike the stodgy, misogynistic, prewar NASA, was creative, economically efficient, and groundbreaking.

Of course, this new quest for crewed spaceflight meant abandoning all prewar technology. The new administration was determined that spaceflight should be economical and reusable. In the past, NASA's primary goal had been "exploration", which really meant a race to the finish line to claim a first-place prize that included a stiff American flag planted in moondust and all the accompanying international praise.

After the initial Space Race back in the 1960s, the folks at NASA almost didn't know what to do with themselves. They took a stab at making space more economical and accessible to everyone by diving headfirst into the Space Shuttle program. The Space Shuttle, an awkward vehicle stuck somewhere between a rocket and a jetliner, turned out to be the deadliest space vehicle to ever fly the not-so-friendly skies of low-Earth orbit. Patrick looked back at that time and could only shake his head, wondering what it was all for. Experimentation? Study? Useless, in his opinion.

It wasn't that Patrick didn't value the need for experimentation and study. He knew it was a critical part of conquering the safety aspect of space exploration. But he was determined that his version of space exploration would be useful first, and scientifically meaningful second. Under him, space exploration would provide jobs, advance creativity in engineering, and, most importantly, bring in cash. His plan was to turn NASA into its own business, no longer shackled to the ankles of the overweight congressional representatives who sat in their big leather chairs only a few blocks away from where he sat now. Space was a commercial goldmine, full of unexplored worlds that contained countless unknown minerals for mining, possibly even a resource that could solve the ever-mounting energy crisis on Earth. Hell, a gram of moondust could sell at auction for millions of dollars. If the rich and powerful could build their homes out of stone mined from the surface of Mars or Titan or even Pluto... the possibilities were endless. Patrick's organization was moving ahead at full speed toward finding out what possibilities lay just outside of Earth's thin, filmy atmosphere.

His first move as NASA administrator was to tighten the belt of public relations. NASA had been pretty tight in the past, during the Space Race era, but had reverted to an "open door" policy in the years prior to the war. Since the organization was publicly funded, prior administrators believed the public should know all that went on within its walls. Patrick did not share this opinion. He believed informing the masses should only occur when absolutely necessary, and, to his surprise (it was rare that anything surprised him), Congress agreed with this policy. The new NASA would be about making money behind the scenes and staying well away from the limelight. Congress gave John Patrick the freedom and funding to make it happen.

For the first time in history, NASA wasn't under a tight deadline to make space happen. They were taking their time, and Patrick couldn't have been more pleased with the outcome so far. Crewed missions were on the near horizon. NASA had recruited an astronaut corps that was deep into training at a high-tech commercial facility built with the joint funds of private companies and the American taxpayers. It was a collaborative effort and a damned good one, he thought.

A tall and lean man, John Patrick was in his midforties, with sandy-blond hair and pale blue eyes. They were the kind of blue that looked shallow at first, like water droplets, but could pierce right through you in a matter of seconds. Before coming to NASA, Patrick was a major in the US Army, serving his time deep in the jungles of Central America, fighting the SA. His master's degree in mechanical engineering from MIT had gotten him his first job at NASA right after the war. It took only a few months for him to rise through the ranks to the most coveted corner office at Two Independence Square, exactly as his father did three decades earlier.

His office overlooked the Washington DC division of forensic science. The building looked like a giant glass cube, shimmering in the morning sunlight. Patrick shuddered to think of what went on in there. He had never been a medical man and the sight of blood made his guts wrench. He preferred working with solid things like aluminum and titanium, bolts, joints, ball bearings, ion engines, and so on. Soft stuff wasn't his thing.

In fact, he found the daily grind of his administration duties almost as gut-wrenching as the forensic science stuff. But despite his aversion to it, he was good at dealing with people. Ever the level head, he could deal with almost anything thrown at him, which was the character trait that earned him the job.

"Mr. Patrick," came the call from his assistant, Tommy, whose office was across the hall. "Jade Stanton is here to see you."

"Thanks, Tommy. Send her in," he said.

A moment later, Jade strolled into Patrick's office. After closing the door, she spun on her high-heeled black pump and took a seat at the chair immediately in front of his steel and glass-topped desk. Patrick swiveled in his chair to face her.

Jade wore diamond stud earrings, red lipstick, a hint of pink blush on her dark cheeks, and a black, pinstripe pantsuit. Patrick still couldn't resist the sight of her. Their affair had occurred ten years earlier when they were both serving high positions in the army. It was a secret, of course, but it had been one of the best times of his life. Now, even though he was married with a three-year-old daughter, he still thought of Jade as one of the most beautiful women he had ever known.

More important than that, Patrick respected Jade. The two had been friends long before their short affair and she was one of his most trusted advisors. It was this trust that earned her the director position overseeing the TDRS launch. The satellite launch was a critical element in the crewed space program time line and he knew he could count on Jade to get the job done.

"Good morning, Patrick," she said, a hint of a smile crossing her red lips. However, as soon as the words left her mouth, the tiny curve in her lips faded and a look of intensity came over her face. "We've got a problem."

Patrick was not at all surprised by her forwardness or that she had almost entirely skipped the pleasantries. Jade was not one to dance around a sticky topic. He returned his gaze to the window overlooking the glass box across the street and said, "Yes, your email mentioned that. What's going on? You were... vague."

"Yeah, well, I didn't want to go too far into detail until I could be here in person. I found out about this a few days ago, but I've been holding on to it so I could get the facts straight," she said, looking around the room thoughtfully. "How about a drink? I could use one."

Before he could speak, she was out of her chair and striding across the room to the small bar that stood in the corner opposite the window. It was obvious that Jade had been to that bar before because she knew exactly how to find the hidden switch that turned the lights on and popped open the door to the liquor cabinet. As she poured herself a drink from a bottle of bourbon, aged thirty years, she looked over at him to get his response.

"No, I think I'll be okay. I mean, it is only 10:30 a.m., Jade," he said, glancing down at the tiny holo-watch on his wrist.

She nodded but ignored the implications behind it and poured another glass of the fragrant liquor before heading back over to the desk. She placed one glass squarely in front of Patrick before taking her seat.

"Trust me, you might want that after I tell you about this," she said, pointing at the cut crystal glass in front of him.

"Well, spit it out then," he said. Her antics did not amuse him. Jade wasn't a dramatic person—that's why he liked her. Whatever this was, it had to be a big deal or she wouldn't be putting on this show.

She sipped her drink and explained the details of the signal that the TDRS had picked up and how they had tracked it to the Delta Space Station, still in orbit after eighteen years.

Patrick listened, still gazing out the window. The look on his face wasn't disbelief exactly; he'd seen enough unbelievable things during his time fighting the SA to know almost anything was possible. But this information definitely threw him off. When she finished, he asked, "How is that possible?" Patrick knew as well as anyone else that it was almost impossible the Delta was functioning after eighteen years, let alone still in orbit.

"Because"—she took another long swig of her bourbon, draining the glass—"there's a girl up there."

"I'm sorry, what did you just say?" he asked, the window forgotten, his pointy blue eyes resting solidly on her face.

"There's a girl up there," she said, slower this time, emphasizing each word.

"You've got to be kidding, Jade."

"I wish I were. There's a girl up there," she repeated, shaking her head as if she couldn't believe it even though she had spoken to the girl herself that very morning.

Patrick opened his mouth to speak, but the words were lost. Instead, he picked up the glass in front of him and took a long drink.

"I told you you'd want the bourbon," she said, getting up for a refill. As she walked, she continued speaking. "I talked to her myself this morning on the damned ham radio." She laughed out loud. "Think about that! Here we are, with all of NASA and its technology at our fingertips, and we're using an amateur radio to talk to a girl on a derelict space station!" She shook her head in disbelief as she tipped the bourbon bottle into her glass. "We've given her instructions to orient her antenna array at the TDRS. That's the only reason we even found her. She noticed the launch from Florida based on some sort of visual scanning program. Then she pointed her distress signal at the satellites."

"Wow…" He drained his own glass and tapped it down on the desk.

"Her mother was Millicent Shepard," Jade said, with a raised eyebrow.

"But Millicent Shepard died." Patrick vaguely remembered the story of the Delta and how the crew had burned up over Kazakhstan during reentry.

"Yes, that's right. She died in the Soyuz crash that killed the others. At least, that's what NASA thought."

"Yes, I remember that," Patrick said.

"They confirmed the breakup of the spacecraft over Russia two days after losing communications with the Delta. But since the whole world was concentrating on fighting the war, nobody really looked into the matter further. They couldn't communicate with the Delta and the crew was dead. End of story."

"Wow…" he said again. "You're telling me Millicent Shepard was not only alive, but she was *pregnant*?"

"I guess so," she shrugged. "She must have gotten pregnant while she was on board. They always tested them, the ladies, before they went up, you know. So, it must have happened on the Delta. Apparently, she didn't make the trip down in the Soyuz. Maybe she knew she was pregnant and didn't want to risk it."

"She carried a baby to term, gave birth, and raised a child by herself on a space station," he said, his mind boggled. He couldn't believe his own words. They sounded like something out of a science fiction movie—a bad one at that.

Jade nodded and stared out the window behind Patrick into the blue sky beyond. "There's another problem," she said after a few seconds. "Her engine quit working. Meaning, the orbit will decay long before we get anyone up there to her. We'll have to focus on troubleshooting the engine. It's the only way she'll make it long enough for us to get up there to her. Project Diamond will need to go into serious overdrive. I know we haven't been on a strict deadline, but we've got one now. We expect the orbit to last six months, max. Possibly four."

Patrick pinched the bridge of his nose and squeezed his eyes shut, letting out a long, slow breath. Project Diamond was the code name for the crewed space program and it was still eighteen months away from human flight tests. "Okay, well, let's get our engineers working on the problem."

"I agree," Jade said. "I'll have the engineering team run a full diagnostic check on the onboard systems. We'll have to set up a temporary Mission Control to keep watch over this. I'll give you an update as soon as I know more, but it's going to take a few days to sort everything out. The computer technology that she's got up there is, well, out of date, to say the least."

Patrick nodded. "Okay. Oh, and Jade..." He stopped her as she stood to leave. "The girl... what's her name?"

"Eta. Eta Shepard," she said, turning and heading out the door.

As the door clicked shut behind her, Patrick turned back to the window and gazed up at the sky. In the span of five minutes, the world he'd built at NASA had changed for good. His jaw tightened as he started to mentally add up the dollars he would need to spend on this rescue mission and the resources that would be taken away from his commercially driven space projects.

But what if there was a silver lining to this? Ever the pragmatist, his entrepreneurial mind kicked into gear and he speculated about the possibilities. A girl who was born and raised in space. She was the ultimate test subject. The perfect specimen to show the world what could be possible from colonizing space.

Yes, there might be a positive to this situation after all, he thought. His piercing blue eyes widened and a hint of a smile spread over his lips.

"Eta," he said, his smile growing wider as his mind twirled around the possibilities.

Chapter 27

I miss you, Eta.

There was a sense of calm that used to run through my brain while I performed one mundane task after another. It was really the only way I could carry on, keeping the schedule and keeping my brain quiet.

Now, I can't seem to do anything without mentally breaking down. The old Eta has been replaced with a sniveling, emotional basket case.

I've become Emotional Eta.

I sound crazy. I *feel* crazy. All I've ever wanted is to have contact with someone. I've spent the better part of my life trying and failing to do that, and now that I have, it's almost like my mind is fighting back, like it wants things to go back to the way they were before, cold and numb and routine.

The thing is, I knew how to cope with the way it was. This emotional stuff is all new to me.

I blame Alé. I've developed some sort of strange affection for him that I can't figure out. I can't seem to keep it from invading my daily life... and it's driving me up the wall!

NASA has spent the last few days reprogramming every computer program on the station to make it more compatible with their systems, and along the way, they're making changes left and right. They have literally taken over control and they're in my ear and in my head constantly. I'm not used to that.

They've put me on a tight schedule, allotting exact times for meals, exercise, and sleep—as if my routine wasn't good enough. I try to tell Alé that I've been working on the same schedule since I was born. I *need* to keep it. He assures me that he will talk to them.

Talking to Alé is now the single most important part of my day. He likes to take the night shifts because there are fewer people around and he feels we can speak more freely. He informed me that his goal is to be my friend.

I can't imagine having a friend. Nix is my friend, I guess, in an artificial sort of way. But that's not the same thing.

Since the first contact a few days ago, I've talked with several people, but I can't say that I like talking to any of them. There's a guy named Nemo who goes on and on as if he's speaking to a computer instead of a person. I think his name is John or Jonathan, something like that, but he told me to call him Nemo. There's also a girl named Gina who was on the radio once. She sounded nervous and stuttered a lot. I'm sure it's intimidating talking to me, not knowing if I'm unstable after being up here by myself for so long. Jade was okay, but she doesn't come on anymore. I guess she's the one in charge.

Alé is the only one who actually listens to me. I like that.

***

"Good evening, Eta. How are things in low-Earth orbit?" Alé asks.

I am in the G running when I hear his voice come through the tiny earbud. NASA has asked me to keep it in anytime I'm awake so they can contact me at all times.

"It's fabulous, as always," I reply, not slowing my pace.

"Fabulous," he repeats. "What's for supper tonight?"

"Butter lettuce with garlic-rosemary peanut oil, sautéed potatoes, and green beans," I say. Garlic-rosemary oil is one of my favorites. There's an oil press in the kitchen that I use to make peanut and sunflower seed oil. I like to season it with various herbs and let it sit for a few days so that the herbs come alive with fragrance.

"Wow," he says after hearing about my meal. "I guess I had no idea there was so much variety in that garden. I'm genuinely impressed that you grow all of your own food. It's not something anyone else has ever done in the history of space exploration. And frankly, it's not something many people do on the surface either."

"Don't you garden?" I ask.

He snickers at this. "No, I'm not a gardener."

"I love to garden," I say, slowing down as I make my way around the module to the kitchen. "I plan to garden every day for the rest of my life."

"Of course! When you get down to the surface, I'll find you a big plot of land, full of fertile, black dirt. The kind of dirt that stains your fingers and feels like coffee grounds. You can garden until your heart's content," he says.

I smile and rummage around in the cellar, pulling out ingredients for my meal. It didn't slip by me that he said *when* I get to the surface. Not *if*.

Alé continues. "Eta, there's someone new here who's going to talk to you for a while tonight. Her name is Dr. Tess Avrakotos. She works in our physiology department."

I let out a long sigh. I don't like talking to others. I say this to him.

"I get it," he says. "It's got to be difficult for you, meeting so many new people at once. But you're doing such a good job! Everyone seems to think you're the equivalent to Wonder Woman up there."

"Wonder Woman?" I say, perplexed by this comparison.

"I'm sorry, you probably don't know who Wonder Woman is."

"No, I know who she is," I say. I've seen the movies and read her comic books. "I just can't imagine why anyone would compare me to her. I'm just... here. I mean, I'm nothing special. She's a *superhero*. I'm ordinary—no flashy bracelets or fabulous boots. I don't even have real gravity. My greatest accomplishment is keeping myself alive."

"You amaze me, Eta. How can you say that you're nothing special?" His voice rises slightly with disbelief. "People down here on the surface are amazed you're alive up there. The fact that you've survived as long as you have is, well, a miracle. Do you understand that?"

I shake my head even though I know he can't see me do it. "I survive because I have to. It's no miracle. There's no other choice."

"Well, I think it's a miracle," he responds. "If there is a god out there, and I believe that there is, then you've done something to get on his good side, that's all I'm saying. Who else besides Wonder Woman could keep a space station going without any help from the ground for over eighteen years?"

"Well, I had help..." I say, my voice trailing off. As soon as the words leave my mouth, I regret them. I do not want to talk about Nu.

"Yes. You did." His tone changes ever so slightly, taking on a sadness that I've never heard before. It sounds like he's going to probe, but he doesn't. Instead, he says, "I'd like you to talk to Tess now. She's an accomplished doctor and she wants to discuss your medical history and cover some basic health information. We're working on a plan to bring you down to the surface, but we want to know for sure that your body can handle the stress of reentry."

"What do you mean by that?" I ask. "What if you determine that my body can't handle it? Will you leave me up here?" I bite my upper lip as I rip up pieces of lettuce for my salad.

"No!" A note of panic rises in his voice. "I only mean that you were born in a limited gravity environment with minimal shielding from solar and cosmic radiation. It's something we've never seen before. We need to get a good idea of your physiological makeup so we can be prepared when you come down."

"Okay, let me talk to her then. Will you still be here? I mean, will I be able to talk to you after she's done?" I ask. As I ask him this, my chest tightens. I do not like it when someone new comes around and I do not like it when he is not there.

"I promise. I will be right here," he says. "Tess just has a few questions for now and as soon as she's done, I'll come back on the radio. You have my word, okay?"

"Yes, okay."

There is a pause. I hear the microphone being passed to someone else. I finish tossing the lettuce and oil together and get to work on cutting up a potato.

"Hello, Eta," says a cool voice. I can tell by her tone that she isn't nervous at all. But there's something about her voice that I can't put my finger on. She almost sounds excited to speak to me. "My name is Dr. Avrakotos, but you can call me Tess. Does that sound okay?"

"Sure," I say, finishing with the potato and dumping the chopped pieces into a pan to sauté.

"Before I begin with the medical questions, I want you to know how much I admire you for your bravery," she says.

"Thank you," I say. I'm never sure what to say when they compliment me like that. I don't think of myself as a brave person.

"Alé mentioned that you're cooking supper," Tess continues. "Can you tell me a little bit about your garden? I'd like to get a better idea of what your diet consists of."

I let out a sigh of relief. I don't mind talking about the garden, so I fill her in on the basics of how I run the garden and what I'm growing. She asks me to describe my typical meal. I'm not sure what she means by this. My meals are different every day. But I do my best. Then she asks some general questions about my health and the machinery available on board that I can use to monitor my health and send readings back to the surface. Finally, she says, "Eta..." she hesitates and I know what's coming. "Tell me about your mother."

"What do you want to know?" I ask. I've finished cooking now and am sitting at the table. But suddenly, I don't have much of an appetite.

"What happened to her?" she asks.

I swallow a lump of lettuce before I speak. "I don't want to talk about my mother right now."

Tess sighs. "Eta, you'll have to tell us what happened to her at some point."

It's obvious she's put off by my cold answer to her question. I know she's not trying to upset me, but I also know that I can't talk to her about my mother. Not yet. Emotional Eta makes her appearance and fat tears roll down my cheeks. I try to keep my voice steady. "I'm sorry, Tess. I'm just not ready yet."

"Okay," she says, the word deflated with disappointment. But she seems to understand because mercifully, she moves on to other subjects. She tells me that she wants to know more about my anatomy. She asks me all types of questions about my body temperature, muscle structure, bodily functions, eyesight, and stuff like like. I have a detailed log of my monthly physical checkups dating back to my birth. I tell Tess about these logs and she asks that I transmit them down to the ground so she can take a look.

Before she signs off, Tess says, "Eta, this is so helpful. Can I tell you how happy I am to meet you? Your journey will teach us so much about life in space."

"Glad I can help," I say, happy that her portion of the interview is over.

I'm ready to talk to Alé again.

Chapter 28

"This is totally unprecedented!" Tess said, shaking her head excitedly with a look of disbelief. "I mean, we couldn't have organized a better experiment if we *tried*." As she spoke, she gestured with her hands, accentuating some of the more exciting points in her speech. "I can't believe all the data these two women have kept on their health over the years. I feel like I should pinch myself!"

Alé watched her from behind his holo-screen, interested to hear about her conversation with Eta. Tess was in her midforties, tall and athletic. She had a quirky sense of style and tended to wear things like bold prints and floral dresses. Today she wore a turquoise-and-white geometric-print dress that looked like it was scooped out of a Picasso painting.

As she spoke, hands flying around her head, she paced aggressively around the conference room table in the Mission Control room at Goddard. In the past, Mission Control was always located in Houston, Texas at Johnson Space Center, the mecca of human spaceflight. However, the complex suffered heavy damage during the war and was no longer in use. So, the crew at Goddard transformed one of the largest conference rooms in the building into a temporary Mission Control.

The room buzzed with movement as engineers worked at their holo-screens and talked on their phones while poring over data transferred from the Delta's computers. Located on the third floor at Goddard, the conference room was an unremarkable place to command such an important mission. The room was long and rectangular, and painted a sturdy "conference room beige." In the center of the room was a large oak conference table surrounded by sleek black ergonomic office chairs. This was the main meeting area where they held daily meetings to discuss the ever-changing plan.

Around the perimeter of the room were twelve double desks, each holding the workspace of two engineers facing each other. NASA had thrown together the temporary Mission Control hastily, stuffing the room with holo-screens, telephones, and network wires. With that came the inevitable litter from a group of scientists working long hours in a cramped space.

NASA administration treated this project as a full-blown mission. Although it was crowded and smelled of commercial carpet, sweat, and body odor, the workspace didn't seem to bother the team. They understood the importance of their work.

The elite engineering team consisted of thirty-two engineers, all taking on multiple roles and working around the clock. Alé was the primary CAPCOM and the flight director. Their main objective was figuring out a way to get the Delta's engine back up and running to avoid a deadly atmospheric reentry. They all signed nondisclosure agreements stating that this mission would remain top secret. Armed guards stood on twenty-four-hour watch over the entrance to the makeshift control room to ensure that only those who were necessary to the mission were allowed to enter. The guards also sent a clear message to those leaving the cramped room that anyone found spreading word of this new mission would suffer grave consequences. They tapped personal holo-phones to ensure private communications made no mention of the mission, and an armed guard followed every engineer when they left the premises.

Tess was the flight surgeon. Her medical research into human spaceflight over the last six years had been pivotal in advancing the crewed space program, and the new information Eta uploaded daily from the station logs was enough for two full years of research material. She couldn't believe her blind luck. So far, she had received almost half of Millicent Shepard's pregnancy data and expected to have the full birthing details within the next few hours.

"Alé, I'm telling you," she said as she continued to pace, "it's literally a miracle that this girl is still alive up there. And so far, she seems healthy. I asked her to do a full body ultrasound so we can check for precancerous cells, but she doesn't exhibit any of the normal signs of radiation illness. It's incredible! Millicent Shepard conceived and carried a child to full term on a space station!"

Alé was much less excited about the medical data. He had bigger issues on his mind.

"Yes, Tess," he said, "I get it. It's exciting. But, remember, if we can't get the engine working, there will be no more test subject to study. You seem to forget that we are still eighteen months away from attempting even an *uncrewed* mission using the Diamond spacecraft. Let's say we can get up there sooner, it's still at least a year out. That's too long." He shook his head in despair.

Tess let out an excited squeal. "I realize that Alé, but the data will still be here. I mean, years and years of records that she can send before the station deorbits..." Her voice trailed off as she spoke the words. She stopped pacing and looked at Alé's eyes, which flashed with anger. She realized how callous she sounded. "Sorry, that was totally inappropriate."

Alé rose sharply and pointed his finger at her as he spoke. "That's unacceptable, Tess. We are going to bring Eta home. Get that through your head." Yes, his tone was harsh, but he didn't care. The odds of saving Eta from the untimely deorbit were growing slimmer by the day. They would need every bit of positive energy they could muster to make this happen.

"You're absolutely right." She nodded, fixing her eyes on the floor. "I don't know what came over me. I apologize."

Alé relaxed his gaze and sat down in his chair, pulling his holo-screen closer to him to get back to what he was working on. "Don't worry about it. Just give me a rundown of what you've got so far."

Tess continued her manic pace along the side of the table. "Millicent had an affair with Andrei Fedorov, one of the other astronauts on board."

"Wait," Alé said. "How do you know that?"

"Because she kept detailed notes in her logs. They had been on board together for several months and during that time, conceived Eta. She wasn't sure when, so obviously it was an ongoing thing." She stopped pacing briefly to let those words sink in.

Alé watched her from his seat on the other side of the table. Her excitement exhausted him. He had been awake most of the night and his neck and back ached. He wasn't really in the mood to listen to her, considering she had just arrived only a few hours earlier and was working with a fresh brain. But he allowed her to continue, taking a break from the project open on his screen to absorb what she was saying.

"When she found out she was pregnant," Tess continued, "she started doing regular ultrasounds and saving the results in her medical logs. She even created a separate file to document the baby's progress versus her own. She was a hell of a scientist!" Tess said, and finally came to a rest beside a tall black desk chair that sat empty at the table, opposite Alé.

Alé rubbed his temples. The historical medical data was great, but he was more worried about the current state of Eta's health. "What can we expect when she does get down to the surface?" he asked. "Any ideas?"

Tess shrugged. "Your guess is as good as mine. I'll know more in a few weeks. My initial thought is that since she grew up with partial gravity, her body will be similar to ours. Just not quite as strong. She states that she exercises regularly, again, thanks to her mother, and although the gravity is limited, it's better than nothing at all. She'll be weak, of course, when she comes down to the surface. But I don't think it will be any worse than any regular long-term astronaut spaceflight."

"Good." Alé nodded.

"Well, that's my initial thought," Tess continued. "There could be any number of issues with her circulatory system, mental cognition, lymphatic function, you name it. But the fact that she's still alive says a lot about her health. Plus, she's eating a vegan diet, arguably one of the healthiest ways to eat. She gave me a rundown of some of her typical meals and it appears she's getting all the necessary nutrients, proteins, fats, amino acids, and so on."

An alarm went off on Tess's holo-watch, momentarily drawing her attention away from the conversation. "I've got to go. I have a meeting with Patrick in fifteen minutes and I want to get a quick walk in before I meet him."

Alé nodded and Tess left the room. He turned back to his screen, having lost track of what he was working on, and decided that perhaps a walk would be beneficial to him as well. He hadn't left his chair in at least three hours and his legs were suddenly stiff.

***

Goddard Space Flight Center stood on almost 1,300 acres of land just outside of Washington DC. The campus contained multiple buildings along with parks, walkways, streets, parking lots, and various other storage and groundskeeping areas. Its facilities included the largest clean room in the world, used to assemble actual space vehicles, several large vacuum chambers that could be heated and cooled to unearthly temperatures, and a centrifuge capable of producing thirty times the force of gravity.

The center was the oldest space center in the United States, responsible for tracking and computer support for early crewed NASA missions, including the space stations of the past. But the primary aim of Goddard was to design and build uncrewed, scientific spacecraft, including the TDRS.

Building Thirty-Six was located between the main gate and the south gate of the complex. A road encircled the center section of the campus where most of the buildings resided. Alé stepped out into the breezy night air. It was summer in Baltimore and all around, he could smell the scent of it.

Thick groves of loblolly and Virginia pines, American sycamores, and pignut hickories dominated the grounds. The trees gave the campus an earthy, fresh scent. Especially now, in the summer when the breeze was warm, the pines cast their scent all around, like a perfume spritzer at a department store. It reminded Alé of an orange grove he had once walked through during a visit to Florida as a child. It was a sweet smell, almost citrusy, and the breeze and rustle of the leaves immediately invigorated him.

He headed down the road toward the campus library. There was a café there, open twenty-four hours, where he could get a strong cup of coffee. Sleep should have been his priority, but he knew that sleep would not come to him now. He had too many thoughts swirling through his mind. As he walked, he worked on sorting out the chaos in his head.

His thoughts immediately shifted to the Delta's engine. Alé had the most talented engineers in the world at his disposal. Over the last few days, they had scanned all of the Delta's mechanical systems. For the most part, the computer and all the mechanics were working as they should. It was all that NASA could have hoped for when building a space station—something that would stand the test of time and survive without help from the ground. It amazed him how well the twenty-year-old technology had held up.

But with the engine, they were not so lucky. The engineers figured that the electrical failure had taken place during the last use, a little less than two months prior. Alé chuckled to himself because Eta had told him that, going off of her own analysis of the situation. NASA, of course, wanted a second opinion from an expert on nuclear ion engines. The experts had come up with basically the same hypothesis as Eta: the engine had a major electronic meltdown during the last orbital maneuver and was subsequently fried. There was no backup.

Could it be fixed? That, of course, was unknown. It probably could be fixed, if they had access to a field expert who could do a spacewalk and look at it, and if that expert had the correct tools and parts to replace. But as far as anyone knew, those parts and tools, and the expert, for that matter, did not exist on the Delta.

The engineering team was stunned at how well Eta had kept the station running, considering the limited supplies she had on board. She'd found ways to push everything at her disposal to its limit. Things like air filters, pumps, storage tanks, controller boxes, antennae, and battery units surpassed their estimated life spans.

Preparing a spacewalk for Eta to repair the damage was considered an unnecessary risk. The NIX unit had taken detailed images of the fried electronics and without a plan to repair them, having Eta go out into the void wouldn't do them much good.

Alé continued walking and eventually turned from the main road onto a small walking path, the thoughts still churning. He struggled with the idea that fixing the engine wasn't going to pan out. The only other option was to go get her, a much more dangerous option. Sending up the Diamond spacecraft, which had never been tested in space, could end up taking the lives of both the crew sent for the rescue and Eta.

The team had briefly considered pulling out some old technology for the job. There was a spare Apollo space capsule on display at the Goddard visitor center. Technically, they could recommission and use it. But that was decades-old technology and they had limited experience with it.

They even contacted the Russians about commissioning a Soyuz. If they had a spare Soyuz sitting around, at least that technology, although as old as Apollo, had been used as recently as two decades before. However, they had no luck with the Soyuz. The Russians had been hit hard by the downslide in the economy after the war. Anything they had in storage from their space program was parted out and sold to help support the war effort.

Alé spotted the cafe across the street in the distance. He crossed the street, staring down at the blacktop with his head full of heavy thoughts. When he reached the door, he found a handwritten sign taped to the inside that said "Closed for Servicing." He grabbed the handle and jangled the door angrily. All he got in return was a loud *clunk* as the locks slammed into the doorframe.

With no other option, he let out a sigh of defeat and turned around to head back to the makeshift Mission Control room. Despite the disappointment about the coffee, the walk had done him some good. His mind felt clearer and his muscles were starting to spring back from hours spent hunched over the screen at his desk.

But all the fresh air in the world hadn't given him what he wanted. He still had no idea how to save Eta. That thought bothered him more than all his other thoughts combined.

Chapter 29

"Good morning, Eta."

The voice is distant and faint. At first, I think I'm dreaming. I sit up and my neck immediately aches from the strange sleeping position I was in. It takes me a moment, but I realize the voice isn't far away at all. My ears clear up a bit and I hear it again.

"Good morning, Eta."

Nix is standing right outside my sleeping compartment. His voice is muffled by the door, which is why he seemed far away in my semiconscious state. I must have been sleeping hard. I shake my head to work the kinks out of my neck and clear the fog from my brain. It dawns on me that I took a sleeping pill last night, which is why I'm so fuzzy this morning. Sleep has been difficult for me since I made contact with the ground. My mind won't stop moving, even for a few hours of sleep. I'm not telling NASA about the sleeping pill. They'll start asking a bunch of questions. They don't need to know everything that's going on up here.

"Nix, what's up? Why are you up so early?" I ask.

"I wanted to let you know that Mr. Alé is on the radio for you," he says. "I noticed the notification as I was preparing to go outside and check the hull."

"Oh yeah." I rub my eyes and yawn. "It's Monday."

"Yes, ma'am," he says. "Anyway, Mr. Alé is on the radio waiting. I spoke with him briefly and I must say, I like him. I assured him that you had a long night and that you were simply sleeping in. He asked that I wake you."

"Thank you, Nix." I did have a long night. I spent the evening going over and over the diagnostic results from the engine checks. I did some math and realized that the station orbit is slipping more than I thought it would. It's going to drop much faster than I originally thought. Like, within a few months. It doesn't help matters that the Sun is particularly active right now. And it's expected to get worse. I'm basically a duck sitting on a pond while a solar typhoon is about to come through. And that is no good for my little station dragging its ass along on the upper atmosphere.

In fact, I sort of had a little fit about it. I know, it's shocking, but I do lose my cool from time to time. Nix must have heard me crying over it.

The thing is, I've never had others around to help me. Nu was different. She was pretty much in charge while she was here. I just did what I was told and trusted in her expertise. But since then, I've been totally on my own. It's difficult to adjust to the idea that I now have people looking after me again.

Plus, I was never on a time line before. I mean, time went along as it always did and I knew that eventually, this would happen. Some huge thing would go wrong with the station and that would be the end of me. It wasn't a pressing issue but was lingering off in the future. Now it's here and I must deal with it.

From what I can tell, these NASA guys don't know how to fix it either. Nobody has come out and said that, of course, but I can tell. If they knew how to fix the engines, they'd have given me the commands by now. There's no way they'd cut a crisis this close.

Anyway, a strange thing happened to me last night. I was humming along like usual, doing my research about the engine, when all of a sudden, I started screaming. Like, *really* screaming. I couldn't stop myself. It exploded out of me. I never have emotional outbursts like that, but for some reason, screaming at the top of my lungs felt like the right thing to do as I sat there by myself in the G. Like maybe if I screamed loud enough, they would actually hear me down on Earth.

It wasn't only the screaming either. I was crying like a baby. It was a full-on, snot-nosed, out-of-breath, cherry-faced bawling session. I'm sure I sounded like an idiot, and obviously Nix took notice of my outburst. So, he is correct. I had a long night. Today my throat is scratchy and I have a screaming headache. My brain feels like it's bulging out of my forehead. It doesn't seem like my sleeping pill-induced coma helped. Sleep was foggy, dull, and dreamless: the kind that does nothing for you but moves from one time frame to the next.

I stand and look in the little mirror on the compartment wall, expecting to see something like an elephant staring back at me with hanging skin and gray eye sockets. But the face that stares back at me isn't so unfortunate. It looks tired but otherwise in good health.

Then I remember that Alé is waiting for me. I quickly dress and head out of the G, pausing a moment by the med cabinet for some ibuprofen. The gravity differential between the G leaves my head pounding even worse. I make my way up to the Service Module and turn the radio up on high so I can hear his voice.

"Good morning, Alé," I say, trying to sound cheerful.

"Good morning, Eta! I had a little chat with your robot pal. He's fascinating. I have a friend who works in the robotics department who'd kill to get a look at Nix."

"Yes, Nix is... special. Tell your friend that I'll gladly trade places."

He chuckles. "I'll be sure to pass along the message. Did you create Nix? I know the robot was part of the original mission equipment, but from what I can tell, it didn't have near the capabilities that Nix has."

"No, I didn't make him. Nu did," I say. The sound of her name makes my pounding head pound a bit harder.

"Nu is your mother, Millicent, right?" He is tentative. He knows I do not like to talk about her, but for some reason, I don't seem to mind that he's asking about her. Maybe yesterday's emotional breakdown cracked some sort of lock inside my head.

"Yes, I called her Nu. That was her nickname. Her specialty was programming and she pretty much built Nix up from scratch. We had the hardware already, but his identity is all in his software, which she wrote. He's been pretty much the same throughout my life. As a child, I remember she made some modifications here and there, but she must have built his core system when I was a baby because he has always been here with me."

"You seem to really like him." It's an observation, not a question, so I don't respond to it. "You mentioned his personality," he continues. "Do you know how she was able to program him with such high-level capabilities? The computers in those nautical units weren't very advanced."

I think about this for a second. I know the answer to the question, but I want to make sure my answer is complete and makes sense. "Well," I say, "the computer that he started with actually had a large computing capacity. More than one might expect in something like him. I'm not sure if they made him as a special unit or what, but he was more advanced than the earlier versions of the NIX systems. That said, you are correct in that she had to add hardware to give him more functionality. She used some of the backup processing units from the Service Module to make him. Nu was handy like that. The station computers had more RAM, faster microprocessors, and so on."

"Very interesting," Alé says. "And yes, my robotics friend would absolutely love to take a gander at that code."

"Well, it's complicated... the code, I mean. But I would imagine he'd understand it if it's his specialty."

"Actually, my robotics friend is a woman. Her name is Mila."

"Oh," I say. "She's your girlfriend?"

"No, Eta, she's just my friend. Not my girlfriend."

I flush with embarrassment. I think he misunderstood my question. "No, I meant to ask if she is a girl who is your friend... I'm sorry, I get confused sometimes."

"No need to be sorry. I understand how that could happen. And yes, she is a girl who is my friend."

"Do you have many girlfriends?" I immediately realize my error and rephrase. "I mean, girls who are friends?"

This makes him laugh out loud. I wonder what he means with that laugh. Was it such a silly question?

"I do have some friends who are girls, yes," he answers. "It's more common than you might think. I'm curious, Eta, how do you know so much about things that happen on the surface? I know that you mentioned the station archives. Tell me more about that."

"The archives contain a little bit of everything," I say. "Movies, music, photographs, scientific studies. There is a comprehensive manual about the station and its various systems. I think it was built into the station computers as a knowledge database for astronauts since the station was meant to orbit farther away with less access to ground communications and internet. They gave the crew a limited version of the internet that would be available all the time and contained anything NASA thought might be useful. That's part of it." Pausing, I cock my head to the side. I'm at the far end of the Service Module. From here, I can see the magnificent views of the VP windows. There's a huge hurricane in the ocean below me. It's a recent storm because this is the first I've seen of it. I can usually see a storm brewing for several days before it becomes its signature spiral. But this one must have formed fast. I gaze at it and continue. "But also, Nu went through the personal laptops of the crew after they left and added anything they left behind. There's a hurricane down there."

"Yeah, that's Hurricane Elrond. I forget that you've got the bird's-eye view. It's going to hit landfall down in the Yucatan here in a few hours. Do you know what the Yucatan is?"

"The Yucatan Peninsula, Mexico. It separates the Caribbean Sea from the Gulf of Mexico. The location of the Chicxulub crater, the remains of the asteroid impact that caused the mass extinction of the dinosaurs."

"Spoken like any well-respected encyclopedia," he says, chuckling.

"I studied geography. And yes, my geography lessons came from an encyclopedia." I don't mean to sound defensive, but it may have come off that way.

"Of course," he says. "No disrespect intended. Just trying to get a feel for what you know about the world. Okay, so you had access to a bunch of information. That's good to know. How much do you know about the war?"

He's got me there. The station archives cover everything before the war. "Very little," I say. "They told Nu about the first bombs. Then she lost communication with the ground. That was when the other astronauts left and she figured out that the communication loss had to do with the satellites. After that, all she could do was watch and observe the surface. There were signs— like the lights going out all over the world, and there were times, especially at the beginning, when she could see the smoke and light flashes from some of the bigger bombings. As time went on, everything started to calm down and for the longest time, it was quiet. That's why she made the tracking program. She knew that when humans launched rockets again, there was a chance we could get rescued."

"That was very perceptive of her," Alé says. "The nuclear bombs were only the beginning. There was a massive hacker attack by the SA a day after the bombs. That's what froze up the satellites. Not only did it disable them, but it also fried their boards, rendering them useless. We've only recently gotten back to a level of communications comparable to what we had before the war. Cell phone networks had to be rebuilt around the globe and we're still trying to get the satellite network up to snuff."

"The SA?" I ask. Since I reestablished communications with the surface, I've heard two different people use the term as if it's commonly accepted—as if I *should* know what it means.

"Oh, sorry," he says. "That's what we call the South Americans. The attacks originated in South America. Although it started in Brazil, many of the neighboring countries were taken over or joined at some point. I'll upload some information about the history of the war for you to look through. That way you can understand the magnitude of what we were dealing with down here."

"Thanks. I appreciate that," I say. Any new information is good. I've been looking through the same old computer files for eighteen years.

"Okay, let's lighten the subject matter," he says. "I want to get to know you better. You mentioned that you have lots of media on board. What's your favorite movie?"

I have to put some thought into that one. "Well, that depends on my mood, I guess. I like the first and second *Avatar* movies. Wasn't so much a fan of the third one though. I'm a sucker for science fiction. All eight of the *Alien* movies were great. I mean, some of them were better than others, but I like a good scare from time to time. Superhero movies. Anything with Iron Man in it because he reminds me of Nix. *The Princess Bride*... because of the love story."

"Huh," he says. He sounds genuinely interested in this topic. "My very favorite movie of all time is *The Shining*. It's an old one, but what can I say—I'm a sucker for Stephen King."

"I haven't seen that one," I say. "I read the book though. My favorite Stephen King book is *Carrie*. When I was younger, I would try to make things move with my mind. Just to see if I could, you know?"

He chuckles. "Yeah, I know. Don't worry, you're not the only one who's tried and failed to make things move. If you could manifest the ability to telekinetically move your space station into a higher orbit... well, that would help us all out a lot."

I am quiet when he mentions this. I know they can't figure out how to fix the engines, but nobody has come right out and said it yet. In a way, I appreciate that he's being honest with me and I understand his frustration. He should have heard me screaming about it last night... no, scratch that. I'm glad he didn't hear that. That would have been *really* embarrassing. I sigh out of my own frustration. "Yeah, the engine problem is a tough one," I say. "I know your people have been working on it as hard as they can. I've tried everything I can think of too. I just don't think the engine can be repaired, at least, not with what I have up here."

He sighs. It's a tired sigh. The kind you let loose when you're mentally and physically exhausted. I can tell that my seemingly hopeless situation bothers him.

"Eta, you don't have to do that stuff yourself. I mean, I agree that you are the expert on the systems of the Delta. But I don't want you stressing out about it. Leave the stressing to me, okay?"

"Is my situation stressful for you?"

"Of course, it is," he says. "I care about what happens to you."

"You care?" It's weird because I can't really wrap my mind around someone caring about me like that. It doesn't seem real to me.

"Probably too much," he admits.

A flash of blood rushes up to my cheeks and I blush hard. I press my hand to my face and feel the heat.

"The thing is, Eta," he pauses, like he's trying to find the right words. "You fascinate me. I want to open up your head and read all the thoughts inside. I know it's strange for me to admit that. I've only known you for a few days, but I can't help myself. Does that make sense?"

"No," I say, honestly. "I don't think there's anything exceptional about me. I'm an ordinary girl."

"But the things you've seen and done!" He sounds frustrated by my response and even lets out an exasperated groan before he continues. "Okay, let's change the subject. I don't know if anyone's talked to you about our crewed space program yet. We've been concentrating on fixing your engines because we don't have the technology up and running to send a ship up to rescue you, Eta.

I want to be transparent with you about this so you're in the loop the whole way. It'll be at least twelve months before we can have our prototype ready to fly. We've tried checking with other space agencies around the world too, but..." His voice trails off.

After a pause, he continues, "One option we've been toying around with is to send a supply ship that could dock with the Delta. It would be equipped with thrusters to push the Delta up into a higher orbit and it could carry the tools and supplies you'd need to fix the engines and other systems on board. It would take us a few months to put together, but it would be quicker than a crewed ship. If we can't get the engines fixed within the next few days, we'll pull the trigger on that plan. Unless the Russians have a spare Soyuz lying around."

"Soyuz?" I say, surprised to hear the word. It occurs to me that perhaps he doesn't know.

"Yeah, the Soyuz was a vessel that—"

"I know what a Soyuz is, Alé," I say. "There's one here." He breathes in sharply as if he means to speak but doesn't say anything. "I'm sorry I didn't say anything before, but I figured you knew."

Now he interrupts me, his voice almost shaking. "Wait... what did you say?"

"There is a Soyuz docked to the station right now."

Part III

Chapter 30

"I want to talk about your mother today, Eta. Do you mind if we start there?" Tess hesitates with these words and shifts back around saying, "Okay, scratch that. We *need* to talk about it, so I'm not asking your permission. I understand that it's hard, and I certainly don't want to push you beyond your comfort zone. But we need to know more about your background and that includes your mother."

"I understand," I say. But I really don't. I don't know what she wants me to tell her. I can give her all the specifics she wants about the station and its workings and my daily routines. But talking about someone else, or even myself, is not as easy.

"Good." She sounds satisfied. "Let's start small. Tell me the very first memory you have."

I close my eyes to dial into my brain and come up with something. It's a shred of a memory, but it's the best I can do after being put on the spot. "I remember crawling through the G, along the rubber running track. The smell of the track is what comes to mind first. It's an industrial smell, sort of like a cleaning chemical but more rubbery, I guess. It still smells that way, but I don't notice it anymore."

"You said you were crawling on the track? How old do you think you were?"

"I don't know, maybe six months old? I couldn't walk yet," I answer.

"That is fascinating!" she says in that perky voice she gets when she's heard something strange about me. "Just so I get this correct in my notes: you remember something that happened before you could walk?"

"Yeah," I say, thinking harder, trying to pry more scraps from the edges of the memory. "I know I couldn't walk yet because I tried to reach up for a vine that was hanging over the edge of one of the garden tables and I fell over. Nu caught me. She was suddenly there. I'm sure she was there the whole time, but it seemed like she appeared out of thin air to catch me."

"Do you know how old you were when you started walking? I assume you would not remember, but maybe Nu told you about it?"

"No, I remember it. I was eleven months old." Again, I close my eyes to find more memories. I know they're there, but I haven't thought about those old times in so long that they're a little slippery in my mind. "I can see her waiting for me at the end of the row of planting tables. In this memory, she was a very long way away from me, but I know now that it was only a few meters. She called to me, and without even thinking about it, I let go of the table that I was standing next to and walked to her. I know it was the first time I walked because of how she reacted. Jumping up and down and throwing me over her head. She was laughing and so happy." I smile at the thought of my mother, beautiful and proud, laughing with me after I took my first step. I squeeze my eyes shut to bring it into clearer view. And when I open them again, the tears stream down my cheeks in the weak gravity of the G.

"Wow," she says, her voice trailing off as if she doesn't believe what she's hearing. "You walked at eleven months and you *remember* it. It's amazing. Long-term memory typically takes several years to become advanced enough to contain a memory like that. But you remember it."

"Yes, I remember it," I repeat. I'm not sure why I remember these things so young, but I've always remembered things. Nu used to say I had a photographic memory.

"Okay, let's keep going," she says. "Tell me about your schooling. How did she teach you?"

"I always had learning hours built into my schedule, even when I was very little. She was picky about that, making sure I was educated, I mean. We covered everything: history, math, geography, reading, writing, art. Pretty much every subject that would have been covered in a school. Nu developed lesson plans based on my age and skill level."

"Where did she get the information from?" she asks.

"From the station archives," I say. "As I got older, we did more advanced math, eventually getting into calculus and thermodynamic theory. She also made sure I had lessons on other things. Geography was always my favorite subject. I learned all of the countries and their capitals when I was young, maybe six years old. Nu liked history best. Well, next to science, of course. If she didn't know something, then we learned together by reading through articles or encyclopedias. Art was a big thing for her. She wanted my education to be well-rounded. I used to draw her pictures and she would tack them up on the wall inside her sleeping compartment. They're all still there, actually. I didn't move anything after she passed away."

"What about the station?" she asks. "How did you learn how to run it?

"Learning about the station was part of my everyday curriculum. Even she had things to learn about it. I know that after the crew left and she realized communications wouldn't be restored, she implemented a number of changes in the computer systems so that the station would be more autonomous. In the past, space stations were pretty much flown from the ground, she said, but the Delta was different in that it had all the capabilities to be on its own. She tweaked some things so we didn't have to spend all our time running it. As the years went on, we continued to make changes when necessary."

"And after she died, how did you keep it up for so long by yourself?"

"I just did it," I say, shrugging even though I know she can't see me. "As I said, she taught me early how to run things. Anytime there were issues, she and I worked on them together. Being up here, being an astronaut, it means you have to problem solve more. That's pretty much what we always did. She taught me to keep up with regular maintenance as much as possible to stay ahead of major issues. Nix helps too, doing outside repairs and maintenance. Because of him, I've never had to go outside the station for a spacewalk. That's why she spent so much time on him. Spacewalks are dangerous, especially when you're alone. Creating him helped take some of the burdens of space life off of her."

"Huh," she says, contemplating my answer. "So that's the secret to your success? Problem-solving?" She asks this like I've produced the answer to some deep and profound question and it's such an ordinary answer that she can't hide her disappointment. "What about fun? What do you do for fun? Or in your downtime?"

Fun? Everything I do is necessary. Even my free-time activities. Nu always stressed the importance of doing things that take your mind off of the station. That's how she kept from losing her mind.

"I don't know," I say. "I guess I do normal stuff like reading and watching movies. I like looking through old social media in the archives. There are lots of old YouTube videos saved on there. Do you still have YouTube?"

Tess laughs at this. "Yes, Eta, YouTube is still around. Social media was, of course, lost to us when global communications went down, but it's come back on strong since the war ended. In fact, I can't wait for you to see the YouTube platform now! You'll be blown away by how much better the videos are and the changes they've made in the interface."

"Wow," I say, truly excited at the thought of seeing something new and fresh. There are millions of articles and videos held inside the archives, but they're all so dated. "Honestly, Tess, that makes me smile."

"I'm glad to hear it," she says. "I'll let Alé know. Maybe he can send you up some new files to watch. New movies, online newspaper articles, history pieces about the war, stuff like that."

"I would love that."

"Great! Okay, well, let's get back to the interview here. What did you and Nu do together? If you had some downtime, I mean."

"Sometimes we would exercise together. You know, run around the track or ride the stationary bikes. We watched movies together and made supper together. When I was younger, she read me stories. I mean, I started reading on my own when I was four, but she still read me stories at night for years after that. When I was *really* young, she sang to me."

"Oh, yeah?" she says. "I used to sing to my daughter all the time. What kinds of songs would she sing?"

"She loved all kinds of music. Some classical. Some pop. Some rock 'n' roll. She didn't like new stuff though. Only the old classics." I close my eyes and imagine her singing "Suspicious Minds" into a cucumber held up to serve as a microphone. "Tell me about your daughter, Tess," I say to her.

"Oh, well…" She's caught off guard by this. It sounds like she's more interested in asking the questions than answering them. But she plays along. "Her name is Cherry. She's not much younger than you are and turned sixteen in April. She has long, dark hair and brown eyes. She's a short girl, like me, but she loves to dance. She's training to be a ballerina at a school in Miami. So, I only get to see her on holidays and over the summer."

"You sound sad about that," I say. "Why don't you visit her in Miami?"

She laughs at this. "Well, I do visit her when I can. But I have a lot of responsibilities here. It's complicated."

"Oh." I drop the subject.

She pauses for a moment before asking, "Eta, can you tell me a little more about when your mother died?"

I scowl at this question, even though she can't see my face. "Well, you saw the medical records, right?" I haven't thought about her death in many years and I don't want to do it now. Especially when Emotional Eta might jump out at any second and overtake my ability to control myself.

"Yes, I saw them," she says. "But I want to hear how you feel about it."

"Well," I say, cautiously, "from the time she first started to complain about the pain in her breast, it took only a few weeks. It was that fast and she was gone. It was terrifying." The emotions well up inside me. "I can't really talk about that right now. It's so far behind me."

I hear her sigh into the microphone. I can tell this is what she has come here to talk about and I feel bad because I've grown to like Tess. She's been interviewing me now for days and I want to do what I can to help her research. But I can't bring myself to relive those days.

"I understand, Eta. Perhaps, in time, you can open up more about it," she says. "Listen, I think we've done enough today. It's been almost an hour and I know the engineers want to talk with you about some upcoming safety procedures they're working on."

"Safety procedures?" I ask, genuinely confused. What kind of safety do they think they're going to give me by mucking up my schedule with safety procedures?

She chuckles. "Yeah, I know, it sounds totally ridiculous now that I hear myself saying it. But hey, I'm not the boss. Anyway, it was good talking to you today. Hang in there, okay?"

I like her choice of words. That's me, hanging around in low-Earth orbit. Waiting for a ride.

"Will do," I say. Before she signs off, I stop her. "Tess?"

"Yes?"

"Say 'Hi' to your daughter for me."

"Will do," she says and signs off.

Chapter 31

Alé rounded the corner of the hallway. Fast. A little *too* fast. At the apex, he had to jump out of the way of a janitor milling along behind a huge cleaning cart. The janitor scowled as he passed Alé who had planted his back firmly against the beige wall and was standing on his tiptoes to keep his feet away from any entanglement with the rubber wheels of the cart. He had moved so fast he ended up knocking his head against the wall in the process. The grumpy janitor pushing the awkward piece of equipment must have realized how close the call was and said, "Watch it!" as he trundled by.

After the cart was gone, Alé took up his breakneck speed again down the long, now-empty hallway, rubbing the sore spot on the back of his head with the tips of his fingers. After a few more long strides, he reached his destination. He pulled the door to Jade's office open without pausing or even so much as a knock and announced, "There's a Soyuz at the Delta!"

He was breathless and still rubbing the tender part of his scalp when he looked around the room and realized that John Patrick, NASA administrator, sat in the chair in front of Jade's massive desk. Both of them looked up at Alé in shock, not so much for what he had blurted out at them, but because his intrusion was so unexpected.

"Oh, I'm sorry," Alé stammered, his eyes dropping down to neatly tiled floor, which, he noticed, was clean enough to eat off of. "I didn't mean to interrupt."

"No, it's no problem," Jade said. Then, waving her long fingers capped with red, impeccably manicured nails, she gestured for him to take the seat next to Patrick. "Sit down. What's up?"

Alé let out his breath, relieved he hadn't interrupted anything more serious. He didn't know it for sure, but he had a hunch that Jade and Patrick had a history. He pushed the thought out of his mind and nodded while making his way to the empty chair. "There's a Soyuz at the Delta," he repeated in a quieter and more stable voice. "I have no idea how NASA missed this detail, but there were *two* Soyuz docked at the Delta when the other two crew members left. It wasn't recorded in any of the NASA logs at the time. Millicent Shepard was up there that whole time with her very own Soyuz."

Patrick cleared his throat. "So, why didn't Millicent take the Soyuz down when she realized that communications weren't coming back? Why would she stay up there for that many years when there was a perfectly good return vehicle available?"

"I'm guessing that was the original plan," Alé said, the sore spot on his head now forgotten. "Maybe she stayed behind to keep

- 244 -

the station running until another crew could arrive and when she found out she was pregnant, she realized that reentry would be too dangerous for an unborn baby. After Eta was born, well, I guess Millicent didn't want to risk her child's life in the Soyuz either. Eventually, they must have figured as long as the Delta was operating, the risk of taking the old Soyuz was too great."

"That's right," Jade chimed in. "Eta has only known about the engine malfunctions for a few weeks. I imagine if that had happened earlier, Millicent would have risked the trip home rather than have the both of them burn up in reentry. It never got to that point, so they continued to wait it out." She cocked her head to one side and gazed out of her side eye. "But what about when Millicent was sick? You'd think they would have tried to leave then."

Alé shook his head. "Not necessarily. Eta mentioned her mother's illness progressed very quickly. It could be that they didn't realize how bad it was until it was too late. Once she was too weak, Eta wouldn't have wanted to put her through the descent."

"Good point," Jade said. She had now moved her focus to the holo-screen on her desk and was pulling up documents with her fingers. Alé assumed she was looking for more information about the Soyuz spacecraft.

"Great," Patrick said. "Let's get her in it and bring her down."

"It's really not that simple," Alé said in a cautious voice. He didn't mind telling the head of NASA that he was wrong about something, but he didn't want to do it too abruptly.

"He's right," Jade cut in, reading intently from the holo-screen. "That ship is old. Like, *really old*. We've got to make sure it's able to survive reentry. They were meant to have a shelf life of six months. Not to sit out in space for nineteen years."

"But it's a much better option than anything we've come up with so far," Alé said. "The engineering team has had zero luck fixing the engine. They estimate that a repair would require multiple spacewalks, which she's never done on her own, and she doesn't even have the right parts on board to fix it. They'd have to improvise. It's too risky."

"How long before we know the status of the Soyuz?" Patrick asked.

Alé pulled up the tiny holo-screen in his hand to check some data. "I already have the flight team looking into it," he said. "The problem is that it's not even turned on and Eta doesn't know how to do it. What we need is an expert. A *Russian* expert. That's the only way to find out what we're dealing with. Eta speaks Russian so she should be able to handle the systems, but let's face it, nobody at NASA knows much about this spacecraft. This is Cold War-era technology. We've got to find someone with actual Soyuz experience."

Jade, who had been meticulously searching through her screen, found what she was looking for and looked up at them with a distinct look of satisfaction. She grabbed the handset on her phone. "I know exactly who to call."

Chapter 32

There was something wrong with Nu's body.

She noticed a sudden sharp, metallic taste in her mouth. Then her skin became cold and clammy, like damp metal. It seemed to her like there was a stream of metallic fluid running through her veins.

Despite the fact that it was primarily made of aluminum, the station didn't normally smell like metal. The air quality systems had strong filters to remove dust and contaminants from the air. She and Eta were diligent about cleaning those filters on a regular rotation. In the past, they would have replaced the filters, but after they ran out of replacements, they had to rely on thorough cleaning.

At first, when she noticed the metallic smells, Nu had investigated it as if there might be a problem. She inspected the consoles in the Service Module and the mechanisms that kept the

G moving, but she wasn't able to find a source. Eta didn't smell it either, which was another puzzle surrounding the smell.

Nu's left breast swelled about a week after she noticed the smells. It became tender and warm to the touch. The swelling extended under her armpit. At first, she thought maybe she was having an allergic reaction to something. The medical journals she consulted said that sometimes allergies could develop over time.

To rule out an allergic reaction, she started experimenting with cutting different foods out of her diet. No matter what she tried, the breast only got worse. The skin became greasy and waxy and took on a pale orange color.

By the time she did an ultrasound, a few days after she stopped eating peanuts, a large lump had developed in her armpit. The ultrasound revealed two other small lumps, deeper within the breast tissue.

"What does it mean?" Eta asked her as they both peered at the ominous ultrasound picture.

Nu sighed. She didn't want to worry her daughter who was only a few months away from her fifteenth birthday, but the news was not good.

"Well, it means my breasts are changing and it's happening really fast," Nu said. Eta, of course, knew about breast cancer. She also knew that because they lived in space under a constant barrage of radioactive particles, that cancer was an omnipresent threat.

"So," Nu continued, "I'll do a little research this afternoon and see if I can't find out what type of lumps they are. They might be benign." She looked again at the ultrasound on the screen in front of her. "As far as the changing color and texture, that could have to do with a blocked lymphatic duct, not necessarily something to worry about, but perhaps something to attend to."

It wasn't a coincidence that the word "cancer" hadn't come up as she discussed the ultrasound results. Nu was a firm believer in the power of thoughts and words. Eta noticed this, of course, but she nodded in agreement that additional research was required and continued on with her work schedule.

Later that evening, she and Nu sat at the table in the kitchen, each researching the archives on separate holo-screens, looking for matches to Nu's symptoms. Finally, Nu slipped her finger across the top of her screen, turning it off, and slouched back in her seat. "Well, I keep getting hits for inflammatory breast cancer. The signs are all there, but we can't be sure without a sample to biopsy." She pulled her chair closer to Eta's and brought up the ultrasound pictures on the screen.

"See, look here." She pointed at the lumps on the ultrasound, specifically the one under her arm. "This is a blocked lymph node. That means the cancer has spread and is now blocking the lymph system to the breast, which is why it's so swollen and irritated. But here"—again, she pointed at the picture, this time at the two smaller lumps that formed below the lymph node—"these two appear to be part of the lobes indicating a lobular malformation. Lobular carcinoma if it is cancerous."

Eta nodded. She had figured this out on her own, but she let Nu explain it. Often, when Nu needed to figure something out, it helped if Eta kept quiet and let Nu talk it out to herself. Eta hoped that she would come up with a plan now that she knew more or less what she was dealing with.

"I have a plan," Nu said, as if on cue. Eta leaned in to get a better look at the ultrasound pictures as Nu's fingers rapidly switched from one to the next, demonstrating the abnormalities. "I will do a biopsy on the lump closest to the surface, here. I can make a small incision here, and after I take out a portion of the lump, I can examine it under the microscope to get a better look. If it is cancerous, I can start chemotherapy treatments. There are multiple rounds of Adriamycin and Cytoxan here on the station for just such an emergency." Eta looked at her mother, who was deep in thought, still staring at the photographs on the screen. A tiny seed of panic planted itself in Eta's belly, making her feel as though she might throw up.

"There is plenty of lidocaine on board," Nu continued, still not taking her eyes off the pictures. "I'll do the surgery myself. Nix can help. He's good at standing around and taking orders. You won't even have to be involved, Eta. I can do it all with his help." Her words sounded sure, but the more she spoke, the more desperate she sounded, until Eta had finally had enough.

"Look," Eta said. "You won't be doing it by yourself. I'll do it." As she spoke the words, her knees bounced up and down under the table. The prospect of performing a breast biopsy on her own mother was terrifying, but there was no way she could sit around twiddling her thumbs while her mother operated on her own breast. No way.

"Absolutely not!" Nu growled. "I'm going to do it. I know more about physiology than you do. It will be easy for me to do it, honest."

It was true. Astronauts were actually required to obtain a bachelor's degree in physiology in addition to an advanced degree in a specialty of their choice. NASA and other space agencies were working on long-term crewed missions to the outer solar system. In order to go way out there, you had to know more about the human body.

"Okay, how about a compromise," Eta said. "You can be awake to help navigate the procedure, but I will do the work." She understood how stubborn her mother could be and she wasn't giving in so quickly. The thought of Nu operating on her own breast made Eta's already churning stomach flip on its side.

Nu sighed and looked into her daughter's eyes. She didn't want to admit it, but the odds of a successful operation were greater with Eta's help. She suddenly felt weary, like the air had been let out of her. "All right," she said. "If you think you can do it, that's what we'll do. Let's take a night to rest and do our research. We'll do it tomorrow."

Eta nodded, stood from the table, and walked to her sleeping compartment. She could think better in there.

Nu watched her go and turned back to her holo-screen to make some notes and do some more research. She knew she wouldn't get much sleep tonight. She only hoped that Eta would.

***

Eta lay in her bed many hours later, the curtains drawn to make it as dark as possible. But she did not sleep. What Nu had failed to mention during her self-diagnosis, was that inflammatory breast cancer was hyperaggressive. By the time symptoms made their appearance, it had already spread, and it was clear from the large lumps forming throughout the breast and armpit that it had, indeed, spread.

If they did nothing, the cancer would spread rapidly and Nu might only have a few weeks left. She shuddered at that thought and closed her eyes tight, imagining that her eyelids were the gateways that kept the terrifying thoughts out of her head.

Even with her eyes closed tight, thoughts swirled around in the darkness. Not terrifying thoughts, but practical ones. She tried to organize them into imaginary folders tucked into the nooks of her brain. She'd spent the last six hours researching the operation and learning every detail of how to perform it. What nerves to avoid. What blood vessels she needed to watch out for. How to recognize the lump from the surrounding tissue and cut as much of it away as possible.

Before long, she fell into a deep, restless sleep.

***

The next morning at 0630 GMT, Nu sat upright on one of the exam chairs in the medical bay, tucked between the kitchen and the sleeping compartments in the G.

The medical bay had one exam table near the wall on one side and two exam chairs on the other. Cabinets holding medical equipment and supplies covered the walls. There was a small sink and a refrigerator-freezer combination on the floor of the room. This was where they kept blood and tissue samples. On the other side of the room was another larger refrigerator that held various medicines.

Nu sat in the chair, staring out the tiny window implanted into the wall next to her, watching the sky and the Earth rotate, her mind wandering. It was Eta who brought her back to the moment.

"We should start," Eta said, working methodically on the countertop, laying out surgical tools on a sterile pad. She wanted to make sure everything was at her fingertips, which were currently trembling. She quickly thrust them under the hot water streaming from the sink faucet so that Nu wouldn't see her shaking.

But Nu understood her daughter too well. "Would you like to take something to keep you calm during the procedure?" she asked. "I think there's some Valium in that cabinet over there."

"No." Eta shook her head. "I'll be okay. I don't want to get drowsy."

Nu nodded and Eta finished washing her hands and pulled on a pair of pale, powdery latex gloves. She thumped on a hypodermic needle, staring intently at the clear liquid inside. It was lidocaine, a strong local anesthetic. She had a large enough dose to numb the entire breast and she prayed it would work for her mother's sake.

As she turned to administer the injection, Eta suddenly felt calm. Her hands steadied and her heartbeat slowed. She had done ample research in the hours before, so she knew exactly what to do. She had located the lumps with an ultrasound and marked their location on the breast using a small black marker that she found in one of the drawers. Although, she did keep the portable ultrasound on the counter behind her, just in case.

Her mother, so strong and seemingly invincible, sat there reclined in the chair with a surgery drape covering her body. A cutout in the drape exposed the breast, which Eta could already see was badly misshapen and a strange shade of orange. Nu looked up at Eta as she approached with the scalpel in hand and nodded gently at her daughter to begin.

Chapter 33

Alé watched wearily as Tess paced back and forth in front of Jade's desk. He wasn't actually listening to what she was saying, although he should have been, considering her medical and psychological observations were essential to Eta's safe return. The problem of the Soyuz niggled in the back of his mind. At first, he had been elated to find out there was a return vessel already docked to the Delta. But the more they delved into the problems with the ship, the more he worried. Tess continued her animated report while Alé imagined cracked shields, unstable atmosphere regulation, and corrosive fuel. The list of issues was mounting by the hour.

"... and from what she told me of her childhood," Tess continued, unaware of Alé's distracted mind, "her cognitive development was off the charts! The sensorimotor stage of mental development generally takes a good two years before preoperational memory and advanced motor skills. Eta actually *remembers* walking for the first time!" As she paced, Tess made big, sweeping motions with her arms to illustrate how exciting this was to her. "It's unheard of! And her mental abilities are far more advanced than a normal teenager. I'd kill to get a look at an MRI. I bet her temporal lobe and hippocampus developed at a much faster rate—."

"Yes, she's outstanding, we get it," Jade said in a rush. "Why do you think she has such vivid memories of her childhood?"

"Hard to say." Tess paused to straighten the wrinkles in her peach dress. "I suppose it could be the gravity environment. You know, the brain has only ever been studied in the developmental stage under the influence of surface gravity. It's possible that under lighter gravity, it develops differently. Of course," she added, "it also could be her unique situation."

Alé had caught the tail end of the monologue. "What do you mean by that?" he asked. "How would her situation affect physiological development? I mean, isn't it all biological? She's still a human, after all."

"I mean," Tess responded, "that every day of her life has been a struggle just to keep things running and to keep her alive. Perhaps her memory developed at a sharper rate in order to protect her. Children who grow up under intense situations such as war, abuse, or advanced illness, develop different mechanisms to cope. Maybe that's why her brain developed at such a fast pace."

She stood still for a moment and continued. "It could also have to do with conception. Studies have shown that brain development is inextricably tied to the environment under which conception takes place. Perhaps the microgravity had its effects as she was actually being formed in the womb."

"What about her social skills?" Jade asked.

"Well, that's another thing," Tess said. "She's detached, meaning she has an analytical rather than conversational nature to her speech. But honestly, that's to be expected. I mean, she's been alone for three years and although her social skills are slightly underdeveloped, they aren't nearly as bad as you might think." Tess paced again.

"For the most part, she's got a good mental grasp on things," she continued. "She has a sense of humor, understands many of our language nuances and even pop culture references. Of course, her cultural references are two decades behind, but she still understands them. She told me that she watches movies, TV, YouTube videos, reads books and articles, and even listens to music from all genres and time frames. Because of her access to the station archives, she knows how other humans interact with each other."

Raising a finger as if to make a point, Tess added, "Plus, she had her mother around for most of her life. Nu's role in her development was obviously critical and it seems like she did a thorough job acclimating her daughter to human life even in those odd circumstances."

"Well, Millicent was a product of NASA, after all," Jade said. "Good work, Tess. Keep up your observations. And for heaven's sakes, record everything. I want to make sure we've got full details so you can publish this."

"Of course," Tess said.

Jade turned to Alé, which was Tess's cue that her time with the boss had come to an end. She took the hint and quietly left the room.

"What's the next step, Alé? How are we going to get her down?"

***

Two hours later, Alé reported to the makeshift control center for his daily chat with Eta. He wasn't a big note taker, but today, he'd compiled a thorough list of items to discuss with her. He didn't want to leave anything to chance.

He slipped on his headset and sent a page through the network. The person who'd been there before him said Eta had been out of contact for the past hour during her supper break. They had done some drills on the Soyuz computers earlier that afternoon and he had good news for Alé. The computer seemed to be functioning as it should. No bugs or issues that they had come up with yet.

"This is Delta," came Eta's voice after a few seconds. They opted to continue using the old Delta call sign to follow traditional protocol. Although it seemed totally ridiculous to Alé since Eta and Delta were one and the same. It's not like they were in danger of mistaking her for someone else.

"How's the garden today?" Alé asked.

"The garden is spectacular. But then, it's spectacular every day," she replied.

Instead of starting in on the details of the plan, Alé had something else on his mind for today's chat. Days earlier, he'd realized he had no idea what Eta looked like. Since then, he had become somewhat obsessed with knowing. It was a curiosity that he couldn't drop and he knew it. He could, of course, ask her to send him a picture. They had the ability to download pictures from Nix's cameras, but they were currently busy downloading so much information from the Delta's database it would be hard to stop the process so Eta could send Alé a picture of herself. Plus, he felt weird about asking this girl to send him a selfie. They had a few pictures of her when she was a baby, taken from Nu's medical updates in the station archives, but nothing recent.

She must have sensed his curiosity because she asked, "What's on your mind today?"

He hesitated, unsure of what she might think of this line of questioning. He finally decided that he couldn't bear the thought of not knowing any longer. So, he asked, "Well... this may sound strange, but I'm curious if you could describe what you look like for me?"

Just saying the words out loud made him blush. Fortunately, most of the night shift was down in the cafeteria loading up on Thursday night's special, chicken enchiladas. A few minutes of banter with her wouldn't hurt.

"You want me to tell you what I look like?" she asked. He listened closely to her tone, waiting for annoyance to pop up. But she didn't sound annoyed by the question, just surprised. "I guess I've never thought about that before."

"Well, I don't mean to put you on the spot. I'm curious is all. You could say that curiosity is one of my weaknesses. If you'd like, I can tell you what I look like too." Okay, he definitely felt strange now. But he was also excited. Telling her more about himself and hearing more about her was honestly more exciting to him than the last two NBA finals games put together. Of course, that wasn't saying much. The Minnesota Timberwolves had taken both games decidedly. Game four would be tomorrow night and he expected the T-Wolves to win the title in a sweep.

Eta was quiet for a moment and when she spoke again, he snapped out of his basketball daydream. "I don't know, I mean, there's nothing all that special about me. I stand one point seven meters when I'm in microgravity and one point six meters when I stand in the G. Tess says that I will probably be shorter than that when I come down to the surface."

"When..." Alé's voice was a whisper, barely audible, even to himself. *When she comes down to the surface.* His heart tip-tapped a bit at the thought of that. Then he said, louder so she could hear, "Yes, gravity does that sort of stuff."

"And I weigh about nine point five kilograms in the G," she continued. "But of course, that will be different too. I have light brown hair and my skin is pale. Too pale, really. I look like a ghost sometimes, almost gray." She paused to clear her throat. "I do have freckles on my nose and cheeks. My mother always told me how much she loved them."

"What color are your eyes?" he asked.

"They are dark brown. Like my mother's."

"Brown," he repeated softly.

Without thinking, he closed his eyes and tried to draw a picture of her in his mind. Based on the diagrams and NASA archival photos, he knew what the Delta space station looked like on the inside. He imagined the interior of the VP as it looked in pictures, covered with windows on all sides, the Earth splayed out in a brilliant display of color below. He pictured her, Eta, hovering above the largest pentagonal window, staring out over the planet. Her brown hair was pulled back at the nape of her neck, with rogue strands standing on end around her head. In his imagination, she was wearing the gray cotton shorts and a matching T-shirt that would have been standard operating apparel for the crew of the Delta.

The Eta in his imagination turned her head and looked directly at him, her brown eyes, dark and wide, and the freckles on her nose giving her face a childlike quality. Then she smiled, her lips pulling up slightly at the edges. Nothing big, but a smile, nonetheless, as she floated toward him. His heart rate picked up, his breath ceased for a second, and she said his name...

"Alé? Are you still there?" Eta's real voice crackled over the radio, making him jump, his eyes flying open.

Even with his eyes open, he could still see her in his mind. "Sorry Eta, I was just thinking about something," he said at last.

"Is there anything else you would like to know?" she asked.

"I guess not. I was curious, that's all. Thank you for that. Now I have a face to put with the voice."

"I'm curious about your name, Alé," she said, obviously ready to change the subject. "It's not a very common name. How did your parents come up with it?"

"It's short for Alexandros, my great uncle's name on my mother's side. My parents are both Greek and their families come from similar areas in Greece. The nickname has been with me since I was a kid."

"Do you have siblings?"

"Yes, my older brother is Nicholas. We call him Nic. He is three years older than I am. I'm not very close to him though."

"That's a shame. I always wonder what it would have been like to have a sibling. Someone to keep me company," she said. Eta didn't often sound lonely to Alé. He figured that she was, given her situation, but he'd never heard it in her voice until now.

"You know," he said, "it's interesting that you say that because even though he was there, I was still lonely. He was older than I was, so he kind of beat up on me when we were little. And then, for a while, he was too cool to be seen with me. But I guess knowing he was there was something I could always fall back on. Even if we didn't get along."

"Tell me about your parents," she said.

"My mother is Christine. She lives here in Baltimore and I take her to church every Sunday. She was a poet and an author before the war. When the bombing started, she went to work in a factory that manufactured parts for battle drones. She came to America when she was only ten years old, but she has all these poems and stories written about her life in Greece. Sometimes I think about getting her to put them together in a book, but she's not interested in it. I think the memories of her family are too painful for her now that most of them are gone. The war was hard on her. It took many people out of her life."

"And your father?"

"His name was Nicholas too, like my brother. He was born in New York, his parents immigrated here before he was born. He moved to Baltimore to go to college and that's where he met my mother. She still cries when she looks at pictures of him." Alé paused and closed his eyes. He never spoke much about his father.

"What happened to him?"

"He was killed in the war. When the bombing started, I was eight years old. He enlisted in the Navy the very next day and we never saw him again."

Eta remained silent. In a way, he was glad she hadn't said anything like "I'm so sorry for your loss" or "Gee, that must have been hard." Her silence somehow meant more than those words would have.

Alé was surprised at how good it felt to talk about his father with Eta. "My father always loved his Greek heritage, but he was so proud to be an American," he continued. "He was on an aircraft carrier in the Pacific off the coast of South America. We aren't sure what happened, but we know the SA bombed the ship and it sank near Santiago, Chile."

Alé glanced at his watch. They had been chatting now for over twenty minutes and he knew he needed to move on. "Um, I should probably get going with the technical stuff now." With a slight smile and a chuckle, he added, "We're kind of on a time line, you know."

He heard Eta giggle at his joke and the sound made his smile widen. "Oh, I am aware of the time line," she said, laughing again.

"We've been doing research on the Soyuz. It's really old tech. And I mean *really* old. Like stuff from the Cold War era. The good news is that even though it's old, it's reliable. That's why they continued to use it for so many years. NASA used various other transport ships too, but the Soyuz was still the primary spacecraft even though it had been around for so long. That thing was built to last. Hopefully, we won't have to make too many modifications to make it fit for reentry."

"Great," Eta said. "Where do we start?"

Chapter 34

The medication made Nu vomit almost constantly. Eta took over primary operations of the station so Nu could rest. The weightlessness was almost unbearable for her so she stayed exclusively in the G.

As the days dragged on, Nu became more desperate. Eta could see her fading. It was as if it were happening in slow motion, although she knew it wasn't. She'd never noticed before, but her mother gave off a light when she was near. You could see it in her skin and in her eyes. But the light had started to fade. Eta could hardly catch a glimpse of it anymore.

Nu's attitude and her actions had taken on a frantic tone. She would forget where she put things and rip apart her sleeping compartment looking for whatever it was. She spent hours propped up with pillows on the cushioned bench in the kitchen, scrolling through her holo-screen, looking pale and determined. No matter how hard Eta tried to get her to rest, she wouldn't think of it. Nu held out hope that she would beat this cancer and the only way she could envision doing that was to do more research. On chemo days, she confined herself to her sleep sack, with a bucket to catch her vomit.

The surgery went as well as could be expected, although, to Eta, it had been comparable to jumping out of an airplane, something she imagined to be the scariest experience possible. She had seen an action movie once where the hero did some daring stunt move, jumping from an airplane and free-falling back to Earth in full gravity, while his backup parachute floundered helplessly behind him, finally busting open and stopping him from a neck-breaking death a mere fifty meters above the ground. It had terrified her to watch it, knowing full-well that the gravity down below behaves nothing like the gravity she was used to.

As Eta prepared to operate on her mother's breast, she channeled her inner daredevil. Despite the fact that it terrified her to make the incision, she knew that, in this instance, fear was good. It would keep her accurate, focused, and on the ball. Before she began, she closed her eyes and imagined that leap out of the airplane. She conjured up in her mind what it might feel like for her legs to actually leave the structure, the feeling of it leaving the soles of her feet. Then she imagined the wind rushing by, the sound deafening in her ears. It was all speculation. She had never actually heard wind before, but she knew enough about wind to conjure up her own version of it.

Eyes squeezed shut, scalpel in hand, she imagined the terror of falling from the sky. Of watching the surface rush toward her, first a muddled landscape, then quickly becoming pocked with ridges, hills, towers, trees, cars, people. Before finally, feeling the astonishingly strong rip of the parachute filling with air, vaulting her back up toward the heavens where she came from and casually letting her drift down to the surface.

At that moment, before she began her mother's surgery, Eta embraced the fear of that free fall. She harnessed the power of it, opened her eyes, and began.

The surgery took approximately two hours. The plan had been to take out three lumps, each about the size of a lima bean. With her studies the night before, she knew more or less what they would look like and how she would tell them apart from the rest of the breast tissue. She knew how much of the surrounding tissue she needed to take and verified this with ultrasound as she worked.

Nu, obviously in pain, guided her as best she could. But Eta handled it well. Her hands steady, her eyes sharp, with her tongue tucked between her teeth.

After she closed the incision with dissolving stitches, Eta gave Nu a strong antibiotic, ten milligrams of morphine, and a sleeping pill, before tucking her into her sleeping compartment, where she would sleep for the next twenty hours. Eta cleaned up the medical bay and preserved the samples. She would analyze some of the cells later and determine that yes, her mother had advanced breast cancer.

When the work was done, she allowed herself to drop into her sleep sack. Exhausted, she fell into a deep sleep. No counting. No dreaming. Just sleep.

Three weeks later, there had been no improvement in her mother's situation, and Eta, desperate for any kind of good news, watched her constantly. As the illness took over Nu's body, Eta took notes, administered medication, made herbal tea, and prayed for a miracle.

Nu was not a religious person, but Eta had gathered, from her mother's actions, that she did believe in some sort of higher power. In the desperate hope that her mother's life would be spared, Eta prayed to this higher power to come to her rescue. She spent her days working on the station systems and maintenance, learning everything she could while Nu rested in the G.

But nothing that either woman did could stop the inevitable. The cancer would not cede its ground so easily. It was highly aggressive, worse than anything Eta had read about in any medical journals, and a short two months after the surgery, the cancer won. It consumed her mother, mind, body, and soul.

Eta had spent much of the last few days holding Nu's hand, reading to her out loud, as Nu had done for Eta when she was a little girl. They didn't speak much. Nu drifted in and out but was mostly incoherent from the high doses of morphine.

"You will make it out of here, my beautiful daughter," she said to Eta the day before she passed away, in her last moment of coherency.

"Mama," Eta said, choking on the word. She hadn't called her mama in ten years. "Mama, I don't know how I will survive without you."

Eta wasn't a crier, but on that day, her eyes weren't strong enough to hold the tears back. They were like those old, ill-fated mud dams she'd read about in history books. One tiny crack from the pressure and they released..

Throughout Eta's life, Nu taught her that she was tougher than any situation. She could figure it out, no matter what. She could solve problems. She could make it work. But Eta was not in control of this one. She couldn't figure out a way to reprogram or redirect or reconfigure something. There was nothing she could do and that, more than anything, brought the tears and the total and utter feeling of helplessness.

"You will survive because you have to, Eta. I believe in you. My strong, beautiful daughter," Nu said, squeezing Eta's hand in her own. Her fingers were like pencils wrapped in translucent skin, thin and taut.

Eta nodded and there was nothing more to say. She curled up beside her mother under the layer of warm blankets, held her hand, and waited.

Eta knew the exact moment her mother passed away. The light, wispy breaths Nu took couldn't have moved a leaf. Yet when they stopped, Eta sensed it immediately. She also felt the tension in the room release. It was sudden, like an air vent had opened, releasing a room full of old, stale air and filling it with fresh, new air. Eta hadn't realized it before, but the tension she felt was in her mother's body. As soon as the air left the room, her mother's body relaxed and she was finally at peace. Eta imagined that her mother had sucked that stale air up out of the room along with her spirit, hopeful that Eta would taste the fresh air and get up. Get moving. Work the next problem.

Eta knew something else too. At that moment, when she felt the air flow out of the room along with her mother's spirit, she knew she had to get off of the Delta. She had to make it to the surface somehow. As she cradled her mother in her arms one last time, frail from illness and growing cold from death, Eta knew she must live long enough to reach the surface. She didn't know how yet, but she knew that she would, because her mother deserved that.

Nix helped her move her mother's body to his airlock. Although the airlock was much too small for a person in a space suit to fit, Nix could fit in there with Nu's body, which had shrunk to half her normal size during the illness. He took pictures for the archives before getting in with her. Eta watched from the VP, a few feet away. After decompression, Nix opened the outer lock door and the cold of space invaded the limp body in his arms, making it solid.

Nix wasn't necessarily sad. Sadness was not part of his programming, but common courtesy was, and there was nobody he respected more than Nu. So, if anything, he felt a sense of loss. Nu gave him his brain. His mind. No doubt, he would miss her.

After clipping his tether to the hook just outside his airlock, he attached a small CO_2 canister to Nu's belt. He pulled the seal on the canister and pointed his dearest companion down toward the surface below. He and Eta hadn't discussed it, but Nix felt like sending Nu's body down to the surface would be a better fate than floating in space forever. It was the courteous thing to do, to send her back to her beginnings, to become part of the Earth once more. Dust to dust, after all.

When he came back in, he said to Eta, "Your mother was a wonderful woman. I will miss her very much."

Eta nodded and said nothing. She wasn't crying now. She had work to do.

Chapter 35

Yuri Medvedev was a grizzled old soul. You'd know this simply by looking at his face, which bore the deeply tanned skin and sun-wrinkled look of a man who'd seen a battle or two in his younger days. His hair, bleached white with age, was cropped short and stood straight on his head.

He sat with his chair cocked against the back wall of the conference room, teetering on the back two legs, shoulders resting on the wall. His feet, wrapped in worn leather moccasins, were propped up on a small desk next to the conference table. Spread out in front of him was an assembly of documents, maps, schematics, and file folders. Sitting open were two old-style laptops teetering precariously on top of the pile of paperwork in front of him. He held a stained, ceramic coffee mug in his left hand. A third old laptop sat on his lap over his worn cotton Dockers. His pale pink button-up shirt had a matching coffee stain on the left breast pocket.

Yuri took a sip of the extra-strength coffee in his mug and replaced it in his lap before checking a small phone that he pulled out of his right pocket. To say that Yuri was Russian would be an understatement. If ever there was a poster child for a rough, Russian upbringing, he was it. He was born and raised on a pig farm near Saint Petersburg and had three PhDs to his name. Twenty years before, he'd been a young member of the corps of astronauts at Roscosmos. His tenure there was, of course, cut short by the start of the war. Doing his duty as a proud Russian citizen, he enlisted in the army to fight on the North Korean front.

Alé, impressed by Yuri's casual entrance into the conference room, corralled a desk and chair for him to set up his own space. Yuri was currently working with the Russian government to start up their space program again, but it would be a long road. The war hit the Russians particularly hard and their programs were many years behind those of NASA.

One rumor floating around the building was that Yuri was part of the underground Russian mafia. Nobody could prove that, of course, and it was highly unlikely that Roscosmos would hire on a true mobster, but Alé could see how the curious eyes at NASA might make such a judgment on the big fellow who sat before him. He looked like someone who fell into the "not to be messed with" category.

When Jade called in a favor from a friend of hers at the Russian Embassy, Yuri was the obvious choice. He flew on the Soyuz twice during his prewar stint with Roscosmos, once as a flight engineer and once as commander. He even spent three months on the Delta as part of the rotating astronaut crew about a year prior to the outbreak of the war.

The Soyuz program dated back to the Soviet Union of the 1960s. It predated the moon landings and the Space Shuttle and represented a time when you could cut the Cold War tension with a knife. Somehow, the Soyuz technology survived.

Born from the mind of one of the greatest rocket scientists of all time, Sergei Korolev, the Soyuz was originally meant to be part of a Soviet moon-landing program. Despite the early success of the Soviet spaceflight programs, America beat them to the punch, setting a crewed ship down onto the gray powder of the lunar surface on July 20, 1969. After this defeat, the Soviets turned their attention to other matters. More practical matters of how to keep humans in space, long-term.

In the mid-1960s, the program underwent its first test flights, only to struggle with limited success. The first crewed flight, intended as more of a public relations statement than an actual test of the equipment, failed miserably, claiming the life of the cosmonaut on board and sending the Soviet engineers back to their respective drawing boards.

After a complete engineering overhaul and more rigorous testing, the Soyuz flew again. This time, the Soviets tasted success. The spacecraft design stood the test of time, outliving the engineers who built it, the spectators who watched its first flight, and even the government that developed it. It became the most reliable vehicle ever to fly the friendly skies of low-Earth orbit.

Through collaborative efforts, the world space agencies built more advanced space stations, leading up to the most important and expensive collaboration of all, the Delta. All the while, the Soyuz remained the primary people-hauling workhorse, with the Russians selling tickets at astronomical prices to any space agency who wanted an astronaut moved into orbit.

Yuri was part of the Roscosmos team that helped build the Delta, so it didn't surprise him when he received a phone call from Jade telling him to get to Baltimore ASAP. Once again, the Americans needed the Russians to deliver them to the surface, and that thought brought a smile to Yuri's lips.

Now, as Yuri pored over maps and schematics, Alé watched him, wondering if his knowledge of the Russian spacecraft, no doubt faded after years of war and life, would be enough to bring this Soyuz home safely. Alé could only hope. This was their best option, considering the age of the technology.

The biggest problem facing them now was the age of the Soyuz parked at the Delta. It wasn't just the fact that it was old. This Soyuz had spent nineteen years *in a vacuum*, the harshest environment known to man.

Of course, the Delta itself was still operational after as many years, but that was thanks to the diligent hard work of its crew members. Although Eta and Nu kept the space station going for many years, they hadn't done anything with the Soyuz. There were no regular power-ups, battery testing, or shield inspections done. It was essentially like a tiny parasite attached to its host, drawing power, yet producing none of its own. Whether it could survive away from the Delta remained a mystery.

"Yuri," Alé said, taking a seat next to the gruff Russian, "good morning. Did you have a good night's sleep?" They had spoken briefly when Yuri arrived the night before but had passed along no pleasantries. Just a quick introduction before Yuri stomped off, his laptop and a stack of debriefing paperwork tucked under his left arm, a haggard, yellowed suitcase hanging from his right fingers.

Hardly looking up from the old laptop in front of him, Yuri set down the coffee mug and grunted in reply to Alé's question. Alé lifted one eyebrow, unsure how to take that. Did the man sleep? It was obvious Yuri wasn't the talkative type, which was fine with Alé. As long as he knew his stuff, Alé was okay with him. It certainly *looked* like Yuri knew his stuff.

"You're aware of the situation, I assume," Alé continued. "Any questions for me?"

"Nyet." The word came out short and sharp. While Alé waited, Yuri finished looking over the document on the desk in front of him before he said, "Mr. Bakas."

"Please, call me Alé."

Yuri nodded. "Alé, I am aware of the situation. I was given a full briefing the day before yesterday." Surprisingly, Yuri Medvedev spoke exceptional English. He had studied at Oxford and knew the language fluently. There was only a slight hint of a Russian accent in his speech.

"Great," Alé said. "So where do we start?"

"Unknown at this time," Yuri replied, turning his attention back to the laptop and making notes in a little purple notebook. "I will have a full diagnostic report by the end of the day. I spoke to the girl earlier and relayed the information on starting up the Soyuz so we can start pulling data from the systems on board." He shook his head and smiled at the mention of Eta. "That girl is smart. She is fluent in Russian, you know?"

Alé nodded in response. He knew that Eta was fluent, but he hadn't actually spoken to her in Russian before.

Yuri continued. "It will take her several hours to bring all systems online. Until that time, we wait. I asked her to send her robot out to take pictures of the outside of the ship. Who knows what type of damage the outside has sustained? But the fact that the docking system has been open all these years is a good sign. It means that the hull of the ship is intact."

"Good," Alé said. "Let me know when you've got more information. I will be in my office."

***

Later that day, Yuri dropped into the empty chair across from Alé's desk. "The Soyuz systems are all operational," he said. "The batteries are dead, but that's to be expected after nineteen years. She is running on power fed directly through an umbilical from the Delta. You mentioned that the batteries on the station are still functional?"

"Yes," Alé said. "The Delta's equipped with solid-state lithium batteries, but when the nuclear power plant is functioning normally, they aren't used. The computer is set to test them periodically and to use thirty percent of their capacity from time to time to make sure they remain functional. But like I said, the station doesn't rely on them for power like it would if it were running on solar power."

Yuri nodded and looked down at the little purple notebook. "The Soyuz batteries are older technology. It's equipped with five lithium-ion batteries here." As he spoke, he pointed to the very bottom of a hologram projection of the Soyuz that stood directly over Alé's desk.

"These serve both primary and backup battery purposes," Yuri continued. "Then there are reentry batteries, also lithium ion, here." Now he waved aside a small panel on the middle portion of the craft to reveal the components underneath. "The solar panels are also not functioning. It appears to be a total electrical failure. I'm not sure why. The electrical systems are working within the craft, but the power generation and storage systems are dead."

Alé's brow crumpled with worry. "That's not an issue as long as we stay docked to the Delta. But once it undocks, no more power."

"Da." Yuri nodded in agreement.

"We'll use batteries from the station." Alé looked up at Yuri and asked, "Will that work?"

Yuri nodded. "It should work. The batteries on the Delta are solid state, but they can be adapted to fit into the Soyuz. She'll have to do a spacewalk though. The compartments are not accessible through the interior of the spacecraft."

Alé dropped his head and pinched the bridge of his nose. The spacewalk was risky. Eta had never done one before. "What about the robot?" he asked. "Could the NIX unit replace the batteries?"

"Doubtful," Yuri said. "It's complicated, especially since the battery types are not the same. From what I know of the robot, it would not be able to. But I could be wrong."

Alé thought about this for a second. Nix had greater capabilities than any robot he'd seen before, but he knew this was a stretch. "Perhaps we should ask Eta. She knows what he's capable of better than any of us."

"It's worth a try," Yuri agreed. "I will come up with the plan to move the batteries. I'll need full schematics on the Delta's battery bank to make sure the connections can be updated, but I don't foresee a problem." He flipped the cover of his notebook shut and stood to leave. As he turned to go, he paused. "Before we change out these batteries, we must be absolutely sure who's doing this spacewalk. If the robot is not capable, it could damage the batteries in the transfer and with a finite number of station batteries to work with, we need to be clean here."

"Understood," Alé replied.

***

Later that week, Alé sat in his apartment in the Baltimore neighborhood of Pigtown. He'd lived in Pigtown his entire life. In fact, his mother still lived there, just a few blocks away from him. The apartment, although small, was perfect for him. He had a good view of Carroll Park and it was only a few blocks' walk to Oriole Park at Camden Yards. The drive to Goddard took easily an hour one way, so he spent a lot of time at work. He had briefly considered moving closer to Goddard after he landed the job at

NASA, but he'd scrapped the idea. Pigtown was home, and it had always been home.

He sat on his couch with a large holo-screen open in front of him. The screen was open to a coding program he was working on for the battery transfer, but he hadn't touched it in several minutes. He was too wrapped up in his thoughts to notice the coding program.

The longer he worked with Eta, the more distracted he found himself. He'd be in the middle of walking or driving or working, and all of a sudden, he'd picture her in his mind, floating in front of the station windows, staring down at the surface. Before he knew it, he'd lose himself in the image and all ability to concentrate escaped him. It was incredibly annoying.

Every day, Eta said or did something that amazed him. Her knowledge of football statistics, or her willingness to share her favorite recipes, or even just the sound of her voice. There was a subtle innocence to her that he'd never noticed in another human being. He left every conversation lighthearted and loopy. He even caught himself smiling like a goofball while he spoke to her.

Now, as he sat on his couch with his eyes closed, he was there with her, floating in front of that window. This time, she was looking at him, smiling. Then she reached out her hand and he could almost feel her fingers graze the skin on his cheek. Blood pulsed through his body as he imagined her touching his skin and a shiver went down his back.

His phone vibrating next to him jerked him back to reality. He grabbed the phone off the table and stared at the time. It was nearly ten o'clock at night and he realized that he'd been sitting in the same spot, dazed, for over an hour. He shook his head to clear away the cobwebbed feeling from his mind and answered the phone.

"Good evening, young one!" came Yuri's voice from the other end. Alé chuckled at the nickname. Apparently, the grizzled old Russian had warmed to him. "I've been going over the schematics and I found another problem."

For two days, the team had worked on the plan to move the batteries from the Delta to the Soyuz. Eta would need a week of practice and prep work before the spacewalk, so the time frame was tight. Eta confirmed that a task of this magnitude probably wasn't something Nix could handle himself, but when confronted with the idea of doing the spacewalk on her own, Eta had shown no sign of fear or doubt. She just asked for the plan and on they went.

It would take her almost four hours to complete the entire transfer, then another six hours of work inside the Soyuz, bringing all systems online and tying everything to the new batteries. The space suits were, like everything else on the Delta, outdated, but both the primary suit and the spare appeared to be in good working order. The suits were approved for use up to a max of seven hours because of their age, so the four-hour spacewalk would be well within their capabilities.

"What's the problem," Alé asked, biting his lower lip.

"It appears that the external covering, the heat protectant material that covers the Soyuz, is flapping in the breeze," Yuri said.

"Right," Alé answered, ignoring the comment about the breeze since there was no "breeze" in space. "Yeah, Eta mentioned that. She says it's always been that way. That shouldn't affect the reentry, right? I mean, that fabric is just there as a precaution. The heat shield does most of the work."

"Da," Yuri responded, "but the damaged material will need to be removed to make sure it doesn't get in the way of any sighting instruments or change the entry velocity. That's not the biggest problem, though. With that material out of place, it's left the heat shield and the skin of the vessel open to extreme temperatures and debris strikes. That type of exposure weakens the metal over time. I found thirteen holes in the outer hull just by doing a quick overview of the pictures taken by the robot. And that's what we can see right now. There could be more. The Service Module protects the bulk of the heat shield, so that probably saved it from further damage, but with at least thirteen holes in the outer shell alone, it could be a disaster."

Alé groaned and slumped his elbows to his knees. It was true—having a compromised hull was not a good idea for a reentering ship. Even if the heat shield was in perfect working order, the heat from the atmospheric reentry could burn right through the remaining layers of shielding and eventually reach the cabin. The occupant would suffocate when the atmosphere rapidly dispensed and would likely get cooked alive.

"What can we do about it?" Alé asked.

"I'm working on that. I think there may be a way to patch it using material from the outer hull of the Delta. Of course, it will require a much longer spacewalk. In fact, we'll probably need to do two of them. Maybe three."

"Okay," Alé said, sitting up and rubbing his eyes with his left hand. "Keep working on it. We'll discuss it tomorrow morning when I'm back in the office."

"I will do that, young one," Yuri said, ending the phone call.

Alé stood, looked out the window over the lights of the city, sighed, and turned toward his bedroom.

Chapter 36

My finger is stuck inside the thumb hole of the space suit. I've been trying to wiggle it free for the last two minutes and it's starting to cramp. Not only that, my biceps and shoulders feel like they're on fire. Literally, they are about to burn a hole through this suit, or at least that's how it feels in my mind.

The thing about being inside a pressurized suit is that it's like wearing balloons around your arms and torso. You've got to squeeze your arms toward your body if you want to keep your hands in front of you. It's basically squeezing against the force of a tiny atmosphere, and although it's tiny compared to, say, the Earth's atmosphere, it's a real pain to squeeze through it. If you don't force your arms to stay close to your body, they float off to your sides, perpendicular to your body. That doesn't do me any good.

Plus, I'm sweating like a pig in this thing. The temperature regulator in this suit is not working properly, I can tell. I'm wearing a liner between my skin and the actual pressure suit. The liner is made up of tiny tubes and it's supposed to pump cool or warm water through the tubes based on the temperature readouts from the suit sensors. It's definitely not working. I can feel the heat rising in here. Sweat creeps down my back. I imagine that's what a spider might feel like crawling along your skin. I've seen too many science and nature movies about insects. One of the perks of living in space is that there aren't any bugs.

I sigh, a long, exasperated sigh so I know they can hear over the intercom.

Alé responds, "How's the cut going? Having any problems?" He knows damn well I'm not cutting. He can see everything I'm doing from the little cameras mounted on the side of the helmet.

"I stopped cutting two minutes ago. My finger is stuck inside the thumb hole." I bite my tongue between my teeth in concentration. Maybe if I straighten it toward the end of the thumb hole, I can wiggle it free from this little lip of fabric. I grunt with the effort, but it works. My finger has now slipped all the way into the thumb hole.

The problem with this suit is that it's much larger than I am. Usually, they customize these suits to fit a specific body size and this one is the larger of the two suits on board. The smaller one, the one Nu used, didn't perform as well in the screening tests and was deemed the backup. So, I sit here fighting with this glove that's too big for my hand. My thumb and forefinger now share the thumb hole of the glove. I breathe in, bite my tongue again, and pull hard with my hand muscles. Finally, my index finger pops free from the thumb hole and I move it back into the correct finger hole.

"All right, got it fixed," I say, "Oh, by the way, this suit is ridiculously hot. Thoughts on that?"

"Yeah, we can see the temp reading is high," Alé says. That's putting it lightly. I can see the temperature displayed on the inside of my helmet. A small lens projects a handful of useful readings onto the glass faceplate: pressure, oxygen levels, humidity, and temperature. The temperature flashes in front of my face: 31.1°C. It flashes again: 31.6°C. Geez, that's almost 90°F. Way too hot. I punch the buttons on the arm pad to change the display. Now it shows me the outside temperature instead: 22.2°C.

"What do you propose we do about it?" I ask, responding to Alé's vague declaration about the temperature being high. I continue my work, cutting the material I now hold in my gloved hands. My arms still burn, but not quite as much since I took a break to get my finger unstuck.

I don't mean to sound irritated when I ask him this, but I've been in this thing for three hours now and it is boring work. It's not actually accomplishing anything. It's only a test run for the spacewalk. I can't help but feel moody about it. Plus, I'm exhausted and boiling hot.

"Yeah, we're looking into it." He sounds tired too. We've all been working long hours to prepare for this spacewalk. But nobody has worked more than Alé. I imagine him dropping into bed at night, exhausted. "Looks like the cutting is going well," he says, no doubt an effort to keep my mind off of the intense heat in the suit. "Keep at it. Once you get that piece cut, we'll work on applying it to the heat shield."

"Assuming that we can get the temperature down," I add. "I can't stay in this thing much longer. I'll pass out."

"Yes, of course," he replies.

The material in front of me is part of the Kevlar insulation that lines the walls of the station. I'm not actually outside right now. I'm in the VP and we're doing a final run-through of the spacewalk procedures. The Kevlar in my hands didn't actually come from the hull of the station. It's part of the failed thermal shielding that came loose from the Soyuz many years ago. Nix went out and fetched it so I could practice with it. According to Alé, it's the same stuff that I'm going to deal with when I actually do take the cutting torch to my station.

The plan is to cut away the outside layer of aluminum on a two-meter square of the Service Module. That's the thickest layer, probably two centimeters thick. Under that, there are twelve layers of Kevlar blankets. This setup keeps pieces of debris from puncturing the hull. Under that, there are some Mylar thermal blankets for insulation, and under that is an industrial-strength wax about ten centimeters thick. The wax covers the actual pressure hull, which is also made of aluminum.

It's a bit more robust than the stations they made in the past, but the guys at NASA told me the Delta was meant to occupy a much farther orbit. Therefore, it needed some additional padding. That's good news for me because their plan calls for me to cut a big hole in it. Once the aluminum is removed, I'll cut out the layers of Kevlar and bond them to the Soyuz to reinforce the strength of the hull.

This project of strengthening the Soyuz hull is actually for the second of two spacewalks NASA has planned for me. The first spacewalk will be to change the batteries. It sounds like an easier job, but not really. Those batteries are complicated. You can't just unhook one of them and plug it into the Soyuz. There's a long process of rewiring, and to do it correctly, it has to be removed from the Delta without fraying or damaging any of the wiring. That's a tall order for a girl in an oversized space suit with bulky nubs for fingers.

All of this is, of course, dependent on the temperature regulator in the space suit. If it doesn't work better than this, I won't last twenty minutes out there. I'll have to take a look at it myself later. Those NASA guys are pretty good at calculating stuff and pulling up old diagrams, but they're not great at working the problem. Most of what they tell me to do is because they ran some advanced computer simulation and it said I would get a certain result. I don't think they do much trial and error on their own.

Kevlar is essentially like duct tape for the space station. It's a great all-around material that's stronger than steel with excellent thermal properties. It works well in a woven-fiber application, and it can be cut and bonded. In fact, the early Delta astronauts had their own patch kit for just such an emergency. I still have some Kevlar patch material along with plenty of the space-grade thermal resin that's used to set the Kevlar in place on the hull of the Soyuz. Unfortunately, there's not enough patch material left in the patch kit, which is why I'll need to cut open the hull.

Cutting a hole in the side of the Delta is dangerous business. It'll leave the station vulnerable to space debris and radiation. It's a risk NASA's okay with as long as I'm on my way to the surface soon after I make the cuts. I'm okay with it too since it means I might actually have a ship that's strong enough to get me out of here.

If I can successfully cut away the Kevlar, then I've got another problem. I must mix the resin perfectly to ensure it will make a quality seal capable of resisting the thermal forces of reentry, and I must do the mixing *fast* because this stuff is no joke. It takes only a few seconds for it to harden and create a permanent bond. This is a process I've never done before with my bare hands, let alone done with big, bulky space suit gloves on. I'll probably end up gluing my fingers together.

During reentry, the Soyuz must survive several thousand degrees of heat. If even one of my patches fails, I'll get cooked alive inside that capsule. So, I guess, this practice run is pretty important. If only it weren't so hot!

"Alé," I say, "it's too hot in here. What can I do about it?"

"Yeah, Eta, I'm looking at a procedure right now. Hold just one second."

"I've made my cuts. Now I'm going to mix the resin."

"Not yet, Eta. We need to get your suit regulated first."

Sweat creeps down my forehead. A drop lands in my left eyeball, stinging it shut.

A moment later, Alé comes back on the radio. "So this may sound a little strange," he says, "but I want you to shut off your oxygen regulator."

"Hmm... shut off the oxygen?" I ask, skeptically.

"Yeah, we're going to reboot the system," he says. "If we shut it off, it should manually reset and then hopefully, the thermal unit will come back online."

I do as he says and, to my surprise, it starts up again in only a few seconds. Almost immediately, it's much more comfortable in my suit.

"Better?" he asks.

"Better," I say.

"Great. Now what can I do to make your life a little easier?" he asks.

"You can come up here and mix up this resin for me," I say, irritated. "Have you ever tried mixing resin with these gloves on?"

"No, but I once built a Jenga tower wearing ski gloves. It was a dare. Does that count?" He must know I'm irritated because he adds, "Trust me, if I could go up there and help you, I would."

"You're a liar. Not one person on the surface would opt to take my place up here and that includes you."

"Oh, you think I'm lying to you, huh?" he says. "Nothing makes me more uncomfortable than knowing you've got to do these spacewalks. I would trade places with you in a second if it meant you were safe."

I'm skeptical of this, so I don't say anything in response. It makes me wonder if NASA protocol says that the guy in charge needs to act like he cares so that the lost soul doesn't give up hope.

He must sense my doubt. "I'm serious, you know. I would do anything to get you here safe. Even if it meant trading places with you."

Now that the suit temperature is regulated again, I know it's not the suit making my face hot. I choose to ignore it and continue to measure the chemicals in the resin. Once I mix them together, that's it. The clock is ticking. During the spacewalk, I'll have to mix resin like fifteen times. So, I'd better learn how to do it right with these stupid gloves on.

***

Later that night, Nix comes into my sleeping compartment. He jokes with me about how well I did at mixing resin while wearing ski gloves. Perhaps he caught that little tidbit from our conversation about ski gloves. Tomorrow, he'll go outside with me to help hold tools and equipment and provide guidance, if necessary. It makes me feel less nervous knowing he'll be there with me.

I'm staring out the small porthole window in my sleeping compartment. The Earth spins slowly in a giant circle. It's bright. The station is in the day part of its orbit and I really shouldn't have my window open. It's after midnight GMT. I should be sleeping, though I can't help but take a peek outside while the station is still in the sunlight.

I wonder what Alé is doing at the moment. Just as I think of him, my body relaxes and a smile spreads over my face. I am closer than I've ever been to leaving the Delta and seeing him in person. That thought makes me happier than almost any thought I've ever had.

The holo-screen next to my bed pings—an email has popped into my inbox. The subject says "Eta..." The email reads:

```
Eta,
Have you ever wondered what they call a space fruit?
A coco-naut :)
Just a little astronaut joke to warm you up. After
all, you didn't get enough heat this afternoon in
that space suit!
You will be great tomorrow. I have all kinds of
faith in you. Now go to sleep! It's late. And you've
got a big day...

Good night, Miss Coco-naut.
Alé
```

Smiling, I blush and hug my knees to myself. I feel like a silly teenager, and that feeling is fabulous. I reply:

```
Alé,
You need to sleep as much as I do. And thanks for
the joke. It made me smile.
Eta
```

A few minutes later, he replies again:

```
Eta,
A smile from you is worth a thousand silly astronaut
jokes. Sleep tight, coco-naut.
Alé
```

I run my finger down the holo-screen to shut it down and close the window shade, turning the room dark. I can hear the rumbling of the G's spin around me. I start counting.

999... 998... 997... 996...

But tonight, the counting is not working like it normally does. My mind drifts back and forth between Alé and the numbers.

He's thinking of me tonight. That thought spins my mind and sucks the breath right out of me. After many more minutes, I drift off into a restless doze.

Alé is in my dream. I can barely see him, but he's there, and I know it because I can *feel* him. I can't remember what happened in the dream, but I know that he was there the whole time.

Chapter 37

I am not an astronaut.

How do I know? Because I'm sitting here, strapped into my space suit, waiting to start this spacewalk, and I am terrified. Astronauts don't let fear tackle them. They spend their lives training and waiting and training and waiting, all for the glory of coming to space and feeling what it's like to be outside of Mother Earth's protective outer layers. I, on the other hand, would like nothing more than to be carefully enveloped into those protective layers. That's how I know I'm no astronaut. A legit space explorer would be thrilled to take the opportunity I have now.

Of course, it's not easy to get inside those protective layers of the atmosphere. Mother Earth does a good job of ensuring that hostiles don't get in, and she won't just open up for one of her own. You've got to earn your way into her inner circle.

So, that's what we're doing now. Retrofitting this old Soyuz so it can stand up to the atmosphere and earn its way inside. The fact that I've been training for this spacewalk for two weeks doesn't make me any less nervous. If the procedures we've decided on don't work, Mother Earth *will* reject me.

Nix is beside me. He tips his Iron Man head in my direction as he remotely downloads data from the station computers. Nix is in charge of keeping me organized and reminding me of the next step while I'm doing the work on the Soyuz. He's also got my backup computer and a whole bunch of tools strapped to his body. He's been practicing too. We ran hundreds of drills, the two of us. He has step-by-step instructions for the spacewalk stored in his hard drive. There are 632 instructions, to be exact.

Alé will be here too. As the thought of Alé enters my mind, my heart speeds up slightly and for a moment, my mind wanders away from the overwhelming task at hand. I'm quickly brought back when the communications link in the suit crackles to life, causing me to jump.

"Just a test, Eta. Only a few more minutes now. I'll come back on when we're ready," Alé says from the other end.

I blink a few times and shake my head inside the space suit to stay active. It's the only thing I can move right in this cramped little airlock. I turn my head to the left and see the hatch. It hasn't been opened in two decades and the pressure of holding in an entire atmosphere must take be taking its toll on the metal and seals. It worries me.

To take my mind off of the hatch, I start to list off all the things that can go wrong with this spacewalk. If I know about them all in advance, maybe the task won't seem so intimidating.

First, I might die. This is true, of course, but frankly, the never-ending presence of death is something I've lived with my whole life. It's no reason to get all worked up about now.

My suit might malfunction while I'm out in space. This suit is older than I am. That's a strong possibility. But so far, the suit has worked fine, other than the glitch with the temperature regulation. Well, there's also the fact that it hasn't been in the vacuum yet. All of the practice runs were done in the pressurized atmosphere of the station and you never know how something will react to the vacuum. To err on the side of positivity, it's been working fine so far and there's no reason to think it will fail now.

If the suit malfunctions, I'll have to get back to the airlock in a hurry. It's not fun or easy to hurry in a space suit. Nix will be there. Maybe he can help me get back quickly.

If I *can't* get back fast enough, the suit might totally fail on me. But again, it's been working okay so far, so why would it fail now? If the suit does fail completely, I'll die for sure, which brings me back to my first point.

The procedures we've practiced might not go as planned. In fact, they probably won't go as planned. But when does anything go as planned?

If the spacewalk doesn't go as planned, I'll have to improvise. I'm no stranger to improvisation. I've been improvising solutions to mechanical problems since I was five.

If the improvisations don't work, then the procedure will fail and the Soyuz won't be tough enough to punch through the atmosphere. If the Soyuz doesn't make it, I'll die during reentry, which, again, brings me back to my first point—I'm always on the verge of dying.

My mind is so full of these buzzing thoughts, it starts to make me feel tired, and I can't have that. I take a moment to push all those negative thoughts back and focus on the positive. I will be okay. I will make it to the surface. I'll do it for Nu. I'll do it for Alé. I'll do it for me.

"Eta?" Alé says over the radio. Again, the sudden noise makes me jump.

"Yes, I'm here," I say awkwardly.

"You ready to do this, girl? I'm giving you a good luck wink from down on the surface." I don't think he's ever called me "girl" before. He's trying to sound upbeat. I can tell by the slight tremor in his voice that it's an act. He's as nervous about this as I am, and suddenly, I believe him when he says he'd change places with me in a heartbeat. The thought brings me comfort.

"Wink when we're done, Alé," I say.

"Whatever you say, boss," he says. "First step, open the hatch. Let's get started."

Chapter 38

I'm sitting in the kitchen eating rice and beans. I'm still alive... for now.

Actually, the first spacewalk went as well as could be expected. I was able to get three batteries detached from the hull of the Service Module. The first one was a beast. For a moment, I thought I wouldn't be able to do it. The casing around the battery was held on by four very tight bolts. After several minutes of sweating wrenching, I was finally able to free them. Then it took me about an hour to unhook the battery and take it back to the airlock.

I repeated the process with two more batteries. Those two came loose much easier after I figured out how to position myself so I could remove the bolts. You'd be amazed at how tough it is to get any torque when you're in microgravity. It's all about positioning. I finally figured out that if I tucked my feet into the hand straps that surround the outer hull, I could push up on the wrench to loosen the bolts.

I've never been outside the walls of the Delta and frankly, it made me uneasy. The outer skin of my station looks like an RV after a hail storm with nicks and dents all over the place. I was shocked to see this at first. Nix assured me that's how it always looks, and I've seen pictures of it from his point of view, but it's different when you see all the little dents in person. It's difficult to see your home, your only source of heat, oxygen, water, food, *life*... all beat up like that.

The battery bank is on the outside of the Service Module, which is where I spent my six-hour-long spacewalk. When I went back through the airlock, it was a tight fit. We did remove the other space suit so there would be room for me and the batteries, but those things are not small. It'll be interesting fitting them into the Soyuz which is even smaller than the airlock.

For now, I'm not concerned about that. I left them in the Docking Module. Tomorrow, they want me to wire them into the Soyuz and make sure they're working right. If they don't work, it'll be back to the very short drawing board. The original plan was to do the second spacewalk right away. But after they saw the condition of the outer skin, they'd rather I get the Soyuz ready to go on the inside before I go cutting off the exterior aluminum.

Alé sent me an email when he got home. He was with me during the spacewalk and afterward he went home to rest. He told me about his night and cracked a few jokes. He talked about how much he hates to do laundry, and how much I'll hate doing laundry when I get down to the surface. He mentioned he likes to grill steak and isn't a huge fan of vegetables, but tries to get them into his diet when he can. He told me how much he admires my strict cleaning schedule and he can barely handle keeping his bathroom clean.

I'm smiling now as I read it. It feels wonderful to have a normal conversation with someone else. As I read his words to me, tears cloud my eyes.

Chapter 39

I was using a laser cutter on the aluminum hull of the Service Module when it happened.

An alarm sounded inside the headset of my suit.

Hull breach.

The alarm made sense. After all, I was breaching the hull of my own station by cutting a big chunk of aluminum off of it. I expected the hull breach alarms. But I didn't expect them to make me so nervous. It also didn't help that I was totally exhausted after the first spacewalk two days earlier.

The first spacewalk was a killer on my joints and muscles. I spent the better part of the day after applying cold packs to my body and chewing ibuprofen tablets. I wasn't even given the whole day off. The batteries I removed from the outside of the station are these big, bulky things and I had to move them into the tiny descent module of the Soyuz. NASA assured me that this was possible. But it was *not* an easy task. Technically, I could have taken them apart.

They're full of a bunch of individual cells, so each bulky container is really more of a "battery pack". But NASA didn't want to risk this because the odds are too great that I'd damage them in the process. Plus, it's easier to wire them into the Soyuz as a whole unit versus a bunch of little cells.

The good part is, the Soyuz is in microgravity, making it easier to maneuver the big batteries than it would have been in full gravity. Still, it took me almost three hours to get them moved from the airlock and settled in place inside the Soyuz. And by "in place" I mean, strapped into the two empty seats inside the descent module. The ship has three seats for three astronauts. I plan to occupy the third seat, obviously. I placed one battery into each seat and then balanced the third on top of those two strapping everything down with duct tape. It took me another four hours to get them wired into the ship, but now they're installed and they seem to be functioning properly, meaning, I will have power on my short ride home.

So, the next day when I was performing the second spacewalk to repair the outer hull of the Soyuz, I was totally exhausted. That's when the suit alarm indicating the hull breach sent my anxiety soaring. Alé sent his team of engineers into the computer system to shut down the alarm, but unfortunately, a hull breach alarm isn't so easily disabled. It's considered a "top priority" alarm.

They eventually got it turned off, but the constant ping in my earpiece gave me the nerves. My hands were shaking and I was sweating like a pig. I kept thinking about how ridiculous I was for actually going forward with this plan to cut holes in the outer skin of my space station.

Fortunately, the rational part of my brain eventually won and calmed my body down. Even so, it took the better part of six hours outside in the void to get enough Kevlar cut from the Service Module to patch up the Soyuz.

And the really unfortunate part is, now I have to go back out there. It took much longer than expected to cut out the Kevlar and I'll have to do a third spacewalk tomorrow to actually patch the Soyuz.

I'm back inside now. I left the harvested Kevlar pieces in the airlock, and to tell you the truth, I'm happy they are there. I closed up the hatch immediately to seal them off. I don't like the way they smell. They smell like space. It's a strange, burnt smell, all smoky and raw. I don't want it permeating the rest of the station. My stay here won't be too much longer, but I'd rather not smell the odor of space while I'm here. It makes me uneasy.

I'm going to sleep now. Tomorrow will be (hopefully) my last spacewalk before leaving this place. Third time's a charm, right?

Chapter 40

Alé paced the center of the room. His headset light flickered bright green in the dim lighting of the conference room. He was in the middle of a heated discussion with one of the engineers. The engineer in question was in charge of the team overseeing the airlock functions.

Eta, on the dark side of the Earth, was pacing in her own way. She was counting backward from one thousand inside her space suit, just inside the airlock hatch. They had a serious problem.

It had taken her a full six hours to get the Kevlar fabric that she had harvested from the belly of the Service Module attached to the outer hull of the Soyuz. The patch was supposed to take no longer than three hours, but everyone, including Alé, had underestimated the sturdiness of the Kevlar.

It was not only thick, but it was fibrous, and after eighteen years in vacuum and extreme temperatures, it had toughened up to the point where it was almost impossible to bend. They knew after the prior day's spacewalk that it would be tough stuff to work with, yet nobody predicted how hard it would be to mold it onto the skin of the Soyuz.

Alé mentally kicked himself for not taking that into account. But, much to everyone's relief, Eta found a way. Using her wrench set, combined with heat from her blowtorch, she managed to figure out a way to wield the material into the necessary shape to fit the sides of the Soyuz.

The key to this installation was that there be no gap between the Kevlar and the Soyuz. If gaps existed, air would leak in once the ship hit the atmosphere. At such high speeds, the air pockets would cause friction, ripping the blankets from the Soyuz and exposing the capsule to intense heat. After some experimentation, Eta found that she could heat a flat-sided wrench with the blowtorch and create a "space iron," as she called it. Nix held the torch and Eta held the handles at the ends of the longest wrench, measuring one meter in length. He was careful to avoid her gloves while they did this. Then she slowly pulled the wrench down the fabric and the extreme cold of space would flash-freeze the unruly fabric into place. Then, once she got the right shape, she welded the seams directly to each other and to the outside of the Soyuz, creating a perfect seal.

These additional steps took time. Lots of time. Before they knew it, the six-hour spacewalk time frame came and went. But she had done it, and that meant Eta would be on her way to the surface in just a few short hours, which made everyone working in the makeshift Mission Control breathe a sigh of relief.

The feeling of relief lasted exactly six minutes and forty-three seconds, the moment Eta entered the airlock and attempted to close the outer door. The airlock was where she now waited, floating just outside the inner door, counting to herself in an attempt to calm herself down.

She had entered the airlock a few minutes earlier and when she turned to close the hatch, she noticed a slight warping of the metal on the outer frame of the hatch. It wasn't a large area, maybe a few centimeters, but the warped metal was just large enough to catch the corner of her eye.

The problem had actually occurred many hours earlier, a few seconds after the airlock depressurization at the beginning of the spacewalk. When she opened the hatch, a silent burst of air popped through the seal, twisting the metal slightly. The Soviets had a similar incident happen once on the Mir space station. An outward-opening airlock became warped and refused to close after a spacewalk. Since that time, airlock doors were always designed to open inward. This design used the natural forces of the pressurized atmosphere inside to help push the door into place and tighten the seal.

In the case of the Soviet airlock failure, the door had been opened before the lock had fully decompressed. This extra pressure forced the door to open outward in an explosive manner. That explosive decompression, as slight as it may have been, caused the frame of the door to warp and the astronauts were then stuck outside. Thankfully, they were able to use a different airlock on the Mir to get back inside.

Eta's exit from the airlock at the beginning of the spacewalk had a similar problem. Although her airlock door opened inward, a tiny amount of atmosphere was trapped between the outer hull and the inner hull because of a hairline fracture in the seal. The fracture happened during the depressurization the day before and was caused by the age of the seals. NASA knew that a seal fracture was a possibility, but they considered it a low risk since the airlocks were not opened or closed for many years.

When Eta came back in from her spacewalk the previous day and closed the airlock door, the fracture allowed a tiny amount of air to seep in between the inner seal and outer seal. Then, when she opened the hatch for her third and final spacewalk, the tiny amount of air caused an explosive decompression, shooting the hatch door inward and warping the metal on the outer casing.

Eta noticed this, of course. The door shot back with much more force than it had the other two times she opened it. At the time, she examined it and found that nothing looked out of place. NASA cleared her to continue with the spacewalk. After she spent the next six hours forcing the aged Kevlar into place, the airlock issues were forgotten.

Until now.

As Alé spoke hurriedly into the phone, sweat broke out around his collar causing him to pull at it with rough, harsh tugs. He fought to loosen his tie before finally ripping it from his shirt and tossing it into an empty chair propped against the wall.

"What can we do?" he said to the engineer on the other end of the line, his voice cracking with desperation. "I mean, we had to consider hatch failure a possibility? Right?"

He paused, listening to the voice on the other end, his face becoming became redder with every passing second.

"Yeah, but just because it worked out before, didn't mean... Yeah... Uh-huh," he said, trying to calm himself.

At this point, one of the other engineers in the room approached Alé with a pad of paper in his hand. He gestured toward the notepad and mouthed something to Alé, who glanced at it and nodded, shooing the engineer away with his free hand.

There was another airlock that Eta could use, but that posed a problem: a large piece of debris had struck the spare airlock six years earlier. Pieces of debris hit the outer hull of the Delta almost daily. Most of them were small and didn't do any harm, other than denting the surface of the hull. But occasionally, there had been larger strikes that caused bigger problems. This was one of those. The debris strike did extensive damage to that hatch causing Nu to seal it from the inside. They considered it a dead option. Opening it would be done only in case of extreme emergency.

But each passing second brought them a second closer to that extreme emergency situation. Eta's space suit was cleared to go for six hours and she was already thirty-two minutes beyond that time. Her oxygen supply was already at a critical point. They figured she had about twenty more minutes. They were running out of time.

The airlock was part of the Docking Module and was made up of two areas, the Briefing Node and the airlock itself. The briefing node was a small room where they kept the extra space suits and where astronauts got ready to do spacewalks.

There were three doors, or hatches, included in this design. The innermost hatch led from the Docking Module into the Briefing Node. Then there was a hatch between the Briefing Node and the airlock. Finally, there was the door to the outside, the one that warped during the decompression.

In case of hatch failure, they could depressurize the Briefing Node, allowing Eta to enter through the inner hatch instead. But at the moment, the innermost hatch stood wide open. They couldn't depressurize the briefing node without depressurizing the entire station. Under normal circumstances, this hatch could be closed by another astronaut inside the station, but with no other astronauts on board, it was a situation they never considered.

Alé continued to listen on the other end of the phone. From time to time, he would say something in short, clipped sentences to the engineer and listen again, letting out exasperated sighs in response. He turned around to see Yuri standing right behind him, so close that it made Alé jump back. As Yuri remained there, arms folded in front of him, he had a strange look on his face. Alé turned back to the phone and said, "Let me call you back."

Yuri cocked his head slightly to one side before saying, "What about the robot?"

Chapter 41

We have a plan. I'm not sure it's a good plan... but it is a plan, so that's good news.

Nix will go inside through his special airlock and close up the innermost hatch so that I can enter through the Briefing Node and bypass the warped door on the airlock. Why can't I go through the robot airlock myself? That would be convenient, but they didn't design it to fit a person, especially one wearing a bulky space suit. It's only big enough for him and even he has to fold up to get in there.

They're discussing the plan right now down on the surface. I keep counting.

538... 537... 536...

I bring up the oxygen reading on the inner faceplate of my helmet. It says I have sixteen minutes of oxygen remaining. I squeeze my eyes shut.

535... 534... 533...

Will Nix be able to close the inner hatch and depressurize the Briefing Node? I have to admit, I'm worried about him. He is a robot, after all. He's meant to perform minor tasks. Depressurizing an airlock is not part of his repertoire of duties and neither is closing up a complicated hatch door. But it's the only option we've come up with.

532... 531... 530...

The low oxygen alarm starts to sound inside my helmet. A slow, steady beep. I let my counting fall into step with the beeping.

529... 528... 527...

I open my eyes. We've been on the dark side now for about twenty minutes. The stars out here look so much closer than they do from the inside. I know they aren't, but it feels like I could reach out and grab one of them. I wonder what it would be like to hold a tiny star in my hand? I close my eyes again and try to keep my heart from racing.

526... 525... 524...

Alé is on the radio again. Nix is at the inner hatch, Alé says. I let him know I heard him. I turn around and look in the tiny porthole window in the center of the hatch. Nix's smiling, Iron Man face is staring back at me. A laugh escapes my lips. I've probably never been in more danger of dying, but the sight of Nix's ridiculous Iron Man head still makes me laugh.

After a moment, I realize he's just sitting there, staring at me. He isn't actually moving to do anything. He still has to close the hatch and depressurize the Briefing Node. I check the oxygen reading again. Thirteen minutes. It could be wrong. Maybe that reading is like the expiration date on a dairy product. I've never had a dairy product, but I've read about them. The government makes all dairy producers issue an expiration date for their products. Just because something expires doesn't mean it's bad. The date is a general idea for when it *might* go bad. Maybe my space suit is set to warn me early as a precautionary measure. Maybe there's still twenty minutes, or thirty minutes, or an hour left of oxygen—enough time for us to think of something else. I close my eyes again.

523... 522... 521...

My radio crackles and I hear Alé say, "Okay, Eta. He's closing the inner hatch now." I nod in reply. I know he can't see me do this, but my voice isn't working now. This is the part that worries me the most. If Nix can't get the door closed, I won't be getting in. At least, not through this airlock.

The three airlock hatches are all the same. The door Nix must close is a round, aluminum door with pressure seals along the edge. A gearbox sits in the middle of the door, just under the window. It opens and closes the six latches that secure the hatch. There's a big handle on the gearbox too. If the electrical components of the box don't work, you can manually open the latches by cranking the handle counterclockwise. Then, once it's closed, the Briefing Node can be pressurized either by a command from the central computer or by manual valves inside the Node.

I watch Nix, but he still hasn't done anything. He's just staring at me.

"Umm..." I mumble, trying to find the words to tell Alé that Nix isn't moving, but before I can say anything, Nix moves. He grabs the handhold on the wall to his right and turns himself around so he's facing the door. Then he pulls the inner door closed. I can see the latches click into place as he works the controls to the gearbox. He turns around and puts one of his thumbs up in the air to let me know that all is okay. I release a long sigh of relief and say, "Alé, he's got the door closed. Do you confirm?"

A moment later, Alé says, "Yes, we confirm. The door is closed and latched. We're running pressure tests now. Should only be a few more seconds, then we'll have him depressurize the Briefing Node."

I close my eyes again and smile, grateful I'm not facing this situation alone. Grateful that Nix is there and that he has the ability to help me. Grateful that Alé is leading me through this.

Alé comes back on the radio. "We're going to have Nix depressurize the Briefing Node now. Stay away from the hatch, just in case." He still sounds nervous.

"Okay," I say. I suppose they want me to stay as far away from the Briefing Node as I can in case the hatches give way and the whole station depressurizes, blowing me and my atmosphere out into space. Frankly, if this happens, there won't be anything left to save me. But I oblige. "I'll hook onto the handholds on the starboard side of the outer hatch. Will that work?"

"Perfect," he says. "Hold tight. He's working on it now."

Within a few seconds of reaching the handholds and hooking on with my tether, the carbon dioxide alarm inside the suits starts to sound too. It's a long, mournful tone, unlike the oxygen alarm's quick beep. It's interesting how different they are.

I close my eyes again and resume counting, trying to take my mind off the suit alarms.

520... 519... 518...

When I get down to 500, I decide that I have to say something. "Alé, what's going on? Why isn't he through yet?"

"He's working on it," Alé says in a short, clipped voice.

"What's the issue?" I ask, biting my lip.

"There's no issue," he says with no elaboration.

A few more seconds tick by and Nix pops his head out of the airlock. I've never been so happy to see Iron Man in my life.

"I'm here. Did you miss me?" he says.

"Not at all!" A laugh of pure relief escapes me. I unhook my tether from the handholds and we head into the Briefing Node together. I turn to close the middle hatch and the latches click into place without issue. Then I open the manual valves to start pressurizing the room with atmosphere. Within a few seconds, I feel the rush of the atmosphere filling the room. After several minutes, the rush subsides and finally stops. I don't ask Alé for an update on the atmosphere. I'm tired of hearing these alarms buzzing inside my helmet. I reach up and snap the helmet locking mechanism open. There's a hiss as the two atmospheres, the one in my helmet and the one in the airlock, meet for the first time. I breathe in and the air smells good. Much better than the air in the space suit.

"How do you feel, Eta?" asks Nix.

"I'm good, Nix," I say. "Feeling great."

And it's true. I do feel great. The spacewalks are in my past. My rescue ship is ready to go. In two days, I'm traveling to the surface. I'm going home to meet my future.

Part IV

Chapter 42

"How are you feeling this morning?" Tess asked.

"Fine," Eta said, her voice heavy.

"Just fine? Care to elaborate?"

"Well," Eta said, pausing for a moment, "I'm feeling about as good as anyone would, considering I'm about to leave my old space station in an old spaceship that I basically duct-taped together."

Tess sighed. Over the last two days, Eta had become increasingly irritated with Tess's questioning and the behavior puzzled Tess. So far, the plans to bring the Soyuz down were going well. No issues had popped up and all systems were working as they should. Tess wasn't sure why Eta was so irritable about it, but then again, there were plenty of things that she didn't understand about Eta.

"So, what's on your mind? Tell me," Tess said.

"Nothing really. I told you, I'm fine." The response was short, precise, and completely inaccurate. Tess was sure of it.

"Look," Tess said, shifting forward in her seat so she could concentrate better on her words. "I don't understand what you're going through, I get that. Nobody does. But I'm *trying* to understand it so I can help you get through this. The more you help me, the more I can help you."

Eta paused. It was the type of pause she took often as she measured her words carefully. "I feel sort of... blank. I don't know. It's not easy to describe. Have you ever mixed paint?"

"Have *you* ever mixed paint?" Tess asked quickly. Then she backtracked. She didn't want to hurt Eta by reminding her of all the life experiences she hadn't had. "I'm sorry, Eta. I just mean that it's an interesting metaphor and I'm curious to hear more."

"Actually," Eta said, "I have mixed paint. We had art supplies on board. The paint is long gone, but when I was young, I painted lots of little pictures for my mother."

"Huh," Tess said, jotting down a note on an open tile in her holo-screen. She learned new and interesting things about Eta every day. The fact she had access to art supplies during her childhood was a great indicator of how her personality developed.

"Anyway," Eta continued, "when you mix paint, you get different colors, right? Like blue and red make purple. Yellow and red make orange. And there are a handful of primary paint colors that all other colors derive from. Well, I feel like there are a certain number of emotions you can feel. Basic ones. Like fear, anger, happiness, sadness. Kind of like that movie... what was it?"

Eta paused, likely working it out in her head, trying to come up with the missing pieces of information. Tess waited, her index finger hovering over her screen, ready to make notes.

After a few seconds, Eta snapped her fingers and it was loud enough for Tess to hear over the comm link. "*Inside Out*," Eta said.

"Inside out? That's how you feel?" Tess asked, confused.

"No, I don't *feel* inside out. *Inside Out* is a movie. It's old, but I've watched it here in the archives before. It's an animated movie about the thoughts inside a girl's brain. Did you ever see it?"

"No, I've never even heard of it. *Inside Out* you called it? I'll have to check that out." She jotted down a note in her memo tile: Find *Inside Out*.

"It's actually a really good movie," Eta said, "It's about the emotions going on inside a girl's brain. There are... let me think... five of them: joy, sadness, anger, fear, and disgust. They each take their turns controlling the girl's thoughts and actions. Of course, there are a lot more emotions than those five, but the premise of the story is that those five make up the "primary" emotions and other emotions are based on them. So, my point is, anything we feel is really just a concoction of these basic emotions. Does that make sense?"

Tess cocked her head to the side, thinking about the idea. "That's actually a great way to look at it," she said after a few seconds.

"Yeah," Eta said. "It's like when you feel excited, it's a mix of fear and happiness, or when you feel dread, it's a mixture of fear and sadness."

"Okay, so, when you're lonely, you might be mixing fear, sadness, and even anger," Tess added, nodding. "Right?"

"Yeah, exactly. So, when I say I feel "blank," it's like I mixed all five of those primary emotions up in one bucket, like paint. When you mix all the paint colors up, you get gray, or brown, or something really dull. That's what I mean. I can't pick any one or two emotions out. It's just... dull."

Tess couldn't have been more pleased with the discussion and a wide smile planted itself on her face. "That makes perfect sense, Eta," she said. "But maybe it's not the whole situation we need to look at. Maybe you'd have a better idea of how you feel if we broke down the experience into small parts."

"Well... that's fine. But I really don't understand why you need to know this," Eta said, genuinely puzzled and slightly annoyed by this line of questioning. She didn't understand why Tess, or anybody for that matter, cared about how she felt. It wasn't something that she considered even remotely important.

"Because, Eta," Tess said, "I'm researching how such a traumatic and unprecedented event affects emotions and I plan to publish this research so that, hopefully, it can help others live through similar situations in the future. If I'm going to do my research properly, I need you to cooperate and let me into your head."

Again, there was no answer from Eta, so Tess continued, "Okay, then let's go through the technicalities of what's coming and you let me know your thoughts about them. How about that? It might be easier that way."

"Whatever you think," Eta said.

Tess straightened her dress and sat in the desk chair, pulling the holo-screen closer to her so she could take notes. "Let's start with the actual flight plan," she said. "How are you feeling about it? You've been a big part of the planning and preparation. What do you think of it so far?"

"It's something new, which is kind of exciting. I'll get to see the Delta in a way I've never seen it before. I have to admit, I am excited to see Earth as it comes closer and closer to me."

"Are you scared?" Tess asked.

"No," Eta said quickly, then backtracked. "Well, yes and no. I am scared. I can tell that because of the tightness in my chest whenever I work on something in the Soyuz. But it's not the blatant kind of fear, like when I was stuck outside the station and the hatch wouldn't close. This fear is further away. You see, to me, it's all just mechanics. The person who's willing to do the work and fix the most problems wins. That's how I've always looked at life up here. As long as I have the ability to troubleshoot, I get to live."

Tess jotted down a few more notes. "Okay, so now what about the surface. How do you feel about the surface?"

"You mean like the ground?" Eta asked, confused.

"Well, yeah, the ground. But, more specifically, the Earth itself. How do you feel about the oceans, the fields, the mountains, the valleys? What do you feel when you think about getting to see those things?"

"Well, I have seen those things," Eta reminded her. "But I understand your question. What will it be like to see them up close and finally know what they smell like, and what they sound like, and how they feel?" She paused for a moment. "It's exciting, but I haven't really thought about it too much yet. There's so much work to be done first."

"Okay, fair enough," Tess said. "What about the people?"

"The people?" Eta asked.

"Yeah, the people. How do you feel about meeting new people?"

"I-I-I don't know," Eta stammered. She took a deep breath like she might continue but released it without saying anything more.

After a moment, Tess tried a different angle. "What about Alé?" she asked. "He was the first person you talked to and he's been your main contact person. What are your feelings about finally getting to see him in person?"

Again, there was silence. Tess could hear Eta breathing on the other end of the comm link—short, nervous breaths. "I'm scared to death of meeting Alé," she finally said.

Tess nodded and made a note about social anxiety in her memo tile. "You're scared of meeting him, specifically? Or other people too?"

"I'm scared of all of it," Eta said. "I've never met anyone before. What if they don't like me? What if I fall short of everyone's expectations? What if I die trying to reach them and they're disappointed because I didn't make it to them alive?"

"You know, Eta," Tess said, bringing a motherly tone into her voice. "It's perfectly normal to be scared of meeting new people. In fact, it's one of the most normal things I've heard you say since I've been interviewing you."

"Really?" Eta asked. "That's really the most normal thing about me?"

Tess let out a chuckle and said, "Sure is. You'd be surprised how common social anxiety is. You've got a heavy case of it, I'll admit that. But it's not abnormal at all. You know something else?"

"What?" Eta asked.

"You won't disappoint *anyone*. No matter what you do. So, if it helps you get into the right mindset, put those fears aside. You've got a long day and a lot of work coming up. Don't worry about meeting new people," Tess repeated. "Can you do that for me?"

"Okay, I can do that." The slight quiver in her voice smoothed out and she took a big breath over the comm link.

"Good!" Tess said. "My time is up with you today. Tomorrow I'll be there to greet you in person after you land. I want you to get some good sleep tonight, so put down your worries, okay?"

"Yes," Eta said. "No worries for me tonight."

Chapter 43

It's finally here. The last night.

This is the last night I will spend here. Alé was not on the comm link today. They said he's resting for tomorrow, but I really wish I could have talked with him, just to hear his voice and know what I'm doing is the right thing.

Of course, I do know it's the right thing. If I don't leave tomorrow, I'll die up here. But it's not dying that scares me. It's the thought that I might never know what it's like to be on the surface that scares me most.

I've been getting antsy about it, knowing the day is so close. Today, I took a little walk through one of my tuber beds to cement what it feels like in my mind. I closed my eyes and pushed my toes into the dirt and tried to imagine I was there, on the surface, doing the same thing. The dirt felt crumbly and moist, almost like chopped up sunflower seeds made into a meal. The action of working my feet into the soil produced a fresh smell. It's a smell I always experience when I'm working with the soil in the garden, but I've never paid attention to it before now. I wonder if that smell is real or if it's only found here at the station. Does the dirt on the surface smell the same way? I'll never know if I don't leave.

Does the planet really want me? Do I belong there? I rotate around the surface, privy to the best views of our planet known to humankind, but I'm not really part of it. I was never there. I'm an outsider. I belong to my own orbit.

These are some of the questions that have popped into my mind lately. Deep, I know. I normally don't think too much into this type of stuff, but recently, I can't help myself. After I took my walk through the tuber bed, I packed a little science vial of soil from the garden and tucked it into the pocket of my spacesuit. I didn't tell NASA about it. They wouldn't have approved. But I needed to bring something back with me. My garden is my greatest accomplishment, and the thought of my plants burning up in the atmosphere makes my heart squeeze in on itself, turning it into a tiny, sour lump. It hurts.

Again, I wish I could have spoken to Alé before bedtime. They had me working all day on preparing the Soyuz and going over the flight plan. They want Nix to ride with me so they can study him. I'm happy with that decision. I'll have my oldest and dearest friend with me on the journey into the atmosphere.

For weeks I've worked and worked and worked, and now, there's nothing left to do. At 1900 GMT, they told me to get my rest and spend the rest of the night doing as I pleased.

I can't say I'm happy about that. I don't know what to do with myself. Maybe I should spend this time thinking about all the things I hate about this station. Maybe that will make me feel better about leaving it. So, that's what I'm doing now. I'm sitting at the table in the kitchen, dictating my final thoughts about the Delta on the small holo-screen in front of me. I'm taking this one with me. It's got my personal journal entries on it and I didn't feel like uploading that stuff for all of NASA to read.

Why is the Delta so miserable?

Well, there's the toilet. How many times can one person fix a space station toilet? The correct answer is 593 times. I *hate* having to fix that damn toilet. I'm hoping that the toilets on the Earth aren't so silly. They don't have suction mechanisms, or storage tanks, or tiny little valves that can get clogged and easily broken. When the toilet breaks on Earth, you can probably find another toilet, or you can hire someone else to fix it for you. That will be nice!

Another reason this place is miserable is because Nu is here. I miss her so much it hurts, and I don't know Nu anywhere else. If the Delta is no more, then she will be gone forever. Everything she touched or researched or worked on will all roll back into the atmosphere as rubble. There are times when I can actually *feel* her here with me, like she's part of the station. She loved this place, and she taught me how to run it and fix it and love it too because there was no other option.

That's what I loved most about her. She knew what we had to do to stay alive. Even when I was little and I wailed about how much I hated that we couldn't run through the poppy fields like Dorothy and the Tin Man, she kept me calm and showed me what there was to love about it.

I miss her. I don't want to leave the memories of her. I can't bear it. But maybe if I leave, I can move on and finally lay her to rest. I have to remember, after all, that Nu wasn't always on the Delta. There was a time in her life when she was on the surface like every other human. I want that for myself.

Perhaps the most important reason I hate this place is because Alé isn't here. He's been my rock through the last few months. I can't imagine a life where I never get to meet him in person. I picture him in my mind and it brings me shivers of joy and tingles of excitement. I think about his smile, his hair, his mouth, his nose, his arms, his chest. Wait... what was I saying?

Chapter 44

"Would you like me to make you some eggs for breakfast, Eta?" Nix asks the next morning.

We aren't in the kitchen. We're floating in the VP, looking down on the surface. It's almost 1100 GMT, which means it's about 0700 in Baltimore. I smile at Nix's joke about the eggs. It's a lame joke, but he doesn't know any better. He's a victim of his programming.

"Oh Nix, your eggs are very good, but I'll pass today," I say. Of course, we've never had eggs here. And if we did, Nix couldn't have made them himself even if he wanted to. "How much longer do we have Nix?"

"Ten minutes and thirty-two seconds," he replies.

"Thanks."

The Earth is displayed below, creeping along under the station as if being pushed by a tiny engine at a snail's pace. There's a huge hurricane over the Pacific, right in the middle of my view.

Fortunately, I'm supposed to land in New Mexico, a good way from it, but I shake my head as I look at it. That would be my luck, to plop down right in the middle of the Pacific. In the middle of nowhere. In the middle of a hurricane.

I close my eyes and force myself to smile again. It's leaving day. I've been waiting for this day for the last six weeks. Well, actually for the last eighteen years and six weeks. It's not easy to describe what it feels like to leave home, knowing you'll never come back. It's almost heartbreaking.

I had my heart broken once, when Nu died, and I'm not excited to go through it again. This old station is going to burn up in the atmosphere in about four days, according to NASA's calculations. We shaved it close, but the NASA guys claim that I'm ready to go. Everything is prepped, fueled, juiced, hyped, and recorded. I've run simulations, safety drills, and escape scenarios. They say we're ready, but I don't feel ready.

I open my eyes again and glance back down at the surface. The station has moved past the hurricane and now I can see the West Coast of the United States below me. It's so much more comforting to look out over that vast, sprawling swath of land instead of the cool, blue ocean, and its frothy storm. Land. That's where I'm supposed to be. That beautiful, brown and green landscape looks warm and inviting.

"Nix," I say, "let's get out of here."

"Yes ma'am," he says in a voice calm as ever.

I pull myself close to the largest window in the center of the VP. It's scuffed and scratched with age and wear, and I press my hands against it. Then I press my lips against it. I will never see this view again. I will never be the girl up in the space station again. At that moment, I know, deep down, that's exactly what I want.

I push myself away from the window, grab Nix by his hand, and pull him through the VP toward the waiting Soyuz.

"Let's go home," I say.

Chapter 45

At 4:37 a.m., Alé jumped straight up in his bed as his alarm buzzed on the bedside table next to his ear. He had been in the middle of a deep dream, and the alarm, set for 4:30 a.m., had been going off for seven minutes without even a flicker of wakefulness reaching his brain.

What he was dreaming about, he couldn't remember. But he knew Eta was there in his dream. Sweat beads crawled down his neck and onto his bare back. He was breathing hard, almost panting. This wasn't a good dream, he realized, and it didn't surprise him because this was a common theme lately. The closer they got to sending Eta on her voyage home, the more desperate his dreaming mind became, pulling up all sorts of absurd problems and mishaps: blown gaskets, torn belts, critical alarms, hull breaches. It seemed as though his dreaming mind was testing his resolve, preparing him for some unfortunate incident yet to come.

"Something's wrong," he muttered to himself in a whisper.

The alarm continued to buzz on the nightstand for a few seconds before he came back to reality. He rubbed his eyes, grabbed the alarm, and hit the snooze button before dropping his head back down on the pillow. He flung the sheets off him to bring some fresh air to his clammy skin. He needed a shower. Slowly, he rolled over the edge of the bed and landed on his feet, steadying himself and stretching his arms up over his head, pulling the stiffness out of his body.

Without another thought about the dream, he walked toward the bathroom door.

***

Later that morning, Alé switched on the comm link to the Soyuz. With static crackling in his ear, Alé said, "Good morning, Eta. How are things on board the Soyuz? Did you get some good rest last night? Or were you up all night dreaming about me?"

"Great," she said. "Things are great on the Soyuz. And yes, I did actually get a decent night of sleep, although, I don't believe you showed up anywhere in my dreams. I could be wrong about that though. You never know."

Alé laughed and a big smile spread across his face. Secretly, his heart fluttered and the blood warmed in his veins. "Well, let's get this thing moving, shall we? Did you go through all the prechecks last night? From the readouts I have, everything looks green."

"Yep, it's all done."

"How are you feeling?" he asked. He didn't have any idea what *he* would do in the same situation, but he was pretty sure he wouldn't handle it nearly as well as she had.

"I'm fine." Her voice sounded choked and short.

He knew right away that this wasn't the case, but he decided not to push the issue. She had her own ways of dealing with things and he'd become accustomed to her attitude twists. "All right," he said, "since we're all in a brilliant mood this fine morning, let's get that hatch closed."

As he ran through the hatch-closing procedures with her, the strange feeling he'd had when he woke from that dream struck him again. The feeling that something wasn't right.

"Hold on one second," he told her as he pulled up a different tile on his holo-screen. The feeling wasn't something he could have described even if he'd wanted to. It was the sort of feeling you get right before a big drop of spaghetti sauce falls on your white shirt. It happens in slow motion and you do your best to get out of the way but you can't move quite fast enough to avoid it. And then SPLAT...

Just as Alé pulled up the tile he was looking for, the proximity alarms started sounding.

Chapter 46

"Whoa!" I say as the spacecraft shifts around me in sudden, jerking movements. Alarms start to buzz on the computers all around me, first on the screen that's still connected to the main Delta computer, and then on the Soyuz computers too. I pull up the alarm on a screen tile and lean in to read what's going on.

Something has hit the station. This happens fairly regularly, but I've never felt an impact this close before—or one this large. In that instance, I felt the shudder as the station walls absorbed the impact.

It's funny how an impact in space reverberates. The force moves like a wave through the metal. The wave moves fast, so you don't really see it, but it *seems* like it's in slow motion when you're inside listening to the metal bend and change. An impact kicks up a smell too, like something burning in a sauté pan. It's the smell of the vacuum, which is worrisome because the smell of vacuum is not a good thing to have when you're *inside* a pressurized spacecraft. That's definitely what's happened here because I can smell it now.

"Nix, what do you think?" I ask him. Nix is linked wirelessly to the station computers and he has access to the data too.

"There must have been an impact," he says, as if he's adding some serious analysis to the conversation.

I nod at him. "Well, the air isn't rushing out of this place. Let's get out of the Soyuz and see what happened."

I pull myself through the hatch into the Docking Module just in time to feel the second impact. And then the third. Again, the walls shudder as the impact waves move through the interior panels and I can see that the Docking Module and the Service Module are moving around independently of each other, putting a lot of torque on the tunnel between them.

"Shit," I say, pushing myself along the tunnel toward the Service Module, Nix close behind me.

"Well, there's no cause for profanity," Nix says. "Imagine what your mother would think." He's right. Nu hated profanity. I immediately regret the slip.

Once I get into the Service Module, I pull up the primary holo-screen bank and run a full ship scan, pulling up separate tiles to give the status of each of the modules and all of the primary life-support systems.

"Shouldn't you confer with NASA?" Nix asks.

"Oh, you're right!" I say. I totally forgot that the comm link I had in my ear inside the Soyuz was specific to that spacecraft only. When I yanked it out of my ear to go back into the Delta, I didn't transfer the feed to the Delta comm system. I pull up another tile on the screen to configure the bud in my ear and almost immediately I hear Alé's voice practically screaming from the other end.

"...space debris! The sensors are going wild. Eta! Where are you?"

"Did you miss me?" I ask him, knowing that he's probably not in the mood for jokes.

But surprisingly, he doesn't sound angry when he replies, "Oh, Eta. You scared me nearly half to death! I mean really, that was scary. We got all these system alarms and there were these loud noises... and you disappeared! I'm just..." He pauses and a little smile cracks my lips when I hear his concern. "I'm just glad to hear your voice. Give me a second. I'll go around the room here and get some answers."

I continue to check the systems on my screen and after about ten minutes of back and forth and system readouts, we all agree there were three pieces of debris, each about twenty-five centimeters in diameter that struck the Docking Module, just above where the Soyuz was docked. Since the engines are toast, moving the Delta to avoid debris hasn't been an option. Because of this, nobody was actually monitoring for larger pieces of debris, or they would have caught these little space rocks coming in for a head-on collision.

After a few more minutes of checking the systems, they tell me that it's okay to get back into the Soyuz, which wasn't hit, thank goodness. Nix and I load back up into the Soyuz and start turning things on again where we left off the first time.

Hopefully nothing more will go wrong...

Chapter 47

Alé hiked his legs up on the desk in his office and loosened the knot on his tie. He'd contemplated wearing jeans today, but opted instead to wear a sleek blue tie and matching tailored jacket. It was appropriate to dress professionally today, he thought, considering the magnitude of what they were about to do.

Eta was in the middle of a long string of commands to get the Soyuz systems ready for hatch closing, giving Alé about ten minutes of downtime before they actually began closing up the hatch and detaching from the Delta. Although he thought about sticking around the command center, he wanted to catch his breath alone for a few minutes. He was trying to get a grip on his frazzled nerves.

Luck hadn't been on their side. The debris hits couldn't have come at a worse time. They'd had to reset their time line, losing about an hour, to make sure there were no structural damages to the Soyuz. A day earlier, two of the engineers detected a malfunction in the station's gyroscopes. The gyroscopes, or gyros, as they called them, were responsible for minor orientation movements of the station. They played a more critical role in slowing the drag on the station since the engine quit working. The gyro malfunction had caused a swift decline in altitude, even sharper than they'd anticipated, before they could get the gyros working properly again. That would have been a big problem if they weren't prepared to leave today.

Because of this, the Soyuz undocking had to go perfectly. They couldn't afford to wait another day. The station was on a collision course for the atmosphere and there was no way Eta would survive if it broke apart with her on it.

As much as he tried to relax and purge his mind of thoughts about the station, that last thought, the thought of Eta burning up in the atmosphere, made him double over in his seat. He dropped his head between his knees in an effort to keep his insides on the inside and took five sharp, deep breaths. When his heart rate slowed and his stomach settled, he stood and left the room without bothering to close the door behind him.

***

"What happened?" Alé asked, his face twisted in a look of total disbelief.

Tess stood behind Yuri's seat in the conference room, the tip of her index finger planted solidly in her mouth. Yuri spoke swift Russian into his phone. He was having a heated discussion with one of his counterparts back in Moscow. Alé could tell by the mad frenzy in the room that his short break had not been uneventful for the control staff.

Tess turned to him, her face tense and her eyes narrowed. "The latches won't release," she said. "They had Eta close the inner hatch on the station from the outside, then she closed the Soyuz hatch. But now, the computer detects a low seal quality and it won't release the hooks. It's a safety precaution to keep the station and the departing ship safe from depressurization during undocking."

"Yuri," Alé began, but he stopped speaking when Yuri lifted his index finger to indicate he was not done with his phone conversation. Alé flushed with anger and clenched his jaw but waited for the gruff Russian to finish.

After another minute, Yuri hung up and turned to Alé. "It must have something to do with the alignment of the ship. The debris strikes moved things around and compromised the connection between the two ships."

"What are the options?" Alé asked.

"That's what I'm finding out," Yuri said. "I talked with a fellow Soyuz expert in Moscow and they're sending me the plans for the latch-hook system. I'll find out more in a few minutes."

Alé turned to Tess. "Does she know what's going on?"

Tess nodded. "She's the one who told us first. She's going to troubleshoot it herself and see if she can figure it out. Sounds like we may need to bypass the computer on this one and open the latches manually."

"Manually?" Alé asked.

"Yes, manually." With a sharp, sideways smile, she added, "She plans to kick it."

"Oh, great." Alé rolled his eyes. "That's all we need—her kicking something loose and losing pressure in both ships." He plopped down in his seat and put his earpiece in.

"Eta, are you there?" he asked.

"Mentally or physically? You know the answer to where I am physically, but mentally, I'm on a beach somewhere watching the waves settle into the sand."

"Well, I'm glad to see your sense of humor is holding up," he said, smiling at the sarcasm. "Let's get to work on troubleshooting this problem."

Chapter 48

"Does that make sense? Eta? Are you still there?" Yuri's been speaking for several minutes and I've heard everything he said, but I haven't exactly been paying attention to him. He lost me after he said, "and the robot stays behind."

The plan they've come up with calls for Nix to remain on the Delta. The low seal quality alarm affects the Delta's seal, not the Soyuz. In a normal situation, if the Soyuz left with a poor seal on the Delta side, then the entire ship could decompress, which is why the computer won't allow the hooks to release the Soyuz. Nix will manually release the hooks and send the Soyuz on its way. NASA figures that the seal quality is good enough to get the Soyuz away from the Delta before any decompression happens. Once I'm at a safe distance in the Soyuz, it doesn't matter what happens with the Delta's pressure. And I'll be leaving Nix behind.

The robot stays behind. That's what Yuri had said.

The robot. *My robot.*

They want me to leave Nix behind. I've had one friend my entire life and now they want me to leave him behind. My heart flutters with a newfound anxiety. When we first decided to leave in the Soyuz, I assumed that Nix wouldn't make the trip. I had made peace with that. But then we brainstormed all the ways he could be useful on the ride back, and the NASA guys wanted to have a good look at him, so they decided he would come too.

For the last few weeks, I've wrapped my mind around the idea that I won't be alone on this journey. Nix is supposed to be there with me. He has jobs to do on board. He's in charge of pushing buttons that I can't reach. He's *supposed* to go with me! How can they think about leaving him here?

The breath I've been holding in my lungs finally leaves my mouth in one loud push. I suck in another immediately and realize I've squeezed my eyes shut and Yuri is still going on inside my ear.

"Are you there?" he's saying, "I understand this decision disrupts the flight plan, but it's the only way I see…"

"The *only* way?" I interrupt, my voice only a whisper. "The only way we can get this thing backed out of here is to leave Nix behind? Can't you think of something else?"

He pauses, then says, "Eta, I see how this might be difficult for you. Please remember that Nix is only a robot. A machine. *You* are the most important part of this mission and your station is slipping into the atmosphere at an unprecedented…"

I reach up and slip the earbud out of my ear. I don't want to hear it. I *can't* leave Nix behind. He's the only thing I have left. My eyes swell with tears. I shut them tight and use the back of my hand to wipe away the droplets that leaked out. I open my eyes again and look over to my left.

Nix sits beside me. He's smiling like Iron Man.

***

I've moved down to the G and am sitting at the kitchen table, staring at the floor. I know they're waiting for me. The window to leave has come and gone, but I haven't talked to them in over ten minutes. I can't leave Nix behind. I just *can't*. If I don't have Nix, I'll be totally alone during this descent. I'm not handling this idea well, which is why I came in here. I couldn't think inside the Soyuz with Nix sitting right there next to me. So, I came back to the kitchen where I could look at my garden one final time and try to come to terms with this.

The station alarm rings for the thirty-third time. I've been counting. It is Mission Control calling me. It's the thirty-third alarm that finally shakes my mind loose. I stand up and make my way to the ladder leading out of the G.

My body shakes with fear. I'll be totally alone. I won't even have a radio link for the scariest part of the trip. Twice, as I climb higher and the gravity lightens, I have to stop and breath, counting numbers in my head to calm me down. I make it up eventually and feel the familiar nausea of lost gravity. This might be the last time I feel that.

I pull myself through the Service Module and the Docking Module and down into the Soyuz for the last time. Then I place the little earbud back into my ear. "This is Eta. I'm sorry I disappeared, but I had to collect myself."

I expect to hear Yuri's husky voice on the other end, but it's not Yuri who greets me. Alé's smooth, rounded voice comes over the comm link.

"I'm glad you're back with us, Eta," he says, sounding much calmer than I would have expected considering I have been missing for the last ten minutes. "What can I do to help make this easier?"

"Alé," I say, the word catching in my throat. His voice is so beautiful, it brings more tears to my eyes. I close them and wipe the tears away. "I'm okay. It's just... It's just so terrifying. I'll be alone." I have to stop and the sobs come to me in thick, heavy waves emanating from my stomach.

"I can't imagine how scary this is for you," Alé says, "but I also can't tell you how important you are to all of us down here. You are the reason we're here, Eta. You. We... I want to bring you to the surface so much, it's almost painful." He stops. I can actually hear the pain in his voice. He sounds desperate, like he thinks I've given up on him.

"You know," he continues, "when my father died, I didn't leave my room for four months. Did I ever tell you about that?"

I shake my head. I know he can't see it, but it's all I can muster.

"I get it," he says. "It hurts to leave something behind for good. That's why I stayed in my room. For some reason, I thought if I left my room or the house or got on with my life, I would be leaving his memory behind. I felt like I was betraying him. If I could only bask in the pain and fear, he would still have a place in my heart. Does that make sense?"

I nod again. He must be able to sense my movement because he continues. "You know what really got me to move on?"

This grabs my interest and I finally get my voice back. "What?" I ask in a whisper.

"My mother sold our house," he says. This catches me off guard. I was expecting some deep, therapeutic reason, not something as practical as a real estate transaction. "I was seventeen at that time and was in danger of losing my high school diploma. But when she decided to sell the house, I had no choice. I had to move on. Sometimes, it's not about choice, Eta. Sometimes, it's about necessity."

My tears have stopped and the realization hits me with the force of a rocket. Hanging on to this old space station won't bring Nu back. It won't give me a normal childhood. It won't keep me safe as I go through life. Having Nix with me is only a crutch to ease me into a brand new and totally terrifying life. I can't live in this station forever. I have to get over that idea.

I love Nix as if he's a real person, but I must remember, he's not a real person. There *is* a real person waiting for me on the surface, a few hundred kilometers below where I now float. I must say goodbye to my dear companion because Nu would want me to, because I am more than simply a passenger on this space station, and because Alé is waiting for me.

"Thank you for that, Alé," I say. "I have one question for you before we go. Is that true? Or did you make that up to get me moving?"

He laughs. "That one was true. But you're right about one thing—I do want you to get moving before it's too late. I want to see you, Eta. I want to know you. I feel like a part of me is up there with you, and I don't want to see a part of my soul burn up in the atmosphere. Understood?"

"Understood," I say.

***

Nix stares at me, smiling like he always does. I tell him about the plan. He will stay on the Delta. We'll reseal everything and make sure the pressure on the Soyuz looks good. Nix will manually dismantle the inner clips that hold the Soyuz in place.

He can do that using a screwdriver tool that attaches to one of his hands. It's not even that difficult. This function was built into the design so that crew members still inside the station could release a Soyuz manually if they needed to. I'm lucky I have Nix here, or there would be no way to release the Soyuz. Thanks, Nu.

After I fill him in, he speaks directly to Mission Control and they make sure he's remotely connected to their systems so they can guide him through the process. Now, it's time for me to get back into the Soyuz.

He and I float next to each other in the Docking Module. He's holding onto a handrail above his head so it looks like he's doing a one-handed pull-up.

"Nix," I say, "I guess this is goodbye."

"Yes, it seems so," he answers. "I hope you have a lovely descent. It's supposed to be sunny in New Mexico this afternoon."

I chuckle. He's been scanning the weather reports sent up by Mission Control.

"I wish," I say, pausing to find the right words, "I wish I could bring you with me, Nix. You know that, right?"

"Of course, I do," he says. "I would gladly come with you if I could, but I'm also not the kind of robot who lies down on the job. You need me here to get the job done for you and that's what I plan to do."

"You're my best friend. You really are, Iron Man."

"Oh, don't make me blush!" he says as the lights in his cheeks flare on to simulate blushing. He's good at creating emotions with the few lighting and facial features he has. "Well now, you've got to get going. Time is ticking." He points to his chest where his control panel clock sits.

"Yeah." I nod, grab his little white hand, and squeeze it. "Take it easy, Nix."

"You too, Eta."

I climb into the Soyuz and start to close the hatch behind me. I see him watching me as I do this and before it's fully closed, he gives me a slight nod and one final smile.

Chapter 49

NIX Unit 3348 Service Log Entry #664532

Date: 22.5.88

Time: 11:52:01 GMT

Internal Note: The hatch to Soyuz MV-49 is now closed and locked on Eta's end. My job is to pry the hooks loose to allow it to exit from docking port 3 of the Delta Station Docking Module.

Incoming Comm Link: "Nix, are you there? It's Alé."

Response: "Yes, Mr. Alé. I am all ears."

Incoming Comm Link: "All ears, huh? How do you manage that? I thought you didn't have ears."

Response: "You've got me there. I'm all external noise detection systems, then." (Slight laugh included in response to his obvious joke.)

Incoming Comm Link: "Good to hear. It's time to get to work on those latches."

Response: "Yes. I didn't want to mention it while Eta was still here, but I see that the station trajectory has taken a turn. Estimated time to reentry dropped with the last debris strike from 312 hours to .495 hours. Do not fret, I'm working on the latches now."

Incoming Comm Link: "You caught that, huh? Yeah, we noticed as well. The strike must have given her a little nudge."

Response: "A little nudge? I'd say that qualifies as a big nudge, don't you think?"

Incoming Comm Link: "Right... How are the latches coming along?"

Response: "I've already dismantled three of them. Six more to go."

Incoming Comm Link: "Good. Great news."

Response: "While I have you on the line, Alé, I am curious. Do you plan to continue on with the plan to move the Soyuz into a parking orbit that's lower than the Delta? If at all possible, I would advise against that. You certainly don't want Eta passing through station debris. I would imagine a higher orbit would protect against that until the station has safely passed into the atmosphere and disintegrated."

Incoming Comm Link: "We've got the engineers working the numbers, but it looks like we don't have a choice. If we don't bring her back now, as soon as possible, it could be days before the atmosphere is safe for her to reenter. The lower orbit puts her on the fast track. Although, she will have to deal with a ballistic reentry because of the timing, that's a risk I'd rather take. I don't want to test the systems of that old Soyuz for too long up there."

Response: "Understood. I agree with your reasoning. Three more latches to go."

Internal Note: I continue to unscrew the latches using the L47 U-bolt driver. So far, they are coming off smoothly, some friction, but not too bad considering how long they have been suspended in orbit. I mentioned to Alé that I agree with his plan, but I don't entirely. For the record of the station log, I'll explain why.

There are two orbital options when undocking a Soyuz from the Delta Station. One is to bring the vessel to a safe distance of twenty meters away from the station before firing the main thrusters to move the Soyuz down to about forty kilometers below the Delta.

The second option does essentially the opposite. It moves the Soyuz above the Delta. This is done to prevent the two spacecraft from colliding in orbit. Both options are viable when the Delta is in a stable orbit. However, the Delta is not in a stable position in the atmosphere at this time.

Putting the Soyuz into a lower parking orbit puts Eta at much greater risk to be struck by debris from the station as it slows down and breaks up in the atmosphere. By my calculations, it's slowing at a rate of 2.1 m/sec and that's increasing exponentially the thicker the atmosphere gets. The station is, of course, much larger than the Soyuz. So, by the laws of physics, it experiences more drag and therefore slows at a much quicker pace. As I see it, the safe distance to which she would need to drop in order to avoid collision with the Delta is three hundred kilometers, which isn't a possibility at this point.

I see Alé's point that bringing her to a higher orbit simply delays her entrance and still puts her at risk of collision with station debris when she finally does reenter. But I do not know that the lower orbit is the best option at this time. I need to do more calculations to know for sure. For now, I will keep this information to myself while I run the numbers again.

Response (cont.): "All latches are released. The Soyuz is ready to undock."

Chapter 50

"The robot has a point," Yuri said, before taking a long swig from the NASA-decaled coffee mug in his hand. "I've been running the numbers and the Delta is dropping much quicker than we thought it would. Even faster than she was this morning before the debris strike."

"Well, that's fine," Alé responded, pacing a few meters in front of where Yuri sat at his desk along the outer wall of the Mission Control conference room, "But she can't live up there in a nineteen-year-old Soyuz for three days while the wreckage clears. It's not an option."

"Da. You have a good point," Yuri said. "But I've got another idea."

Alé paused for a moment. "What's that?"

"We've been looking at bringing her orbit either below the station or above it, right?" Yuri said.

"Yeah, that's right," Alé replied.

"Well, what if we brought them in at the same time?" Yuri tipped his mug all the way back in his mouth to grab every last bit of the liquid inside.

Alé had the feeling that it wasn't coffee, but he was curious enough about Yuri's idea to set the thought aside. "What do you mean by that?" He stopped right next to Yuri's desk and crossed his arms, eyebrows knitted together.

"We could shoot the Soyuz a few hundred kilometers ahead of the Delta in their existing orbit," Yuri said. "Then we could manually force the Delta into reentry. Eta's spacecraft will reenter at approximately the same time, but she would be well ahead of it and out of the way of debris. Plus, she'll get to see the station break up for the first few seconds, something we've never seen before. Could be a good photo op." He leaned his chair back against the wall behind him and propped his feet up onto the scattering of paperwork on his desk.

Alé nodded but remained silent.

Jade, who had been watching this exchange from a chair at the main table chimed in. "So, you're saying that instead of dropping her into a lower orbit where she might get hit by the station as it reenters, you think we can use the Soyuz engine to push her out ahead of it. Then direct them both into reentry at the same time, a few hundred kilometers away from each other?"

Yuri nodded. "That's the best option, in my humble opinion."

Jade raised her eyebrow. "Since when has your opinion ever come with a side of humble?" This comment brought out a raspy chuckle from the old Russian's lips and a tight side smile from Jade's. She turned to Alé. "I agree with the Russian. This sounds like the best plan."

"Okay," Alé said, nodding. "How will we push the station into early reentry? We don't have any power in the ion engine. There are some smaller course correction thrusters, but they've been out of fuel for years, according to the maintenance logs." Alé moved away from the other two and sat at his workstation, pulling up the holo-screen and flipping to a schematic tile of the Delta. "The gyroscopes could work." He turned to look at Yuri, then Jade. Yuri nodded his approval of the idea.

Alé continued. "The Delta has five gyros that run on electric power instead of propellant, and we have plenty of electric power. We use them to course correct, change station orientation, and so forth. If we could get all five of them going, pushing in the same direction, it should push the entire station farther down into the atmosphere."

Jade looked satisfied enough. She stood from her seat. "It's worth a shot. Run the numbers and let me know when the show is on the road. I'll be in my office."

Chapter 51

NIX Unit 3348 Service Log Entry #664533

Date: 22.5.88

Time: 12:02:02 GMT

Internal note: NASA sent a new plan. I believe they have gotten it right this time. I will do one final task to keep Eta safe during reentry. The solar cell arrays on the Delta Station are equipped with standard-sized Control Moment Gyroscopes (CMGs). Inside each CMG is a spinning rotor and gimbal, which, when tilted in a certain direction, causes torque. This torque is strong enough to move the station substantial distances, especially if they are all used at the same time.

As per Alé's request, I initiated the program to start the CMGs spinning. It can be done via ground-link communication with Mission Control, but it's faster if I do it directly from the Delta computers, and time is of the essence. It takes approximately three minutes for them to spin up to full velocity. Each CMG needs to be pointed at a specific angle in order to get the maximum amount of torque. Enough torque should push the Delta into the atmosphere within six minutes of the initial spin. NASA provided angle calculations and I ran them through my systems to check for errors. The angles are correct.

This action will bring the Delta down into the southern Pacific Ocean and away from almost all populated areas. Eta will continue ahead of it and land over New Mexico as scheduled in approximately thirty-four minutes. I've lost communication with the Soyuz, but I still have a link to the ground. The CMGs are almost ready.

Outgoing Comm Link: "Alé, are you there?"

Incoming Comm Link: "Yes Nix, I'm here."

Response: "I brought the CMGs up to full power and am now set to move them into the correct position. Do you agree with that move?"

Incoming Comm Link: "Yes, that's what we need you to do. Thank you. How are you doing?"

Response: "I am doing just fine and dandy. And thank you for asking. I appreciate the friendly gesture. I have a final thought to share with you. I realize that these are my final moments and I just wanted to let you know how beautiful your planet is. I don't believe I've ever noticed before. The view is spectacular."

Incoming Comm Link: "I'll bet it is, Nix. You're a lucky man for getting to see that."

Response: "You called me a man. That makes me happy, Alé. If you could see me now, I am smiling. I also got the pleasure of knowing Millicent before she passed away. She was a beautiful person. She made me. If I could cry, I would have cried when she died."

Incoming Comm Link: "I'm sure she appreciated you too, Nix. You stayed up there with her daughter, after all."

Response: "Ah, yes, beautiful Eta. I was there when she was born and I watched her grow up. She is the very best friend anyone could ask for. I hope you will agree, Alé."

Incoming Comm Link: "I agree, Nix."

Response: "Good. I know Eta will be in your capable hands now that she has left mine. I dearly wish I could hear her voice again... but I suppose that is not meant to be. Thank you, Alé, for letting me have a few final words with you. You treat me like a real person, and I appreciate that more than you know."

Incoming Comm Link: "Nix, I am happy to have known you. You gave your life so that Eta could survive, and that makes you better than many of the humans living on the surface. Take care, Nix, and God bless."

Response: ...

Response: ...

Response: ...

End log transmission: signal failure.

Chapter 52

I am alone for the moment, staring down at the beautiful swirling white cloud tops below. I'm counting to pass the time, trying to keep fear and nerves at bay. Right now, the Soyuz is tilted in such a way that one window points to the black universe and the other window points to the brilliant Earth. It's an angle I've never seen before, totally unlike any of the views on the Delta.

After Nix released the clamps, I blew the explosive bolts that held the Soyuz to the bulkhead. Those little guys give me a heck of a push. They sounded like someone driving nails into the side of the ship with a sledgehammer. Once I was about two hundred meters from the Delta, they had me light up the primary engine of the Soyuz to put me into my reentry corridor. I'm now the farthest I've ever been away from my home.

"Eta?" I hear Alé's voice come through the comm link. His voice sounds clearer now, almost like he's in the next room, speaking through an open doorway.

"Yes, I'm here."

"Just a few more minutes before we lose radio communication. How are you?" he asks.

In my mind, I can see his expression. I close my eyes to get a clearer view of him. He has dark curly hair and dark eyebrows. I imagine his eyebrows rolling up, meeting the little smile lines in his forehead as he asks me how I'm doing. I smile thinking about him, knowing that if I survive the next twenty minutes, I'll get to see him in person.

"I'm great, Alé. I'm doing great."

"That's good to hear," he says. "I thought you might like to know that we're tracking the Delta over the Pacific, just behind you. If you want, you can probably catch sight of it before it's gone for good."

I turn to the window, but I don't see the horizon because the window is facing down toward the ocean. I'll have to rotate the Soyuz using the attitude thrusters. I touch the screen panel in front of me and punch in the proper codes to roll the craft. I can hear the chemical thrusters pushing pressurized gas outside the vessel. It's hissing next to the metal skin of the Soyuz.

As the vessel rolls, the Delta comes into view through the small bulkhead window. I'm strapped into the middle seat, so I can't get right by the window, but I crane my neck up and out to get a better view.

It's interesting how you feel when you leave the only home you've ever known. I've seen news articles and read books about people who were abducted and held captive for years inside someone's basement or backyard, and I wonder if this is the same feeling they got when they were finally rescued... when they finally saw that place where they were trapped for so long, drifting off into the distance behind them.

Nostalgia is an interesting thing—a wistful affection for the past, a sentimental yearning. I can't say that I feel sentimental, but I do have a deep yearning and an affection for what I've left behind. I can see it clearly out the window, a little world of its own hovering just above the horizon. The last few weeks, I've been so busy preparing to leave, I never noticed how close it was getting to the Earth. But now, from a distance, it looks so tiny and vulnerable, like the Earth is about to reach up and swallow it whole in a fire-breathing display of superiority.

As the thought of fire passes through my mind, the Delta starts to spark. It's not sparking like you might expect a flint to spark into a campfire. It's a different kind of spark. It looks like the ship is wobbling and the reflective metal surface is spinning bits of light all across the universe.

I look down at my hands and hold them up in front of me. I can see the flashes of light flying over them. I move as close to the window as my straps will allow and see that the Delta is, in fact, wobbling. It's gyrating back and forth, a small disk of movement from where I sit, but it's there, nonetheless, pulsating through the upper reaches of the atmosphere.

I can't actually see the station windows because it's too far away from me, but in my mind, I see Nix staring out the windows of the VP, holding up his hand, smiling his Iron Man grin at me through the thick glass. He would, I think, be looking out. He was so much more than a robot, after all. He would want to see the fireworks as much as anybody.

I wonder if Nix feels fear? I'm almost certain he doesn't feel it the way I feel it. But, then again, nobody feels fear the way I feel it, right? Fear doesn't work that way.

Nix may not feel fear, but he surely is aware. He's aware that within the next few minutes, the Delta will crumple up into a twisted blob of metal. He's aware that the atmosphere will pop out of it faster than a bullet from a gun. Nix doesn't need air or pressure or any of that to survive, so he may even survive as the station breaks up around him. Maybe he'll survive the fireworks. His skin can survive in the vacuum, after all. Maybe he'll get to feel the fresh air before he falls into the ocean.

A sudden burst from the Delta jolts me out of my wild thoughts and back into the present. Like splinters flying out of a piece of wood that's been snapped in half, the solar panels that lined both sides of the truss structure fly off in all directions, scattering more light my way. I see the truss has broken completely in half and the primary engine, the one that left me high and dry only a few months ago, is now lulling about, totally separate from the main structure of the Delta. The entire structure has gone into a wicked spin. I see the G. My garden. My life. It's now flopping around the station as it tumbles head over heels.

As I watch it tumble, I think of Nu. What would she have thought if she could have seen this? Her home, her life's work, the reason she lived and the others died, now flipping around uncontrollably, flailing through the dense atmosphere.

Suddenly, a bright light flares in the window. One of the massive solar panels has just smacked into the atmosphere, flaring up and disintegrating in less than two seconds. The atmosphere doesn't begin right in one spot. It's a gradual, funky sort of barrier. It has waves in it, some taller and thicker than others, all waiting to bring you into their fold.

That's when I realize my own spacecraft is feeling a bit like it's on an ocean, bumping about slightly. I check my altitude. I'm eighty-five kilometers above the surface. The comm link buzzes to life in my ear.

"Eta, are you watching it?" Alé asks.

"Yes," I say. "It's beautiful." Tears well in my eyes and my vision clouds. Trying to focus, I clear my throat and shut my eyes. I face forward and leave the Delta to it. For some reason, I don't want to watch it anymore. It's time for me to look ahead.

"Eta, listen to me," Alé says. "You're going to start your own reentry very soon. I won't be able to contact you through the blackout portion of the fall. We're at one minute until expected loss of signal. But you'll be perfect. I have no doubts."

"I'll be perfect," I repeat. I don't know if that's true. I'm only repeating his words because they sounded so sweet coming into my ear from his beautiful voice. They don't sound as great when I say them though. My voice is soft and nasally. His voice is deep and broad and full of warmth.

"Eta." He pauses and I wonder if the radio is cutting out, but when he comes back on, I can hear that his voice is catching, almost like he's choking something back. "I need you to make it down here, Eta. I *need* you to make it through this. Do you understand that?"

I nod. I know he can't see it, but it's all I can do. There are no words to ease his pain or make this easier on him.

"It's just that... well," he continues, choking on the words. "If it gets to be too much for you up there, the gravity, I mean, close your eyes, okay?" He sounds desperate as he continues. "Close your eyes. Count your numbers. Think about beautiful things like sand on the beach, or needles on a pine tree. Think about dogs and birds and butterflies. Think about whatever you need to push through, okay? I mean it. You *must* survive. If you have to, go deep inside yourself to do it. Okay? Do you understand? Tell me you understand."

"I do," I say in a whisper. And I do understand. I know exactly what he's asking me to do.

The odds of this old spacecraft making it through reentry are slim. Probably lower than anyone at NASA would ever share with me. But he's holding out every last ounce of hope in his soul, and he's asking me to do the same.

"Good," he says. "Ten seconds to expected signal loss."

"Alé," I say.

"Yes?"

"I'll think of you."

"Five seconds until loss of signal, Eta. You've got this. And I'll be here, waiting," he says.

With a crackle, the radio signal cuts out and silence takes over.

Chapter 53

Now, I wait.

The ship bumps around beneath me. It feels like what I would imagine a roller coaster might feel like, right at the moment the coaster car creeps over the top of the first drop. After the comm link cut out, there were several seconds of pure, complete silence. But now, I hear a rumbling all around me. It's getting louder and deeper.

Suddenly, flames shoot past the windows on both sides of me. The windows are starting to burn, slowly at first, and before I know it, they're glowing orange. As each second passes, they get darker, turning from bright red, to deep crimson, to almost black, like the color of blood. It seems like I'm inside the head of a dragon and the windows of the Soyuz are its two black, fiery eyes looking out over the world.

I've been so preoccupied with the fire in the windows, I've forgotten about the rest of my body. Gravity is starting to pull on me. Hard. I feel it deep in my gut. There's the sensation of a taut string pulling my spine down, right in the center of my chair.

I take this moment to tighten up the belts holding me to the seat. Alé told me to do that when gravity started to take hold. It does no good to tighten them when you're still in space because you can't get a good grip on the seat with your body. But now, my body is firmly rooted to the seat and the belts tighten easily.

With each second that passes, the gravity pulls harder. It no longer feels like strings, but rather like I'm covered in big straps pulling me tighter and tighter into the chair. I can't lift my head. It feels like it's bolted down.

The altimeter says I'm at sixty-eight kilometers above the surface. The Soyuz is spinning! This realization comes to me suddenly. It's spinning to my right, counterclockwise. I hadn't noticed it before, but now that the gravity is biting down hard, I can feel the spin. I don't think it's supposed to spin like this—not this fast.

The fire surrounds the ship. Heat comes at me in waves. I've never felt heat this intense. Sweat drips down the side of my forehead and cheeks. My lungs won't inflate. I struggle to pull in the thick, hot air from inside the cabin. I see the control panel in front of me with all its technical screens and switches, but I couldn't reach it even if I wanted to. My arms are bolted to my sides and they feel like they'll never move again.

My bones are giving way. My poor, brittle bones are crumbling under my skin. The pain is intense.

I close my eyes. My escape comes quickly. Instead of looking for the numbers, I picture the beach. I'm surrounded by dusty yellow sand and ahead of me, the water flows in loose, frothy waves. The sun is setting, all big and burnt orange on the horizon.

I see Alé standing in the tide. He's been waiting for me here. He holds out his hand and smiles.

Chapter 54

The girl tumbled through the atmosphere as fast as a bullet from a gun. The gravitational pull from such a fall was much stronger than she could have imagined.

Her lips fell to the sides of her mouth, exposing her teeth and giving her an odd grin. As she'd been instructed, she clamped her teeth shut to avoid accidentally biting her tongue. This precaution, as it turned out, wasn't necessary. Her tongue slipped back in her mouth and coiled at the base of her throat, nowhere near her teeth.

At sixty kilometers above the surface, the gravitational forces were six times that of those felt on the ground, or thirty-six times the highest gravity she had ever known.

The Soyuz spacecraft was designed to keep its occupants awake by positioning them faceup, with their backs facing the Earth during reentry. As the blood in the body gains weight, it pools in places it shouldn't. If an astronaut were to sit up during reentry, they would undoubtedly pass out because their heart couldn't push the blood up to their head though the strong gravitational pull. Their feet would balloon with the now-thickened blood, trapping most of it in the lower half of the body. A normal Soyuz passenger would feel plenty of gravity but would remain awake and alert during their descent.

The girl on board Soyuz MV-49 was not so lucky. At fifty-two kilometers above the surface, she lost consciousness. Her seat was not fitted to her body as it would have been if she was a normal astronaut. Because of the ill-fitting seat, her body pressed against the restraints on her sides in an unnatural way. As the capsule spun, the pain in the side of her body worsened. Fortunately, the girl was unconscious when the number eight and nine ribs on her right side cracked nearly in half under the force of the straps digging into them.

As she dreamed, she could sense the pain. She knew that something was bothering her, but she couldn't quite understand it as she escaped further and further into her own mind.

The capsule continued on its sharp trajectory, down, down, down, spinning all the while as the Earth's atmosphere forced it to slow down. The gravitational forces topped out at a stunning eight times the gravitational pull that one experiences on the Earth's surface. Eight minutes after reentry began, the first of two sets of parachutes deployed from the aged spacecraft.

The girl continued to sleep.

The first chute caught the wind and pulled up so sharply on the craft, she experienced a split second of zero gravity before crashing down to the end of the rope. It held, and the craft slowed further.

At five kilometers above the surface, the heat shield jettisoned from the bottom of the capsule, falling to the desert below. The decreased weight caused the capsule to slow more, swaying gently beneath the huge, purple parachutes above it. Had she been awake, the girl would have seen the helicopters standing by outside the craft, waiting for her arrival.

She continued to dream.

The pressure on her broken ribs eased up as the spacecraft slowed and the heavy gravitational forces relaxed. Her heart thudded in her chest, working harder than it ever had to pump her blood. Her brain wavered in and out of oxygen deprivation as her lungs struggled to suck air. The veins in her legs and arms strained under the new weight of her blood and many popped because of the pressure. Her eyes sank heavily into her skull, putting pressure on her optic nerves. Had she been awake, she wouldn't have been able to see.

The second set of parachutes exploded from the craft. These chutes were red and they could easily be seen from the ground, a mere twenty thousand meters below. If she'd been awake, the girl would have heard the loud push of air as they let loose from their holding tanks and then she would have felt a sudden jerk as the capsule slowed further.

Inside the capsule, it was quiet except for her breathing— light and fluttery. Shortly before the capsule touched the ground, six retrorockets fired violently into the red dirt of the New Mexico desert in an effort to slow the spacecraft even more. The girl's seat raised up on shock absorbers to help lessen the blow as the capsule touched down on the surface. If she had been conscious, it would have felt like a truck ramming into her body from beneath.

After touchdown, there was total silence.

The girl on the Soyuz had one important job after landing. She was supposed to release the parachutes by pulling down on a ripcord in the control panel above her head, cutting them free from the spacecraft so they wouldn't drag it around in the case of high winds.

But she continued to sleep and was unable to do this task. The parachutes remained attached and the wind howled outside the burnt windows of the Soyuz.

All remained quiet for a few moments, and then the capsule started to move, rumbling and shaking in the wind. One big wind gust tipped it onto its side. The next big gust sent it tumbling down a small, scrub-covered dune, the parachutes tugging it farther into the desert.

And still, the girl slept.

Had she been awake, she would have felt the seat restraints digging into her side with each tumble of the Soyuz, forcing her broken ribs farther and farther into the soft tissue of her lungs.

Chapter 55

It's amazing what you miss when you can't wake up.

The last thing I remember before passing out was the bloodred color of the capsule windows. That, and the gravity. I remember trying to keep my lips closed and I physically couldn't pull them up around my teeth. Then it all went black and I was on the beach with Alé.

I didn't wake up again until three days later, according to Tess, who's been here with me since the landing. She tells me that after I landed, the parachutes got caught by the wind. The rescue crew wasn't able to get to the capsule until twenty-five minutes after it landed because it went on a violent roll through the desert. Tess said it looked like a blackened ping-pong ball, rolling and bouncing over the dunes. They hadn't told me this before I left the Delta, but the wind was gusting over forty kilometers per hour on the ground. They knew this was a possibility, but they didn't want me worrying about it.

It turns out that of all the things that could have gone wrong, it was the wind that ended up almost killing me. The Soyuz, a true workhorse, performed exactly as planned. Even the spinning during descent was supposed to happen to keep it more stable in the reentry corridor during a ballistic reentry.

I have pictures of the spot where the capsule came to rest. It was in a small valley between two hills. The rescue crew had to wait until the Soyuz quit rolling before it was safe enough to cut the parachute cables. They found me crumpled in my seat, covered in blood and vomit. There are pictures of this too, but I don't have the nerve to look at them.

I landed in the southeastern corner of the Navajo Nation Reservation near a small town called Standing Rock and was immediately taken to a NASA research hospital outside of Albuquerque. The surgery took twelve hours. They repaired my punctured lungs and put pins and supports in the broken ribs. They also repaired my shattered pelvis and left femur.

Tess tells me it's a miracle I made it. With the intense gravity and my fragile body, it could have been a lot worse. She believes that since I've been exercising in limited gravity all my life and subsisting on a plant-based diet, my body was healthy enough to withstand the forces.

I survived and that seems to surprise her. But it doesn't surprise me. I was with Alé. As soon as it became too much, I did exactly what he told me to do. I retreated into my mind and found him there, waiting for me with open arms. That's why I survived. Of course, I needed the Soyuz to do its job too, which it did, but I believe it was his presence that got me here alive.

They kept me in a medically induced coma for three days after surgery. When I finally lifted my heavy eyelids, I was only able to keep them open for a few seconds before the weight of sleep and gravity closed them again. But before they closed on me, I saw Tess sitting on a stool in the corner of the room.

I had never seen Tess before, so I didn't know it was her for sure, but somehow, I did kind of know. She looked pretty much like I imagined her, with curly red hair cropped just below her chin. She wore a beige turtleneck dress and sat with her legs crossed. It was her face that I remember most. I must have made a noise when I woke because she immediately looked my way and the look on her face was pure joy. A huge smile spread across her lips and her green eyes brightened. Just as soon as I got a glimpse of her, I was out again.

As I said, you miss a lot when you can't wake up. Every time I would fight my way out of the heavy fog of sleep, I would open my eyelids and the weight of them would pull me back down into the cloud.

The longer I lay there, the more often my body tried to wake, and the more I tried, the longer I could keep my eyelids open. So, that's how I started to win my battle against gravity—with my eyelids. The other parts of my body were so heavy, they wouldn't budge a centimeter if I tried to move them. But I could move my eyelids. I would try to keep my eyes open one second at a time. Before long, I could last fifteen seconds, then thirty seconds. After a few days, I could keep them open for a whole minute, then two minutes, then five minutes. Eventually, I could keep them open long enough to observe the room around me.

It was a small white room. The walls were white. The ceiling was white. The furniture was white. The bed where I lay was white. In the beginning, I couldn't see the floor, but I soon learned it was white too. There was a white couch on the wall next to my bed, and a white stool in the corner next to a little window. They kept the shades drawn for fear that the sun would hurt my eyes. The shades were white too.

Tess started talking to me a few days after I first opened my eyes. She told me how excited she was to see my beautiful face. She even cried once while she held my hand. I started to look for her every time I opened my eyes, and she was there, every time.

Eventually, I tried to lift my head. It felt like an elephant sat perched on the top of my neck and I wouldn't budge at first, but I kept trying. I also worked on my fingers and toes. Tess told me how important it was for me to start moving. When you've been without gravity (or with so little gravity) for as long as I have, you must start moving around or your body will never heal itself, she said. So, I wiggled my fingers and toes. Then I lifted my hand a few centimeters. I was able to make more and more progress with each passing day.

Gravity wasn't the only thing limiting me from moving. The pain from my shattered pelvis and leg was almost unbearable and I had a difficult time breathing because of the punctured lungs. They kept me heavily medicated.

It was around day seven when I asked the doctors to hold back on the pain medications. I didn't like the way they made me feel: foggy and frail and totally out of it.

After they began to wean me off the pain medications, the nightmares started. I could feel the pain in my sleep and it played games with my mind while I dreamed. Sometimes, I felt like I would die from it. But eventually, the pain started to relent. I kept telling myself if I stood up to it for another minute, it would back down. And soon, that's what happened. After two full weeks in the hospital, I was able to stand up for the first time on the surface of the Earth. I only lasted a few seconds before crumpling back down onto my bed, but it felt amazing. I can't wait until I can run again.

I hope to be able to leave this small white room soon and go somewhere with bigger windows and perhaps even some color on the walls. Maybe in the next few days, Tess says whenever I ask her.

***

"Eta, there's someone here to see you." I hear Tess's voice from outside the door. I'm still in the white room. Even the door is white. I've asked Tess several times now when they plan to move me from this room. She keeps telling me to have patience.

I'm supposed to be sleeping, but I'm reading a book on my holo-screen instead. It's called *The Color of Me* written by someone who survived the SA attack on Buenos Aires during the war. I know so little about the war and I've essentially lived my whole life in the past. But now I'm living in the present and I have access to everything that's come along since the Delta lost contact with Mission Control. I've got my work ahead of me to catch up.

"I'm awake, Tess. Come in," I say.

She steps through the door. Today's outfit is a blue-striped pantsuit and she has her red hair pulled back behind her ears. A man steps through the door behind her.

Plenty of men come in and out of my room every day: doctors and nurses and physical therapists. But I've never seen this man before. He doesn't look like the rest of the NASA guys. They show up and peek in on me when they think I'm sleeping. I sometimes pretend to be just to see what they're up to. I've seen them jotting notes down on holo-screens and whispering to each other. They're always stiff, wearing crisp white shirts and blue ties under white lab coats.

John Patrick, the administrator, came here one day. He introduced himself, and when he said the words, "You might know me as the administrator of NASA," I got a strange feeling. Something about the way he said the word *administrator* didn't sit right. It felt sharp, almost boastful, as if this was something I should be impressed by. Like the others, he had a stiff, unnatural way about him. He wasn't wearing a lab coat, but his clothes were starched and impeccable. Rather than the typical blue tie worn by other NASA guys, Patrick wore a red tie, which I thought was interesting. He was only in my room for a brief moment to introduce himself before stepping out. I heard him outside the door speaking in hushed tones with Tess and another woman who I believe was Jade. For some reason, I get the feeling I'm not being moved to a larger room because of Patrick. He's keeping me here for something, but I'm not sure yet what that is.

The man standing in front of me now has his white shirt open at the neck with no tie. His sleeves are rolled up, showing the tanned skin on his forearms. His left hand is in his pocket while the other hangs casually at his side. His hair is short on the sides with dark curls hanging over his forehead. His eyes are wide and dark brown.

My breath catches in my throat and the holo-screen falls out of my hands and into my lap. My eyes fail me and drop shut. I focus my attention and force myself to work the muscles that keep them open. I want to see this man.

When I manage to pry my eyes open again, he's still there, looking at me with his head cocked slightly to the side. He's so beautiful that my face crumples and tears flow freely from my eyes. For once, I'm grateful for the gravity that allows the tears to fall down my cheeks, keeping my eyes clear.

He stands tall next to Tess. He has a good six inches on her. She smiles at him, but I only see her in the periphery of my vision. He takes up the entire screen in front of me and everything else has faded into the white background behind him.

"I'll just step out and give you two a moment," Tess says and slowly closes the door behind her with a soft click.

He has the strangest look on his face. It's not quite a smile, yet it's not an unhappy expression. If I knew his face, which I don't because I've only seen it in my mind, but if I did, I might think he was about to cry too.

The man moves toward me slowly, gently, then stops. I can tell he's not sure how he should approach. Maybe he's afraid that if he moves too quickly, he'll scare me or cause me pain.

"Come here," I say, my voice quiet but direct and unwavering.

He obeys and moves forward. He reaches the bed and drops down to a squat next to it so his eyes are level with mine. He has not moved them from my face since he first entered the room. To my surprise, he puts his hands over his face, resting his elbows on the side of the bed, and begins to sob.

"No... please don't do that," I say. I want to see his face. He is more beautiful than I could have ever imagined.

He looks up, his eyes red and watery, the sobs still choking in his throat, and he touches my arm. Then he moves both of his hands down to take my hand in his. His hands are solid and powerful and his skin is dark and smooth. My hand looks like a child's compared to his, pale and fragile. He strokes the back of my hand gently with his fingers. Each touch sends pulses of blood up and down my arm. The feeling is so strange, I look down at my forearm, wondering if the skin might explode.

He's still crying and so am I. He puts my hand down on the bed and moves his right hand up to my left cheek. He cups it gently and runs his thumb across it, right under my eye. I let my head fall into his hand, knowing it will support me. Knowing *he* will support me.

"Alé," I say, "you saved my life."

Alé pulls his face close to mine. He's so close, I can feel his breath. It smells like peppermint.

"Eta," he says. "I have waited my whole life for you. There is so much I want to show you."

"Show me, Alé. I want to see everything," I say.

Acknowledgments

A huge thank you to all the people who stood by me during this long and often tedious process.

To my parents, John Ted and Lucy, for your never-ending support no matter where I've gone in life.

To my Minnesota family for showing me lots of love when I was so far away from home.

To my husband, Tim, who always believed that this was the best book ever written (even though I know that's not true, but it's nice to be told from time to time).

To my son, Jack, the most talented baseball player I know, who provides an endless supply of made-up words and silly song verses to encourage my creativity.

To my daughter, Lillian, whose imagination and beautiful spirit inspired the character of Eta and helped bring her from half-baked bedtime story to full-fledged heroine.

www.ingramcontent.com/pod-product-compliance
Lightning Source LLC
Chambersburg PA
CBHW030546180626
46816CB00005B/1421